THE ART OF Healing

Coastal Dreams Book Two

ALEXA ASTON

USA TODAY BESTSELLING AUTHOR

OLIVERHEBERBOOKS

DALLAS

Even though it was a Sunday, Keaton Maxwell awoke at four. His body had long been tuned to rise well before the sun made an appearance. Usually, he headed for the shed in Miss Peggy's backyard and worked for an hour. She had given him use of the shed years ago so that he had a place to paint. It was small, only ten by twelve feet, but it was a place he could create to his heart's content.

Today, he had high hopes that he would sell some of his paintings.

He had always had an artistic bent, sketching in class when he should have been listening to his teachers. Because his attention wandered often, he had earned poor grades and had been labeled troubled. His parents hadn't pressed him about grades because they were drug addicts. Their only interest was where their next fix came from. Keaton was some vague afterthought.

Because of that, he had grown resilient early. He fed himself with whatever he could find in the apartment or from the garbage can he scoured regularly. He'd learned to check the trash at restaurants, especially at closing time. The help dumped all kinds of things, and he reaped the benefits of what patrons had left on their plates. He also washed himself and kept his clothes as clean as he could. As he got older, he learned about the free breakfast and lunch program for disadvantaged kids. He asked someone in the attendance office for the forms when he was eight and filled them out, forging his mom's signature.

By that time, his dad hardly ever came around. When he did, his parents fought. Not just verbally but knock your teeth out kind of fights. Keaton learned to avoid being around them when they were together because all they did was fight or get high. His big mistake had been calling out his dad when he came home after dumpster diving for dinner one night and caught the old man going through his worn backpack. Keaton kept what little money he earned in the backpack, collecting and selling lost balls from a local golf course. When he came home that night and found his dad stuffing money from the backpack into his own pocket, he lost it. He cursed at him. Tried to take the money away, knowing it would just go for the next fix. The next line of coke.

Even though his dad looked like a cadaver from his drug use, he packed a wallop of a punch. Keaton was used as a punching bag for several minutes, trying to fight back. His mom jumped into the fray, trying to steal the money while she was striking them both. Some neighbor called the cops, and the next thing he knew, he was being carted away and placed in temporary foster care. Temporary became permanent after a court case that dragged on for almost two years. His parents lost parental rights to their own flesh and blood when Keaton turned ten and entered the foster system permanently.

No one had to tell him that ten-year-old troubled boys weren't the kind of kids who were eagerly adopted. He went from home to home. From bad to worst. Finally, he landed in a place with six foster kids, all boys. He stayed there for two years, until he turned eighteen and aged out of the system at the end of April. The asshole caregivers didn't even let him finish out his final month of high school before they cut him loose. If it hadn't been for Miss Peggy, who lived across the street and took him in, Keaton wouldn't have earned his high school diploma.

Not that he had many options once he graduated. He'd sleepwalked through school, doing the bare minimum to get by. Though he loved his art classes, he couldn't afford to go to some fancy art school. He was good with his hands, though, and Miss Peggy had a friend who ran a construction crew. Frank Peterson did remodeling jobs in Highland Park, an exclusive enclave surrounded by Dallas. Highland Park folks were mostly white, obscenely rich, and had a penchant for constantly having their homes redone. It didn't take long for Keaton to learn how to do all kinds of physical handiwork. He painted interiors and exteriors. Learned how to put in kitchen sinks, backsplashes, and new countertops. He laid wood flooring and then learned to build cabinets, which also led to jobs redoing people's closets.

That had been the last dozen years of his life. Living in a room he rented from Miss Peggy. Working on Frank's crew. Getting up early to paint mornings and reading books Miss Peggy checked out for him at the library after she fed him dinner at night. She was interested in all kinds of topics. History. Architecture. Art. Politics. When she saw how little education he had retained, Miss Peggy embarked upon a crash course of educating Keaton. He read the books she brought home. They talked about them.

That was his life.

Now, though, he had begun testing the waters with his paintings. He'd signed up and paid for the booth space at two arts and crafts shows this spring. Surprisingly, he had sold five of his paintings. Today he had space at a festival held downtown at Klyde Warren Park, a public park built on top of a freeway by some billionaire. It was an oasis of green space, running three city blocks, and dedicated to the public. It had children's areas. Reading spaces. Fountains and game areas. Food trucks of all types were always parked around its edges. It was the cool, go-to place for many Dallasites and even people from the surrounding suburbs.

And Keaton hoped that today his art would be noticed.

Klyde Warren was on the edge of Dallas' Arts District. It also had some fancy restaurants on its perimeter and nearby. He'd heard some art galleries sent employees to scope out new artists. If someone recognized that he had talent, he might be able to hang up his tool belt and finally devote himself to his art. Of course, that was the pipe dream. In reality, he simply wanted to sell some paintings. Maybe cut back from working on Frank's crews from six days a week to five. Having Saturdays to himself in order to paint would be a luxury.

He dressed quickly and went to the shed, loading paintings into his ten-year-old sedan, then locking it. Returning inside, he showered, putting on fresh clothes, and shaved. When he went to the kitchen, Miss Peggy was already seated at the table, sipping a cup of coffee.

"Got the car loaded?" she asked.

Keaton nodded. "I'm taking twenty paintings to display. Have easels for two."

"And payment?"

"The last couple of shows I let people Venmo or Zelle me, but I talked to a guy about Square. I got the app, so I can use it to sell today. People can just tap their card."

"I hope some good comes out of today, Keaton. You've devoted yourself to your art for a long time."

He put a pod into the coffeemaker. "Yup. A dozen years now."

She got up and went to the counter, lifting the lid off something. Lifting it, she brought it toward him.

It was a cake.

"You remembered," he said, his eyes misting over.

"I would never forget your birthday, young man. Although can I say young? After all, you are thirty today," she teased. "Should I start looking for gray in your hair?"

He laughed and then grew serious. "Thank you, Miss Peggy. Not just for the cake, but for everything. You gave me not only a place to live. You gave me a home. You've been both friend and mentor to me."

She set down the cake. Making light, she said, "I'm just glad you put up with my foolishness. I know I've tried to cram a ton of info into you over the years."

"You have," he agreed, taking his mug of coffee and turning off the coffeemaker. "But I've learned about everything from the Renaissance to how Wall Street works to how to make an omelet. The cooking lessons have fed me physically. The book knowledge has fed my soul."

Miss Peggy touched his cheek. "I wish I had money. I wish I could give you some so that you could travel. See places around the world. Draw inspiration."

"Hey, we watch Rick Steves all the time on PBS. He's shown us everything from cities along the Danube to the Hagia Sophia. It was a helluva lot less expensive that way, watching from the couch."

Keaton took a sip of the coffee. "And if I do start selling my paintings, who knows? Maybe I'll make enough to up and move to Italy for a year and paint. You could come with me. Learn how to make pasta and drink really good wine."

"I'd like that," she said wistfully.

For a moment, he caught something in her eyes. Something she was holding back. He didn't press her, though. If Miss Peggy had something to share with him, she'd do it in her own sweet time. She'd always respected his privacy, and it was something he had done, as well.

"Well, I'm going to get ready for church," she declared. "It's my turn in the rotation to set out the coffee and donuts after Sunday school this morning. Good luck today."

"Thanks."

She left the room, and he whipped up some scrambled eggs and toast for himself. Miss Peggy never ate breakfast. In fact, she didn't eat much, despite being a fine cook. She never had much of an appetite, but lately, she seemed to not eat at all. Now that he thought about it, she was thinner than usual.

A sense of dread filled him. Keaton told himself not to go there. To focus on one day at a time—and today was all about his art.

He left the house and drove to downtown, parking in a lot which had been designated for vendors. Another guy had a flatbed dolly cart and even let him borrow it, saving him trips to and from his car. Keaton set up his paintings and took in the table display stand with his name and prices listed on it. If today proved to be a success, he was even thinking about claiming a domain and creating a website for himself.

The festival started at ten, but people already roamed the park. Throwing frisbees. Dancing to music. A tai chi class was taking place nearby. He found a pretty girl in her mid-twenties and watched as she gracefully executed the moves.

Slowly, others began to arrive, the ones meant to take advantage of the festival. Glancing around, he saw booths with grapevine wreaths. Candles. Children's clothing. Jarred salsas and jellies. Several other artists were also present. One guy was drawing caricatures. Another displayed black and white photographs. A woman in her early forties had crafted silver and turquoise jewelry, while another was a sculptor. He also counted two other painters, one who seemed to specialize in places throughout Texas, while the other displayed quirky cityscapes.

Everyone seemed way more prepared than Keaton. They displayed signs with QR codes for their websites. They passed out business cards and swag such as stickers and pens and magnets. Some vendors even had brochures spotlighting their work. All of that took extra cash, though, and he'd rather sink his money into his art. Still, the idea of having a website was looking better and better to him.

Fortunately, two individuals stopped by his booth, perusing what he offered. Each bought a painting, and pride swelled within him as he completed the sales. He watched the pair, who were friends, leaving with his paintings in tow. Hope filled him, and he thought this festival might be the beginning of a new chapter in his life.

"Keaton? Is that you?"

He swung his gaze to a woman who had stopped at his table. She was dressed casually in a sleeveless silk shirt and capris, with blood red on her toenails and dozens of bangles on each arm. Her engagement and wedding ring set cost more than he had made in his lifetime.

"Mrs. Winslow. It's good to see you," he said politely, giving the Highland Park housewife a smile.

"Monica, please," she insisted. "You did enough work in our house, we should be on a first-name basis. Well, it *was* our house. It's mine now." She flashed a satisfied smile.

"Divorced or widowed?" he asked.

She laughed, a deep, throaty chuckle. "Well, it was going to be number one—until my husband dropped dead on the golf course. He'd initiated divorce proceedings. Found a gal who resembled me from twenty years ago and was ready to trade me in for that newer model. Thankfully, the paperwork was in the early stages of being drawn up. Since it was never completed, much less filed, I got everything—minus the trust funds for our two children."

"Well, being single looks good on you," he complimented.

Her gaze turned to one of his paintings on display. "I didn't know you were a painter. Of landscapes, that is. I know you painted the house more than once. And I simply love the cabinetry you designed and built. I recommend you to all my friends."

"Let me tell you about this one," he said smoothly, transitioning from his work on her house to his art.

For the next few minutes, Keaton showed her the paintings he'd brought with him. Monica seemed impressed.

"I'm going to buy that one with the bluebonnets and sunset." She glanced around. "And I think I'll also take the one which looks like an English garden." She frowned, her eyes looking at his sign. "Is this what you're charging?"

"Yes, ma'am. I didn't want to overprice myself."

"Why, that's criminal, Keaton. Your work is worth ten times that—and that's how I'm going to compensate you."

A thrill ran through him. He'd always thought he had talent, but he had no idea how to market himself.

"Is this the first time you've sold your work?" Monica asked.

"I did a couple of arts and crafts shows last month. One in Plano. Another in Richardson."

She looked at him shrewdly. "You don't know the gold mine you are sitting on. All my friends would buy your work. Joy. Evelyn. Persephone. And Jacqueline. Definitely, Jacqueline."

Keaton was familiar with every woman she named. They

were all friends of hers who had houses he had worked on in one capacity or another over the last dozen years. All had more money than they knew what to do with.

"Have you ever heard of an artist-in-residence?" she asked.

"Traditionally, the concept can be traced back to the sixteenth century and the Duke of Florence, a Medici," he immediately responded and then paused. "But you don't want a history lesson, do you?"

"Certainly not. But I do know talent when I see it. You shouldn't be working construction, Keaton. You should be spending your time devoting yourself to painting. I'm actually part-owner in a local gallery a few blocks from here."

Monica pulled out her phone and sent a quick text message.

"I know the manager is there now. I've told him to come and meet us." She paused. "I have more money than I know what to do with, Keaton. My kids are both in college and rarely come home. I'm looking for something to fill my days." She grinned. "And I've decided you're my new project."

An hour later, Monica had insisted that he quit his construction job. She would be bankrolling him as her personal artist-in-residence. The gallery's manager would view any completed paintings and have the first option to purchase them or pass, then Keaton would be able to sell them on his own if he wished. Monica said her lawyer could draw up the contracts and asked Keaton to commit to a two-year period of association with her gallery.

"You'll want your own lawyer," she advised. "Mine is good, and he'll favor me. I want you to also be taken care of." She dismissed the manager and then smiled at Keaton. "I don't need to make money off you. I just recognize your talent and want to help you learn how to sell your work—and yourself."

Monica said that he would need studio space to work from

and that she would fund that portion for him. They could look together for a place to rent once he turned in his notice to Frank. He fought her on the idea of simply going in and quitting tomorrow, though.

"Frank gave me a job straight out of high school. I'm not going to do him dirty and walk away without notice, Monica."

"Okay, I get it. But once you have an end date, we'll start planning for your future. I'm going to make certain Dallas—and beyond—learns who Keaton Maxwell is."

He shook hands with her. "I can't thank you enough."

"I haven't done anything yet, honey." She smiled. "But I will. I love a good project, and you will be easy to sell. You've got mad artistic talent, plus you're easy on the eyes. And I'm not flirting with you. Actually, I'm already seeing someone. He's a few years older than I am, but he makes me very happy."

"I guess I'll go now and drop off the rest of these canvases at the gallery," he told her since she had told the manager that Keaton would do just that. "I'll be in touch."

They traded cell numbers, and he borrowed the dolly again, taking the paintings which had yet to be sold back to his car. He'd moved two of them before Monica had shown up, and he couldn't help but think now that those individuals had paid a pittance to what a Keaton Maxwell painting would go for in the future.

He returned the dolly to his new acquaintance and grabbed the tabletop sign. Deciding he didn't need it anymore, he tossed it in the trash. On his way to the car, he stopped at a food truck and ordered a Cuban sandwich and Dr Pepper. He ate the sandwich on the way to his car, washing it down with the cold, canned soft drink, then made his way to the Clifford Gallery three blocks away. The manager was waiting and helped Keaton carry in the canvases.

"I'd say it's a case of right place, right time," the older man said. "You're really good. I'll be able to move all these quickly, but I think I'll only make three or four available to begin with. Whet the appetite of the art-loving crowd."

They discussed a few subjects for future paintings he might attempt, and then Keaton said goodbye. He drove home, on top of the world. His days in construction were over. He was going to actually make a living being an artist. He couldn't wait to tell Miss Peggy.

When he got home, though, an ambulance was sitting in front of the house. Neighbors had gathered on the sidewalk and across the street. Keaton leaped from the car and saw two EMTs carrying a stretcher.

The body and face were covered.

Choking on a sob, he rushed over. "Is that ... Miss Peggy?"

"Yes," one replied. "Are you a relative?"

"No. I've rented a room from her for over a dozen years, though, and she's like family to me."

The EMT gave him a sad smile. "Then I'm sorry to tell you that she passed away. It was sudden. A heart attack. Nothing could've been done."

"Where are you taking her?" Keaton asked, feeling lost as never before.

"To the morgue," the other guy replied. "Hold on a minute, and we'll get your contact information. They'll be in touch with you."

He watched them carry the stretcher to the ambulance as dozens of people looked on. Their next-door neighbor, Alicia, came over and slipped an arm about him.

"I was with her, Keaton. She was watering the roses. One minute, we were talking, and the next? She let go of the hose and crumpled to the ground. I called 911. Tried to do CPR." Her eyes welled with tears. "I'm so sorry for your loss."

He squeezed her hand. "Thank you for what you did, Alicia."

"Let me know what I can do. You know she didn't have any family. She's been renting this house for over twenty years. I'm sure the landlord will be here and take possession as soon as he can. If I were you, I'd remove whatever you want of hers, otherwise that greedy bastard will keep it and sell it."

"Okay," he said numbly, heading toward the EMT who now approached him.

He received a sheet of paper, and it contained a number to call for more information. Keaton also provided his name and cell number to the health worker.

"Again, sorry for your loss," the EMT said.

"Thank you," he said faintly, looking around and seeing the crowd dispersing. It included the couple who had fostered him. They still lived across the street, and he had never spoken to them since the day they told him to leave.

Keaton returned inside, the good news he had been ready to share now seeming like nothing at all.

"No," he said aloud. "Miss Peggy would've been proud of me. She always told me I would make something of myself as an artist. Now, I'm going to do just that."

The last word faded, and Keaton gave into the tears. He had lost his best friend today. The door was closing on his past.

And he needed to look to his future.

Chapter One

DALLAS—FOUR-AND-A-HALF YEARS LATER …

Layne Larson removed her two diplomas from Southern Methodist University from the wall behind her desk and placed them in the small box sitting on her desk. This day was bittersweet. The company she had worked for since obtaining her BBA in accounting from SMU had been sold an hour ago. She was making out like a bandit, being given a severance package worth two years' salary, plus COBRA health benefits for a year. While she had started in accounting at the small firm, she had quickly moved over to the tech side. Several of her innovations and creations had caused the company to increase in profits and prestige, and she would be leaving with a sterling reputation as its CFO and enough from the buyout to take her time before deciding where she wanted to work next.

She would like to take some time off and travel. She came from a small town on the Texas coast, twenty miles from Corpus Christi. Driftwood Bay was a sleepy place, and she had been eager to leave it. Everyone knew everyone's business in a small town, and she had been thrilled to win a Presidential Scholarship to SMU. She had hoped for a sports scholarship since she was a terrific soccer player, but the academic full ride to a prestigious university such as SMU was too good to pass up.

Knowing this day was approaching, Layne had taken home a few things here and there over the past two weeks. She pulled a few photos from the walls now, adding them to her box. Pictures of her at various charity events with players from Dallas' professional sports teams. One of her and the city's mayor. Another with her and fellow board of trustees members at SMU. Though she was only thirty, she had packed a lot of business into her twenties.

Now, she wanted to play a little. Maybe go to Europe. See Paris. Rome. London. Take a river cruise down the Danube. She'd love to see the pyramids of Giza and the Northern Lights in Iceland. Every day—weekends included—had been work, work, work. It was time to take a step back and reassess her life. Aim for more of a work/life balance.

She only wondered if Jeremy would be a part of this next chapter.

Jeremy Riggs had been her boyfriend the past five years. They had lived together three of those. While Layne had gone to night school at SMU to earn her MBA, Jeremy had taken two years off to attend classes during the day—with her footing the bill. Jeremy was forever broke, despite working in several high-profile, high-paying jobs. He never seemed happy at any of them. He never remained employed long, always complaining about his boss or the workload or anything else he could think of. Everything was always someone else's fault, and he never seemed happy in his professional life.

Layne was the one who had bought the house in Lakewood. She paid all the bills, from utilities to streaming services. When she asked, he would kick in half of that month's mortgage, but plenty of months had gone by without Jeremy contributing a cent. At least she had only put her name on the deed.

She slipped into her wool coat and gathered her box in her arms and stood at the door, saying goodbye to her corner office with its spectacular view. Her assistant was wiping away tears as Layne hugged her and passed over her keys to the leased car which had been provided to her.

"Here's the keys to the Lexus. I'm going to miss driving that car."

Her assistant accepted them, as well as the office ID badge. "I'll miss you, Layne."

"I'll miss you, too."

As she made her way to the elevator, she waved at various people. Some, like her assistant, would be staying on. Most of the higher ups were being let go. They had built the company from its infancy to world player, but now their baby had outgrown them. She knew she would find a new challenge after she took a much-needed break.

In the elevator, she heard Christmas music playing. Christmas was on a Sunday this year. Her dad had hinted about her coming home to Driftwood Bay for the holiday, but she had told him that she needed to stay in town and finish up all her obligations to her company. Her dad was the only person she had confided in regarding the company's sale and her compensation package. He had told her how proud he was of her and all her many accomplishments and how much he loved her.

Maybe she and Jeremy could catch a flight tomorrow and join her parents for the weekend. Then again, flights were probably booked. They could drive, but Jeremy whined if any car trip lasted over an hour. Besides, her parents didn't like him and made no secret about it. Dad had told her Jeremy was using her as a sugar mama.

As she was slowing down and reevaluating her life, Layne was beginning to agree.

Her mom had been acting distant lately anytime Layne called. She couldn't quite place her finger on what was wrong, but Mom just wasn't acting like herself. Maybe she could go down to the coast for a week or so after Christmas, minus Jeremy, and get in a good visit with her parents. Hopefully, she could spend some time with Mila, too. Her longtime friend had just married Driftwood Bay's basketball coach three weeks ago. Layne had flown down the morning of the wedding, played maid of honor, celebrated briefly at the reception, and then returned to Dallas, where she and Jeremy had then spent Thanksgiving with his family two days later.

PIPER, her other good friend from kindergarten, wouldn't be in Driftwood Bay. She performed in musical theater and was always crisscrossing the country. Piper had worked her way up the ladder from chorus to secondary to leading roles ever since graduating from college. She was now touring in a production of *Chicago*, which had just finished a run in Chicago and would be heading to the West Coast. Seattle would be its first stop, with shows starting two days after Christmas. Layne thought the company was headed to Sacramento next.

Layne owed both Piper and Mila a long FaceTime chat, especially since she was now unemployed. Maybe they could take a girls' trip somewhere once Piper's latest tour ended. Or she and Mila could surprise Piper and fly out to the West Coast. Since Mila's volleyball had ended, hopefully she could take a few days off from school. Then again, her friend was a newlywed and probably wouldn't be interested in leaving Carson and Lily for a few days.

In the lobby, she brought up her rideshare app and placed

an order for a car since her company car was a thing of the past. Living in Dallas, she would need a vehicle to get around. She added car shopping to her to-do list as she waited in front of the building for four minutes. Her driver arrived, and she gave him the code texted to her to confirm he was the correct driver for her trip.

As he drove through downtown Dallas, decorated with Christmas wreaths, Layne faced a reality she had put off for far too long. She and Jeremy had become more like roommates than lovers. When she got home, she would confront him about that and see if she really wanted a future with him.

Her gut told her no. That moment of clarity let her know it was time to cut ties. Enjoy being on her own for a while before looking for a new partner.

She thanked her driver, giving him a five-star rec and tipping him generously as she headed up the sidewalk and let herself inside. As she shed her coat, Layne heard rap music blaring and knew Jeremy was already home. Setting her box on a table in the entryway, she made her way to the kitchen and poured herself a glass of Moscato as she slipped off her black stilettos. She promised her feet she wouldn't put on a pair of heels for at least a month.

Jeremy wandered into the kitchen, barefoot, wearing nothing but sweatpants. She recalled him saying that he had Friday and Monday off for Christmas, but this was Wednesday. Her gut told her that he had probably quit another job and had yet to tell her.

"You're home early. It's just now three. I can't remember the last time you left work in the middle of the afternoon."

Suddenly, everything about him bothered her. Yes, he was definitely easy on the eyes, his body being the only thing he was truly dedicated to. Jeremy worked out religiously, lifting weights and running on alternate days. He had toned muscles and a handsome face, but for the life of her, Layne couldn't remember what she had seen in him. It made what she was about to discuss suddenly easier.

"I've got some news," she said loudly. "Can you turn the music off?"

He slipped his cell from his pocket and hit a button. Blessed silence filled the air.

Going to the fridge, he took out a beer and popped the top before taking a seat at the kitchen table.

"What news? A raise?" he asked, his eyes gleaming with interest.

"No."

Suddenly, Layne didn't want to tell him about the severance package. About wanting to take some time off to relax. All she could see was greed in his eyes.

"My company was sold earlier today," she announced.

His eyes narrowed. "Did you know that was coming?"

"Yes. I've been a part of the plans."

Anger sparked in his eyes. "Babe, we could've made a killing. Sold your stock. Make a tidy profit. I'm pissed you didn't say anything."

"Uh, that's illegal, Jeremy," she pointed out.

He shrugged. "No one ever cares about that stuff."

"Well, I do," she said, downing the rest of her wine and setting the glass on the counter. Layne leaned against it, deciding to test him, wanting to see if he would respond differently from what she expected.

"Where do you see us in a year? Five years? Ten?"

A scowl immediately appeared. "I don't need that kind of pressure coming from you," he said flatly.

"Do you at least think we'll be living together? Engaged?" she pressed.

His jaw set stubbornly. "Marriage is old-fashioned. We don't need that."

"Then what about goals? For our relationship. The direction we're headed. Have you ever thought about having kids?"

"No way. Kids are messy. They take up all your time with sports practices and tournaments. Music lessons. School programs. I like it just being us."

It struck her that they never did anything as a couple. True, she was always working, but he went out for drinks. Dinners. Football games and movies with his friends.

"When was the last time we went on a date?" she asked.

"Date?" He looked at her blankly.

"Yes. Just the two of us. Going to dinner. Seeing a movie. Walking in the park."

He rolled his eyes.

And that caused something to snap in Layne.

"Give me your key," she demanded. "Go to a hotel tonight. I'll pack up the rest of your things, and you can pick everything up tomorrow."

"What? Are you serious?" he asked, shooting to his feet. "What brought this on? Wanting to get engaged. Having kids. Losing your job. This is upsetting me, Layne. I don't like how you're pushing me."

She placed her hands on her hips. "You bet I am. Right out the door. We're done, Jeremy. We've been done for a long time. I just didn't see it or want to acknowledge it. You don't care about me. I can't remember the last time you told me you loved me. The last time you did a little something special for me. Instead, you ride my train, letting me pay for everything."

"You are such a bitch," he said, hate flaring in his brown eyes. "I do plenty for you."

"Name one thing. Just one."

She glared at him defiantly. He glared right back, but she saw he had nothing.

"See? You've used me. I paid for your MBA. I'm sympathetic when you complain about work. I've watched you quit job after job, trying to find yourself. I've been nothing but supportive, financially and emotionally, and you've given me nothing in return. I can't believe I've wasted so much time on you."

Jeremy threw his beer can at her. Layne ducked in time, and it hit the wall, beer splashing everywhere.

"You're never home," he shouted. "You are the most emotionally unavailable person on the planet. All you do is work. You've never even taken time to put up a Christmas tree. You say you've been here for me, but when's the last time we had sex?"

She frowned—and couldn't come up with an answer.

"See? That's why I've been screwing around on you. For years, Layne. Years! And you haven't even noticed. You're a coldhearted, selfish—"

"Enough!" she shouted, humiliation filling her, learning he had been with other women.

And that some of what he said about her rang true.

"Keys," she said. "Now. You've got five minutes to get out before I call the police. And don't think I won't. My name is on the deed. I've asked you to leave. I never want to see you again, you asshole."

He stormed from the room, cursing the entire while. Layne willed herself not to cry, knowing he would view that as a victory over her. Jeremy had always thought crying was a sign of weakness. She used to cry at movies they watched or books she read. He had made fun of her enough times that she finally stopped. She had become what she thought he wanted, something that was so far from who she was that she didn't even recognize herself anymore.

All she wanted to do was curl into a ball and sob. Her twenties were gone. At thirty, she might be thriving professionally, but her personal life had just imploded.

Layne went to wait by the door. Jeremy appeared with his gym bag. It wasn't even zipped. Clothes spilled from the top of it.

"I'll have your clothes sitting out front in boxes by nine tomorrow morning," she told him. "Don't bother ringing the doorbell."

"What about my other stuff?"

"What other stuff?" she demanded. "I've paid for every stick of furniture in this house. Every dish and glass in the kitchen. The food in the pantry and refrigerator."

"My golf clubs," he threw out.

She didn't bother pointing out that she had paid for those, as well, although they had been a Christmas gift for him. It struck her that she'd been so busy with work that she hadn't even shopped for a present for him—and she knew he hadn't gotten anything for her.

"The clubs will be waiting," she said, deflating, the anger leaving her, replaced by an emptiness.

Jeremy threw the kiss at her feet and left without another word, slamming the door behind him. She would need to change the locks because she didn't trust that he didn't have another key squirreled away somewhere. Oh, she needed a change. A big change. Traveling sounded good. Going places and being anonymous. Eating great food and drinking even better wine. And when all that was done, she was selling the house and leaving Dallas. Maybe she'd find work in Houston. Or somewhere really different. Chicago. L.A. Even New York.

She'd gained contacts and wouldn't be shy about using them. Her life was going to take a whole new turn, and she was ready to end her time in Dallas for good.

Layne wanted to call Mila and Piper, but she was afraid she would start bawling like a baby when she saw their concerned faces. Instead, she told Alexa to play Christmas music and spent the next hour packing Jeremy's things. She wanted every trace of him gone from the house. She decided she'd sell the house as soon as she could. Everything here reminded her of her ex. She'd picked out furniture he liked. Painted the walls in colors he wanted. It was time to take charge of her life and find out who she really was.

The doorbell rang, surprising her. She bristled with anger, thinking Jeremy was crawling back, ready to make nice with her and try to win his way back into her good graces. Hell, no. That was *not* happening. Not now. Not ever. Any argument he brought up, Layne would shoot down. She'd been on the debate team in high school and could argue logically and passionately.

She would make toast of him.

When she opened the door, ready to let Jeremy have it, she froze.

Elmo Roberts stood on the porch. Piper's dad. From Driftwood Bay. The moment was surreal, as if he were a mirage. She hadn't a clue why he would be standing on her porch four days before Christmas.

"Layne?" he said, his voice deep and rumbling.

"Mr. Roberts? What are you doing here in Dallas?"

"Can I come in?"

"Of course," she said quickly, ushering him into the foyer and closing the door to the cold air coming in.

"Layne, honey. I've got some bad news," he began. "The kind of news you need to hear in person."

She shook her head. "You're not making any sense, Mr. Roberts."

He took her elbow and led her into the den. She took a seat on the sofa, and he sat next to her.

"There's no good way to say this. Your mama and daddy are gone."

"Gone?" she asked, still confused by his sudden appearance.

"Layne," he said more firmly, and she realized he was speaking in his police chief voice. "Your parents are dead."

Shock reverberated through her. "Dead?" she echoed, repeating—but not comprehending—the word.

Mr. Roberts took her hand, squeezing it. "Yes, honey. I thought you needed to hear it in person and not over the phone."

"You drove all the way up here to tell me," she said dully, reality beginning to set in. "What ... happened?"

"I think this might explain things," he said, removing an envelope from his coat's inner pocket and handing it to her.

With trembling fingers, she opened it, withdrawing the single page and unfolding it. Layne recognized her father's writing and began to read.

> *Layne –*
>
> *I know you're going to have a lot of questions, and I'm sorry I won't be around to answer them for you. The most important thing to know is that we love you.*
>
> *Your mama has a brain tumor. The doctors said it's the inoperable kind. It's been pressing on her brain, and I've watched her becoming a different person. Not the warm, loving gal I married all those years ago, but a stranger. Distant. Unemotional. The doctors said her personality might change, and it has. The last few days,*

she's become angry. Out of control. And it was only going to get worse.

I couldn't stand by and watch her become something she would loathe. I also couldn't lose her and be left alone. Lark has been my everything, from the first night we met and danced together, every step matching, even our heartbeats in sync. She's my whole world.

Because of that, I decided to take matters into my own hands. By the time you read this, we'll both be gone. She didn't suffer. I crushed up a bunch of pills she's been taking and put it in her tea. I didn't have enough for me, but I looked on the internet and figured out that one shot, aimed at the right place, was all it would take and that it happens so fast, it wouldn't hurt.

I'm just sorry we didn't get to see you one more time, baby. Know that we're both proud of you and all you've accomplished. You are the best thing we ever did together, and I only hope that you'll find your soulmate, the same as we did.

Everything we have went into the Bay Breeze. The inn is now yours to do with as you wish. Keep it and hire someone to run it. Sell it and not have to worry about the responsibility it brings. The decision is yours to make.

We love you, Layne.

Daddy

Layne looked up to Mr. Roberts, tears streaming down her cheeks. She would never see her parents again. Never share good news or bad with them. Smell Mama's perfume or Dad's aftershave. They were gone, a murder-suicide. Guilt flooded her, and she wished she had taken more time to call. To investigate and press harder when her mom seemed off.

She'd spent too much time wrapped up in work. It had become everything to her, and now she was left with nothing.

At the same time, Layne realized that she'd been given a second chance, with the Bay Breeze Inn going to her. She would make the most of this second chance.

And start a new chapter of her life in Driftwood Bay.

Chapter Two

DRIFTWOOD BAY

Immediately upon rising, Keaton made his bed. It was just the way he rolled. Living alone, he could've let lots of things slide, but he preferred to behave the same way when others were watching him as when they weren't. That meant he used the shower squeegee on the glass door. Never left dishes in the sink. Always picked up and kept his rental neat.

He also felt it was important to tip service workers, and he did so generously, from the barista who made his coffee at Coastal Roast to servers in the restaurants he patronized in the Bay. He wasn't so far removed from living paycheck to paycheck and knew tips were not a luxury for them. They were a necessity.

Dressing in sweats, he left the house for his daily, five-mile jog. It was a time he looked forward to every morning. The run cleared his head. Centered him for the day. And it let him indulge in drinking beer. Bayside Brewery, a local craft beer hall, had become a place he enjoyed going to sip beer and people-watch.

Once he returned home, Keaton showered, shaved, and

dressed for the day, deciding to go into the gallery and catch up on paperwork. He had opened Gulf Coastal Gallery six months ago, not only to showcase his own art, but that of local artists along the Texas Gulf Coast. The gallery was only open three days a week now, due to it being post-tourist season, but it was still thriving. He enjoyed displaying all kinds of art, from paintings and sculptures to photographs and textile art, as well as highlighting other artists.

Keaton made himself a cup of coffee and a bowl of cereal and scrolled through his phone over breakfast, seeing what had happened in national and international news overnight. He wasn't into social media and had no profiles on any of the popular platforms. Just as he had learned the ins and outs of creating a website for himself as an artist, he had also built a website for the gallery, updating it regularly. He took pride in being self-sufficient and learning new things.

Rinsing his mug and bowl, he placed them in the full dishwasher and started it, turning the magnet from clean to dirty. He would need to stop at the grocery store later today to pick up a few things for Christmas dinner, which was two days away. Keaton had no family, but he had made some friends in the seven months he had resided in Driftwood Bay and would be sharing Christmas dinner with Mila's parents and family. Mila and Carson lived across the street from him, in a house they were caring for while its owner professor was on sabbatical in Australia for a year. The couple had also broken ground on a house down the street, having first razed the dilapidated house sitting on the property. His other friend, Sullivan Shepherd, had designed the house and would help oversee its building. Sullivan had returned to New York to spend Christmas with his family, something he hadn't been looking forward to.

Keaton was eager to also be in his own place instead of renting. Money was no object because of his soaring career, but he was picky when it came to real estate. He wanted to be on the water, which soothed his soul. It was the reason he had moved to Driftwood Bay on a whim after living for two years in the Wyoming mountains at Jackson Hole. House inventory in the Bay was low, however, and his realtor, Hillary Horton, had broadened the search from existing homes to open waterfront property, where he could build from scratch. If he didn't insist on having an art studio on the grounds, he might have decided to live on a houseboat, but that wouldn't be conducive for painting. He just hoped Hillary would find something soon. He was ready to work with Sullivan and build his dream home, sinking roots into a community which had welcomed him.

Before he headed to the gallery, he made a stop at Coastal Charms Boutique, a shop on the town's square, which was owned by Mila's mother. He picked up a pair of silver hoop earrings, having the clerk wrap them in Christmas paper before he drove to the waterfront. The area was full of restaurants and shops, and he had lucked into renting space at the end of a long row of businesses for Gulf Coast Gallery.

Pulling up to park, he saw Stacy's car. He had been fortunate to land Stacy to run the gallery for him, freeing himself up to paint. She had been an art history major in college who had taught art at the local middle school for several years. When he first opened his gallery, she had come in to peruse the art, telling him that she was a former painter who no longer had time to paint. Keaton was a good judge of character, and his gut told him that Stacy was the answer to a question he didn't even know he was asking.

He had flat out asked her during that first meeting if she would be interested in managing his new gallery, saying she could hire as much help as she wished. Keaton explained he wanted it open seven day a week during tourist season, from ten to seven, but after summer ended, the gallery times would cut back to three days a week. Stacy had leapt at the chance for a career change and resigned from her teaching position. With her two teenagers busy with school and extracurricular activities and a recent divorce behind her, she had thrived both as a manager and now artist, taking time to reacquaint herself with her passion for painting.

Stacy had two paintings on display at the gallery now, along with some shell art she had created using local shells and driftwood found along the shore. She was balancing her time and making the most of it, and Keaton could tell she was a much happier woman than the one he had met back in June.

He entered the gallery, and his employee gave him a smile, rising to greet him. She worked the three days a week herself during the off-season, deciding to only hire additional help during the long summer hours. The rest of the time she painted in her converted garage, which now served as her studio.

"Haven't seen you in a week, Keaton."

He handed her the small package. "Merry Christmas, Stacy."

"Why, thank you, Boss."

She went to the desk she had been sitting at and opened a drawer, handing him an envelope with Christmas stickers adorning in. They both opened their gifts simultaneously, with her exclamation of pleasure over the earrings, while he thanked her for the concert tickets to see a country artist whose music he had mentioned to her that he enjoyed. Case Wellborne had been a part of Keaton's construction crew years ago, as well as an inspiration to him. Case began playing shows around Dallas and eventually landed a recording contract. He'd left the crew to pursue music full-time. Since Case had made it, Keaton had pushed himself, hoping he could follow in the other man's footsteps. Now, he owned his own gallery and commanded hefty prices for his landscapes. It was nice to think that both he and Case had made something of themselves.

Glancing at the date on the tickets, he saw the concert was in Houston.

"Houston?" he asked.

Stacy shrugged. "I knew you said you liked Case Wellborne's music. He wasn't coming to Corpus on the tour, and the San Antonio date was sold out. Houston was as close as I could get." She paused, studying him. "I insist you go, Keaton. Not because I gave you the tickets but because you need to get out. Think about more than painting."

He looked at the tickets again, seeing the concert wasn't for a few months.

He wondered if he would ask anyone to accompany him to it. Maybe this would motivate him to look for a date.

"I can't thank you enough for changing the trajectory of my life," Stacy told him. "I existed all these years, teaching art to uninterested students, putting my own art on a back burner. Working at Gulf Coastal Gallery has not only given me the opportunity to step back into the art world again, but I also have time now to pursue painting."

"I'm thankful we connected," he said. "Now, why don't you go on and leave? Nobody is shopping for art two days before Christmas. And remember, I'm closing the gallery until after New Year's."

"I'm so grateful for the time off. Blake is playing in a basketball tournament after Christmas, and I'll be able to make every game with the gallery closed."

"I'm going to stay and play with the books a while," he said. "Enjoy Christmas with your family."

"Have a Merry Christmas, Keaton," Stacy said, slipping

into her jacket and claiming her purse from the bottom desk drawer.

After she left, he flipped the sign on the door from open to closed and retreated to his office in the back, beyond the storeroom. He put the tickets in the lap drawer and then went through the books for the last month, making a few payments and handling some dental insurance for a claim with Stacy's son. He also emailed three artists about which pieces of work they would like to have on display at the gallery come the new year. Each had sold a piece or two in the past few weeks. When the gallery reopened after the holidays, he wanted the public to be greeted with fresh art, from paintings to sculptures to mixed media pieces.

He heard a loud banging on the door and figured someone must be desperate for a last-minute Christmas present. Glancing at his watch, he saw it was almost three o'clock. He made his way back into the gallery showroom and saw his real estate agent on the other side of the glass door. Unlocking the door, he let her in.

"Do you ever answer your phone, Keaton Maxwell?" she chided gently in a motherly tone.

He tapped his hand against his pocket, realizing he had left his phone on the breakfast table. He wasn't a person glued to his cell as others were, texting every five minutes and scrolling through and posting on Instagram.

"Sorry. What's up?" he asked.

"Since the gallery is closed, you have time to come with me now. I found it. The property you've been wanting."

His heart quickened. "Where is it located? Does it have enough acreage to build a good-sized house, plus an art studio in back?"

"It's definitely waterfront property, but you won't need to

build. A house already sits on the land, along with a gatekeeper's cottage, which would be ideal for your studio."

He frowned. "Where? Whose house?"

"John Smith."

"John Smith, the tech guy?"

Smith was the most famous resident of the Bay. He had developed a dating app which had gone viral and was still popular fifteen years later. He had also created a new social media platform which teenagers and young adults flocked to.

"Why would John Smith want to sell? I've driven by the house, and it's gorgeous. He'd be crazy to leave it."

"It's Anna Smith who is wanting to move. Both their children live in the Houston area, and that means their grandchildren do, too. Anna has been working on John to move ever since the third grandbaby arrived this spring. She's finally convinced him the time is right."

Excitement rippled through him. "So, they've put the house on the market."

"No. It's a pocket listing. That means it's not on the market just yet, but I'm allowed to show it to whomever I choose." Hillary grinned. "I choose *you*. The Smiths closed on a house in Houston three days ago, and I just got off the phone with Anna. They've also bought a summer beach house in Galveston. That way, the entire family can spend long weekends together by the water."

She smiled. "I'm sorry I couldn't share anything about the listing with you before now. Anna and John are very quiet, private people, and they didn't want word getting out about the sale. Now that they've purchased something new, I have permission to show the house. You were the only person I thought of."

"Then let's go see it," he said, not hiding his enthusiasm.

Keaton retrieved his jacket and told Hillary he would meet her at the property.

When he pulled up in front of the house, his gut told him this would be his forever home, based on the outside alone. He had salivated when driving past this house ever since moving to the Bay. It was a mixture of wood and glass, with beautiful landscaping.

He wanted it.

Hillary was getting out of her sedan, and Keaton joined her.

"Let's walk the exterior first while I tell you a little about the house," she suggested.

As they moved about the property, he learned that it was over four thousand square feet, with five bedrooms and six bathrooms. A three-car garage. It had a private beach area at one end and a dock and boathouse at the other.

"If you decide to move forward, the cigarette boat will be included in the purchase price. Anna said it would be simpler for them to buy a new boat in Galveston rather than transport this one up there."

The backyard also included a long, rectangular pool and a sleek, covered patio running the entire length of the house. It had various sitting areas cooled by ceiling fans, along with an outdoor kitchen. He couldn't have dreamed up something so perfect.

They entered from the rear of the house and stepped into the great room. The entire wall of this room which faced the ocean was made of glass, making for a spectacular view. Hillary escorted him through the first floor of the house, pointing out various things, and he saw there would be no updates needed.

Reading his mind, the realtor said, "Anna redid the kitchen and all the bathrooms two years ago, anticipating this move. It really is turnkey, Keaton."

"Let's see the rest of it," he said, knowing in his heart that the realtor had already made her sale.

Once they had seen the upstairs and returned to the first floor, Hillary said, "Oh, I forgot! We didn't go to the caretaker's cottage. It's actually on the east side, and we didn't go around that way."

As they exited through glass doors onto the deck again, he asked, "Will the caretaker mind us going through it?"

"Anna just called the structure that. They've never had a caretaker. The previous owners did. Anna simply had housekeepers come in for cleaning. A landscaping company tends to the grass and flowers. If you're interested in using the same crews, I can pass along that information to you."

She looked at him hopefully. "That is, if you're interested."

"You know I'm interested. This is everything I was hoping for. More, actually. I can't think of one box on my list which this doesn't check. Hell, it even added things to the list that I didn't even know I wanted. Like the coffee bar."

She opened the door to the cottage, and they went inside the empty structure. The entire space was probably twenty by thirty feet, with a small kitchen area running along part of the back wall. The farmer's sink would be perfect for rising his brushes. He also could put in a fridge so he would have drinks and snacks available and not have to return to the main house when he was working.

Hillary showed him a full bath which was off the kitchen, along with a large closet where he could store his art supplies and completed canvasses.

"How much will this set me back?" he asked.

She named the price, which Keaton thought was reasonable for a type of property this size in this market and location.

"If everything passes inspection—which I'm certain it will —you can count me in," he told her.

"It's too late to have anyone out today, especially with tomorrow being Christmas Eve. I'll set up the inspections for Monday. Tuesday at the latest in case they already have something on the books. Do you mind if we call the Smiths now and give them the good news?"

"Sounds good to me," he said, grinning from ear to ear.

Hillary put the call on speaker. "Anna, it's Hillary. I've found a buyer for your house."

"Oh, Hillary, I am delighted to hear that. You did it so fast. Is it someone local?"

"Yes, and you know him. Keaton Maxwell. He's with me now on speaker, Anna."

"Mr. Maxwell, I am so happy our home will go to a good person. I'm sure you noticed one of your paintings hanging in my husband's study."

"Yes, ma'am, I did. I remember you coming into the gallery this summer and purchasing it. I believe you said it was a birthday gift."

"Well, I know Hillary will need to set up things on her end. Inspections. Paperwork and whatnot. John and I will need to contact a moving company on our end. Oh, I dread all the packing. Are you eager to close quickly?" Anna asked.

"Take as long as you need, Mrs. Smith. I'm in a rental and extending month-by-month while I've been looking for my permanent home in the Bay. As of now, I'm contracted through the end of January."

"Then that should be plenty of time for the sale to go through and us to be out," Anna assured him. Again, I'm thrilled the house is going to you. I hope you will enjoy your time in it."

Hillary said, "I'll return to the office now and get the paperwork started. I'll message everything to your attorney in Corpus. Have a wonderful Christmas with your family, Anna."

"The same to you, Hillary, dear. And Merry Christmas to you, Mr. Maxwell."

"Goodbye, Mrs. Smith. And thank you for entrusting your home to me."

He beamed at his realtor. "I'm actually going to be a home-owner in Driftwood Bay. Want to go for a celebratory drink?"

"No, I'll let you do that, Keaton. I want to get these inspections scheduled and the paperwork rolling. Knowing the Smiths' attorney is a workaholic, he'll be in his office for at least part of tomorrow and want to review everything. I should have things back from him come Monday."

"Just text when we need to meet. For inspections and the closing. I'll contact my landlord and let him know I won't be renewing beyond the end of January."

Since they were so close to the Pelican Porch, Keaton decided to have a drink there before going home. He had some leftover pizza from Pizza Perfecto that would serve as dinner tonight. But for now, he wanted to sit in a classy place and celebrate his decision to purchase the Smiths' home.

Usually, Ben Chastain, the owner, greeted customers, but a woman in her mid-twenties was serving as hostess tonight. He approached the stand as she scrolled through her phone.

Glancing up, she said, "Sit anywhere. We're not busy."

He looked around, seeing only one couple in a booth and a guy he thought might be his mailman at the bar.

"I'll head to the bar," he told her as her eyes returned to her phone.

Keaton took a seat, and the bartender asked, "What'll it be?"

"A Sazerac."

"Going fancy tonight, I see. Coming right up."

He watched the bartender mix the drink, which was basi-cally an Old Fashioned, with whiskey and sugar, but with the added element of absinthe, which gave the taste of black licorice to every sip.

"Here you go," the bartender said, sliding the drink over atop a napkin.

Keaton took it and spun his stool so he faced out.

Then he saw her.

She was sitting on the opposite side of the room, but he recognized her right away.

Layne. The woman from Carson and Mila's wedding. He remembered hearing that she and Mila were tight since kindergarten, along with another friend who couldn't make the impromptu ceremony. Though they'd only spoken briefly, he'd been taken with her quiet beauty. The bob-length caramel brown hair. The moss green eyes. The slender build with a hint of curves. In their short conversation, she had mentioned her boyfriend, who hadn't been able to come to the wedding since it was the Tuesday before Thanksgiving and he had just started a new job. Keaton, who had been ready to flirt with her, got the message and backed off.

What was she doing back in Driftwood Bay already? He was positive she had mentioned going to the boyfriend's parents for Christmas. Yet here she was, all alone.

He decided it couldn't hurt to go and say hi and took his drink, moving quietly across the bar. Sliding into the opposite seat of the booth, she looked up. Immediately, he knew she had been crying. A lot. Her eyes were swollen and red. So was her nose.

"Are you all right, Layne? It's Keaton. Keaton Maxwell. From the wedding."

She bit her lip, nodding woodenly at him. "I remember you," she said softly.

"What can I do to help?" he asked, seeing she was clearly distressed. "Can I call Mila for you?"

"No," she said emphatically. "I just need some time to myself."

Reluctantly, he pushed himself from the booth. "Okay. I just wanted to see if there was anything you needed."

Her gaze met his, tears swimming in her eyes. "Oh, I need a lot of things, Keaton. Most of all ..." Her voice faded out.

He knelt beside her. "Tell me. I'm here for you."

"I could use a friend right now." She gave him a crooked smile. "Even if it's a new friend. Of course, if I start dumping on you, you may run screaming for the hills."

He reached for her hand and squeezed it, finding it cold. "Try me. I'm a pretty steady guy. Not much scares me—or scares me off."

For some reason, holding her hand felt like the best thing in the world. Different from any other time he had ever touched another woman.

Reluctantly, he released it and rose before taking a seat across from her again. "Fire away. Anticipating torpedo number one," he teased, hoping to lighten her mood.

She eyed him sadly. "For starters? My dad killed my mom and then himself."

Her words stunned him, like a punch in the gut. Keaton was rarely left speechless, but he had no idea what to say to her. Layne pulled an envelope from her purse. "He left me this. Chief Roberts came to Dallas and gave it to me. I've read it at least a dozen times since Wednesday. Every time, I keep hoping what's in it will change. That this nightmare loop I'm stuck in will dissolve and everything will go back to normal."

She gazed at him, her eyes brimming with tears, sadness radiating from her. "But then I have to realize that this *is* my new normal."

His heart ached at her words. Reaching for her hand again, he took it.

"Let's read it together. Then we'll go from there."

Chapter Three

Layne hadn't needed Keaton Maxwell to introduce himself to her.

She knew exactly who he was.

When they had met at Mila's wedding a few weeks ago, she had experienced a surprising attraction to the handsome artist, drawn in by his penetrating azure eyes. It had been years since she'd felt a sexual spark of such magnitude, and she had quickly mentioned how her boyfriend hadn't been able to accompany her to the coast for the quickly arranged wedding on the Tuesday before Thanksgiving. Keaton had picked up on her subtle message that she was taken, and she sensed he backed off, continuing their brief conversation before excusing himself.

Layne was thrilled that Mila had landed a good guy in Carson, and her gut told her that Carson's friend was also cut from the same cloth. Especially now, with him holding her hand and offering to read the letter Jack Larson had penned. Her hand cradled by his brought not only warmth, but a comfort, and she was badly in need of a little sympathy.

She held her breath as he read the letter. Layne was aware of the tang of his citrus cologne, a subtle scent which suited him. He resembled the stereotype of a surfer, with his dirty blond hair, deep tan, and lean frame. She told herself to tamp down the attraction she was feeling. Having just gotten out of a long-term relationship with Jeremy, she was not in the market to replace him with a new man in her life anytime soon.

But as she had told Keaton, she could use a friend.

He placed the page on the table and took a sip of his drink. Then he turned to her. His crystal eyes held empathy.

"I can't imagine the world of hurt you're in, Layne," he said, his hand tightening slightly around hers. "To lose both parents at the same time in such a way is rough. Were you close to them?"

She nodded. "More to Dad than Mom these past few years, but we've always been tight. I never went through a rebellious streak in my teen years. I made good grades. Played soccer. Was a debater. My parents came to every event and supported me. I'm an only child, so they took Mila and Piper in, knowing my best friends were like sisters to me."

"Have you talked to either of them?" he asked.

"No." The word came out as a whisper. "I'm afraid to."

"Why? I've gotten to know Mila through Carson, and she's an incredible woman. You need to lean on her. And Piper. They're the sisters of your heart for a reason."

"I know," she acknowledged, tears misting her eyes. "It's just that everything has crashed and burned. I'm confused. Hurt. Lost," she admitted.

Keaton studied her a moment. "This isn't just about your parents' deaths, is it?"

"No," she said softly. "I broke up with Jeremy, the guy I told you about. We'd been together five years. Living together the last three. I finally realized that I'd fallen out of love with him a long time ago—and that he never really loved me. I kicked him out of our house. No, my house," she corrected. "I bought it and it's in my name. And now the thought of living in it turns my stomach."

He squeezed her hand reassuringly. "You don't have to make a decision about it yet. What's important is to give yourself some time. Don't rush into anything." He paused. "How about work? Can you take a leave of absence?"

She shook her head. "That won't be necessary. As of two days ago, I'm unemployed. Long story short, my small company was bought out by a larger one. I was given a terrific package to leave. So, I can move anywhere I want. Take my time before I take the next step professionally. I'd thought I might want to travel a bit." Layne bit her lip. "After I came down to spend Christmas with Mom and Dad."

Tears welled in her eyes again, spilling onto her cheeks. Keaton removed a handkerchief from his pocket and instead of offering it to her, he brushed away the tears himself. The tender gesture nearly did her in.

"Cry for your parents—but don't you dare shed a tear for the sorry asshole who took you for granted," he advised.

She couldn't help but chuckle. "Understood."

"Okay, anymore bombshells to drop on me? We've covered your parents' deaths. Your jobless status. And your ending a long relationship. You should probably get to the really big stuff now."

Layne saw the teasing light in his eyes, and it was just the medicine she needed. "I think that about covers it. Other than wanting to sell my house and inheriting the B&B, that is."

A shadow crossed his face. "Have you been there yet?"

"No. I drove by when I got into town, but I had already scheduled a meeting with the funeral director. I went to that and then came straight here." She swallowed. "I'm afraid to go inside. Chief Roberts told me that he would take care of things for me. That there would be no crime scene tape when I arrived and everything would be … cleaned up. He'll notify me after the autopsies are completed in Corpus. Then I can plan the actual funerals."

"That was kind of the chief to come to see you in person," Keaton noted. He dabbed at her eyes again.

"It really was. I've always felt as if I had a second and third set of parents in the Roberts and the Perrys. Growing up, I was at their houses as much as my own. They say it takes a village to raise a child, and my village included Mila and Piper's parents."

"What do you need to do next?" he asked. "You said you'd met with the funeral home."

"Yes. Mom and Dad planned and paid for everything years ago. That was just a formality, with me checking on the arrangements. I'm supposed to meet with the preacher at First Baptist Church once the bodies have been released. To set a date and time for their service."

A fresh wave of sorrow filled her, and she choked on that last word. Keaton released her hand and wrapped his arm about her. Layne buried her face against his hard chest, hot tears flowing again. He took her hand and simply held her. This man was practically a stranger to her, yet he'd shown more kindness in the last quarter-hour than Jeremy had during their entire relationship.

Finally, her tears subsided. She lifted her head. "I'll be all right."

"I know you will. You are a confident, accomplished woman."

She frowned. "You don't even know me."

His gaze pinned hers. "I think I do."

Layne saw that was true. "I suppose your artist's soul sees more than the average person."

"It does. I've been a person who studies people my entire life. I listen. I observe. I learn."

"I'm grateful you were here now. I feel you've gotten me over a hump. I really should call Mila and Piper."

She pulled her cell from her purse and turned it on. Immediately, it exploded with pings of text messages and voicemails.

"I guess the news is out," she said dully.

Keaton brushed a kiss against her hair. "Driftwood Bay *is* a small town."

"Would ... would you stay with me another few minutes while I listen to my messages?"

Determination filled his eyes. "I'm not going anywhere until you tell me to."

"Thank you."

First, Layne read through the texts she had received. Then she listened to concerned messages Mila, Piper, and others had left. It touched her how many cared for her and wanted to help in any way they could.

Placing her phone back in her purse, she looked to Keaton. "I'm ready to go see Mila now."

"Would you like me to drive you?" Keaton asked.

"No. I'm good." She hesitated. "But I wouldn't mind if you came with me. I know you live across the street."

He gave her a crooked smile. "I can do that."

Keaton paid for their drinks and escorted Layne to the car she had rented at the Corpus airport, opening her door for her, another thing Jeremy had never done.

"I'll see you there," he told her.

As she left the parking lot of Pelican Porch and drove to Mila and Carson's house, she felt much stronger than she had half an hour ago. Keaton had a calming effect on her. She hoped that he would become a friend.

She was afraid to think she might want more from him.

That would mean staying in the Bay, and Layne wasn't sure if she wanted to make that kind of commitment. Of the three of them, she had been the one most eager to spread her wings and leave their coastal hometown. She had come to love Dallas, with its incredible restaurants, and she enjoyed wearing high fashion ensembles. The Bay was the complete opposite of the cosmopolitan city.

And yet suddenly Layne found herself yearning for a more simple life.

Could she be happy in Driftwood Bay? Should she consider running the B&B? Then she remembered Keaton's advice. Don't move quickly on any decision. He was right. She was on an emotional roller coaster right now and in no way capable of making decisions of this magnitude.

She pulled to the curb and texted Mila that she was outside, asking if she could come in. Keaton had pulled into the driveway across the street and was crossing it when Mila came bursting out of her house. Layne threw open her car door and hurried to meet her friend.

They crashed into one another, their arms going about each other, both sobbing and babbling. It felt good to be with one of her two best friends. Even though they rarely saw one another, due to their jobs, the trio had remained the closest of friends ever since they had each left the Bay, heading to different colleges and different jobs and lifestyles, even arranging FaceTime calls a few times a month to catch up on what was happening in each other's lives.

"I was so worried when I didn't hear from you," Mila said. "Oh, hi, Keaton. Do you remember Layne?"

"I do," he said, his voice a low rumble, causing that attraction she was feeling to pull her invisibly toward him. "We've been talking at Pelican Porch for a little while."

Mila didn't question either of them. Instead, she said,

"Come on in. It's chilly. I have enchiladas about to come out of the oven. We can have dinner and talk."

Mila took Layne's hand and led her into the house, Keaton following them. Carson greeted her, wrapping her in a bear hug.

"I'm sorry about your parents, Layne," he said. "They were good people."

"They were," she said, her throat thick with emotion. "Sorry I'm interrupting your dinner."

"You're not," he assured her, glancing to Keaton. "You want to stay for dinner?"

"Mila said there were enchiladas. You're not getting rid of me."

His words caused Layne to laugh. She let the laughter flow from her, knowing it was cathartic.

"Come and sit," Mila urged, motioning them into the kitchen. "I'll have everything on the table in a jiffy."

Layne and Keaton moved to the table, and she asked, "Where's Lily?"

"She's with her cousins," Carson said. "They're having a sleepover."

"Lily adores Bobby and Gina," Mila said, opening the oven and taking out a casserole dish. She set it on the table, and Layne inhaled the rich smell of beef enchiladas. "They're all worked up about Santa coming tomorrow night."

"Remember the year we all wanted Barbie sleeping bags?" Layne asked. "I think we were five. No, six."

The conversation flowed easily as they ate. Layne and Mila told stories from their childhood, entertaining Carson and Keaton. In turn, Carson talked a little about his basketball team and the tournament they would be playing in after Christmas. Keaton shared with her a little bit about Gulf

Coastal Gallery, which he'd opened just as tourist season began this past June.

"Keaton hired Miss Reed to be its manager," Mila informed her.

"Miss Reed the art teacher from middle school?" Layne asked. "She was always so nice. I remember she encouraged you, even when everything you painted sucked."

Mila laughed. "I was hopeless at art. Piper wasn't bad, but you were actually pretty good if I remember correctly."

"Miss Reed said I had talent, but Dad said art would never pay the bills. He told me not to bother pursuing it. To stick with making good grades and playing soccer."

"Stacy Reed is an excellent manager," Keaton said. "She's an artist herself, and I have some of her work on display. She's also organized and friendly. She doesn't pressure anyone coming in to buy, and yet a good number of them do."

They finished eating, and Carson told them he'd take care of cleanup. Keaton offered to assist, allowing Layne and Mila to go into the den. They sat on the sofa together, and Mila took Layne's hand.

"What can I do? I know there must be tons to do."

"Mom and Dad already had everything arranged and paid for, so I don't have to make any decision regarding caskets or plots. Chief Roberts explained to me how they were taken to Corpus." She paused. "Because of how they died, autopsies are required."

"And with it almost being a holiday, that probably will delay things," Mila fretted.

"Yes. He's running point for me. They'll contact him, then he'll get in touch with me. He told me I probably wouldn't be able to schedule the services until at least next Thursday or Friday."

"I'm glad he's helping you."

"He flew up to Dallas to break the news to me. I was so shocked to find him on my doorstep." Layne hesitated and then decided to plunge ahead. "I'd just kicked Jeremy out a few hours before that."

"You did? Finally?"

Layne smiled ruefully. "I know you were never a Jeremy fan."

"Neither was Piper," Mila pointed out. "But we tried to support you."

"I was blind to so many things." She let out a long sigh. "I also don't have a job."

"What?"

Briefly, Layne explained her buy-out and how she was planning to take some time off. Possibly travel. Just get to know herself again.

"I guess it's a good thing because I'll need to deal with the B&B now. Thank goodness Mom and Dad always closed it the last two weeks of December for the holidays, but I need to look at the books and see about reservations for the new year. Figure out if I need to hire someone to run it or cancel the upcoming reservations and shutter it until I decide what to do."

"You know you can count on me to help you with anything," her friend said.

"I do know that."

Then Mila asked, "What's the deal with Keaton? I was surprised when you turned up with him. You seem really comfortable with one another."

She shrugged. "I stopped at Pelican Porch to have a drink. I was dreading going home, even though Chief Roberts said everything would look the same. Keaton was there. We talked. He's a good listener."

"He really is," Mila agreed. "He and Carson are both loners. Or at least they were. They've become good friends, along with Sullivan Shepherd. He's the architect who designed Tidewater."

"Oh, the new resort being built, right?"

"Yes. Sullivan flew back to New York for the holidays. He wasn't looking forward to it is all I know. I think he's at odds with his family."

"I'm sorry I ignored your calls," Layne apologized. "I was just trying to wrap my head around everything. I'd suggest we call Piper now, but I know tonight was the last performance of her show before she had a break for a few days."

"Promise you'll call her tomorrow," Mila insisted.

"I will."

Carson and Keaton joined them, and Layne said, "Thanks for letting me invite myself to dinner. Keaton, too."

"Keaton does that enough as it is," Carson joked.

"You need to enjoy the rest of your Lily-free night," she told the newlyweds. "I'll talk with you tomorrow," she assured Mila.

Layne and Keaton walked out together, and he opened her car door for her again.

Before she got in, Layne said, "Thank you for rescuing me. I'm not prone to being a damsel in distress, but I appreciate you stepping in and calming me down."

"I was glad to be there for you," he said, his tone sincere. "Are you heading to the B&B now?"

"Yes," she said, dread filling her suddenly.

"I want to go with you."

His words surprised her. "You don't have to do that, Keaton. I've already taken up enough of your time as it is."

He took a step toward her, slipping his hand around hers. "Let me do this for you, Layne," he said, his voice husky. "After all, you said you needed a friend."

It meant so much to her that he offered to accompany her home.

"I have been reluctant to step inside. I would appreciate you coming with me."

"I'll follow you in my car," he said, letting her get into her rental and then shutting the door.

As she started the car and headed to her childhood home, relief swept through Layne.

And something else which she refused to put a name to.

Chapter Four

Though he followed Layne, Keaton knew exactly where they were going. He had stayed for a few days at the Bay Breeze B&B when he had first arrived in Driftwood Bay.

He had chosen moving to the Bay almost randomly, deciding he needed a change after having lived in the Grand Tetons for two years. He had never seen an ocean. He had missed Texas during his time in Wyoming and decided to move to somewhere on the Gulf Coast. It had been the right decision. Water soothed his soul and centered him. Especially now that he would be living directly on the water in his own house, he was glad he had chosen the Bay as his permanent home.

And glad Layne Larson was here, as well.

Keaton had been taken with her upon their first meeting. Now that he had spent the last several hours with her, he felt even more drawn to her in some inexplicable way. It wasn't simply the sexual attraction. Layne appealed to him in other ways. She had a vulnerability about her now because of the deaths of her parents, but he also sensed the strong core which ran through her. He liked that idea of strength wed with fragility. He told himself to hold back, however. More than anything, Layne needed a friend at this time.

That's what he would be for her now.

He had quite a bit of respect for Mila and enjoyed being around her. Since Layne was a lifelong friend of Mila's, Keaton knew she was what folks in the Bay termed *good people*. He would be her friend as long as she needed him in that capacity. If the time came when she could put her failed relationship behind her and want something more from him, he would be more than willing to give it a try. That in itself surprised him because he, too, was coming off the only serious relationship he had experienced—and it had ended in disaster.

They reached the B&B, both of them parking in front of the large structure. He had found it online after he had perused countless websites and decided Driftwood Bay would be the next chapter in his life. Keaton had been slightly disappointed during his stay at the Bay Breeze, though. The pictures on the website showed a much more vibrant place, but he had found the small inn to be faded, as if it had seen better days. Though outdated, his room had been airy and clean, and the food quite good.

Lark Larson, Layne's mom, had been kind if a little distracted. Knowing now that she had an inoperable brain tumor, he thought her condition must have affected the person she had been and that she had probably been warmer and more outgoing prior to her diagnosis. On the other hand, Jack Larson had been friendly, telling Keaton a few stories about Driftwood Bay's history and asking him about his work as an artist. His artist's eye had noticed a small tremor in the B&B owner's right hand. Every now and then, Jack had also hesitated before he spoke, and Keaton wondered if the man might have Parkinson's disease. If that were the case, he could almost understand why the Larsons had done what they had done, choosing to leave this world with one another, on their own terms.

Getting out of the car, Keaton joined Layne, who stood eyeing her childhood home with trepidation.

"Do you have keys to get in?" he asked.

She nodded, pulling a small key ring from her purse. "Back in the day, I never had a key to the place. No one in the Bay locked their doors. It's only in the last few years that Dad said things had begun to change, and he gave me this set of keys. I assume Chief Roberts has keys to the B&B, as well. My parents and the Roberts were close friends."

"It was kind of him to have everything put back into place for you."

She looked to the porch. "Yes, I'm grateful, but I have no idea where anything took place, as far as their deaths are concerned. That creeps me out a little bit. To be frank, I'm dreading walking through those doors, imaging where Mom and Dad spent their last minutes. That's why I asked you to come with me. I didn't want to face walking in alone."

His fingers found hers, lacing them together. "That's why I'm here. So you don't have to do this alone."

Their gazes met.

"Why are you being so good to me?" she questioned. "You don't really know me."

"I think I have a good handle on who you are, Layne. I've enjoyed the time we've spent together today. I hope you were serious about wanting us to be friends."

"I am," she replied softly.

"Good. Friends are there for one another, in good times and bad. You happened to be in need of a friend now, and I'm happy to be here for you."

"I've never been the needy friend," she admitted. "I've

always been the strong one. The person who everyone leaned on, be it professionally or personally."

"I can understand that," he said. "I'm not much of a leaner myself. More of a loner, truth be told. Things are changing for me, being in the Bay now. I'm more sociable. Making friends." He smiled. "And that includes you."

She signed. "All I wanted to do was get out of my hometown when I turned eighteen. I wanted nothing to do with the Bay. I knew there was this great, big, beautiful life waiting for me, and all I had to do was be brave enough to leave. Spread my wings and fly away. I enjoyed my twenties. I'll openly admit I liked the fast-paced life I led in Dallas. The reputation I built. The fun I had—until I allowed work to absorb too much of my life. That's one thing Jeremy was actually right about. I became a workaholic. Whatever I do next, I want to focus on actually having a work/life balance."

He squeezed her fingers gently. "Remember, you don't have to make any big decision regarding your future in the next day or two. Things that may seem important to you now could change significantly in a week. A month. A year. That's why you shouldn't rush into anything."

Layne laughed. "How old are you, Keaton?"

"I'm thirty-four. Why?"

She studied him a moment. "I'm thirty, not that much younger than you, yet you seem to have this worldly wisdom that I'm sorely lacking."

He smiled. "It's all for show. I'll always be that insecure, undiscovered artist deep inside."

"I want to see your work. I want to hear your story. Not now, but over the next few days." She smiled. "Week. Month. Year," echoing what he had just said to her.

Though he never opened up to others about his past,

suddenly it became important to Keaton for Layne to know exactly who he was.

"Stick around the Bay, and I may just give you access to my deepest, darkest secrets," he teased.

"I suppose we should go inside," she said.

He led her up the porch stairs, and Layne inserted a key into the lock. They entered the foyer and turned on a light. He sensed the staleness in the air, a place which had no occupants anymore.

"It looks ... a little sad," she noted, her gaze sweeping across their surroundings.

"How long has it been since you've been here, Layne?" he asked.

She thought a moment. "Four years, I think. I told you I was a workaholic. I got caught up in my job in Dallas. Jeremy thought Driftwood Bay was boring. We only came down together once, and he told me he had no intentions of returning to such a lame place. I tried to get my parents to come up and see me in Dallas, but they were tied to the inn and taking care of their guests. Even when I came for Mila and Carson's wedding a few weeks ago, I flew in that morning and flew back out early evening. I talked to Mom and Dad at the reception, but I didn't have time to stop by the B&B."

She shuddered visibly. "I feel like I was such a bad daughter. I did stay in touch. I called and talked with Mom once a week. Lately, though, she had only said a few words to me and then passed the phone over to Dad. I tried to get them to Face-Time with me like I do with Mila and Piper a few times a month, but they weren't very tech savvy. Mom didn't even have a cell phone, and Dad refused to give up his flip phone."

Layne cursed under her breath. "I should've visited more. Come back more often. Why didn't I make them a priority?" Tears welled in her eyes.

He released her hand and placed both his hands firmly on her shoulders. "You were a good daughter," he assured her. "Beloved by them. You called weekly. Not many kids take the time to do that. Don't blame yourself for what happened. Your mom couldn't help the diagnosis she received. She couldn't change the outcome. If anything, they were trying to make things easier on you."

She bit her lip, causing a rush of desire to flood Keaton. Quickly, he tamped it down.

"I wish they would've been open with me and let me know what was happening," she said wistfully. "I would have taken a leave of absence from work. Come down and cared for Mom during her last weeks. Part of me is so angry at my dad for taking matters into his own hands. For not letting me come and help."

"A lot of people don't like others to see them vulnerable, especially those they love," he said gently. "Besides, you don't know what was happening in your dad's life. The role of care-giver can be draining. It might have affected his thought process."

Keaton hesitated and then decided to share what he suspected with her.

"I think your dad also might have been ill."

"Why do you say that?" she demanded.

"I stayed here for a few days when I first came to the Bay. I noticed a couple of things about your dad. Things others prob-ably hadn't picked up on yet."

Her eyes widened. "Like what?" she pushed.

"I can't say for sure, but I believe he may have been diag-nosed with Parkinson's. You know I observe others. It's simply second nature to me. I noticed a tremor in his right hand, one which he would cover up by slipping it in his pocket or placing his left hand over it to still it. He also would be talking and then suddenly grow very quiet in volume or hesitate before saying something."

Keaton shrugged. "I googled and found those are some early symptoms of Parkinson's."

A single tear rolled down Layne's cheek, and he wiped it away with the pad of his thumb. Understanding filled her eyes.

"That's why he did it. He knew he wouldn't be able to take care of both of them—and he didn't want me saddled with their care."

Her voice broke on that last word, and Keaton enfolded her in his arms, a fresh round of sobs coming loose. He let her cry it out, knowing the tears were cathartic, enjoying the subtle scent of lavender which clung to her.

Finally, she pulled away from him, shaking her head. "You aren't going to need to wash that shirt. I've cried on it so many times, it's probably soaked. I don't know why you want to be friends with me, Keaton. I don't even recognize who I've become in the last forty-eight hours. I'm a hot mess."

"I specialize in hot messes, Miss Larson. I think you could use a cup of hot tea now."

She smiled through watery eyes. "That's what Mom would always say. Time spent with a hot cup of tea solves everything. Let's go to the kitchen and find the tea bags," she suggested.

They made their way through the house, turning on lights as they went, finally arriving at the kitchen. He had eaten a couple of breakfasts at this very table and told her, "Sit. I know where your mom kept the tea bags. She made tea for me every morning I was here."

He retrieved two mugs and filled them with water, putting them in the microwave to heat before going to a cabinet and removing two tea bags.

Layne said, "I didn't figure you for a tea drinker. You look more like a coffee drinker to me."

"I like to go for a run every morning and then come home for coffee. Sometimes, I make it at home. Other times, I head to Coastal Roast, and they know my order. I do, however, unwind with a cup of hot tea about eight o'clock every evening. A good friend of mine was in the habit of drinking tea at night, and she got me started doing so. I like sitting with it, thinking about my day."

Layne's eyes sparked with interest. "Ooh, tell me more about this friend. Are you still friends—or more?"

He laughed easily. "Miss Peggy was a good fifty years older than me and my best friend. She's the woman who saved me. In every way."

The microwave dinged, and Keaton placed the tea bags in their cups and placed them on the kitchen table. He took a seat to Layne's left. As the tea steeped, he decided to tell this woman a little about himself.

"I won't sugarcoat my childhood. It was pretty rough. Drug addicted parents. Loss of parental rights. Shuffled from foster home to foster home. I aged out of the system a month before high school graduation. Miss Peggy was a retired teacher who lived across the street and was kind enough to take me in. That allowed me to earn my diploma."

She looked at him quizzical. "You mean ... your foster parents just kicked you out?"

"I was no longer any good to them. If the state wasn't paying, they had no more need of me. Miss Peggy helped me find a job with a friend of hers from high school. I worked construction for the next dozen years, and I painted on the side. She had a small toolshed out in her back yard, and that's where I worked on my art."

He took a sip of his tea, and Layne opened the sugar bowl sitting on the table. She rose and retrieved a spoon, dumping two healthy spoonfuls of sugar into the hot brew.

Stirring, she asked, "You loved her, didn't you?"

"I did. She was the only mother figure I ever had. I didn't have a chance to go to college or a trade school, so she gave me books to read. She had been an English teacher and decided I was another project for her in retirement. I'm actually very well read now, thanks to the recommendations she made over the years and the discussions we had about all those books, everything from *The Scarlet Letter* to *The Handmaid's Tale*."

"What did you do in construction?" she asked, looking interested.

That surprised him. Keaton had never had a woman interested in his blue collar job. Even Frankie had dismissed the idea he'd supported himself working in construction, telling him it had eaten away at his soul.

"I'm what you might call a jack-of-all-trades. I started with the basics, painting the interior and exterior of houses. There's actually an art to doing that, you know. Then I progressed, graduating to learning how to frame houses. Lay flooring and insulation. Put in sinks and backsplash. I even got into building cabinetry. That was my favorite thing, and I got really good at it."

"And how did you make the switch into Keaton Maxwell, professional artist?"

"I had a little help with that, one of those being in the right place at the right time situations. I had rented a booth at a local arts and crafts fair to try and sell my paintings. One of my boss' former clients, whom we'd done a lot of work for, stopped by when she recognized me. She'd liked the work I had done for her in past remodels and had recommended me to several of her friends. She bought a couple of paintings I had on display and then introduced me to the manager of an art gallery she had a financial interest in. Sidney was onboard right away once he saw my work. His investment in my work allowed me to quit my construction job in order to paint full-time."

"I can't wait to see your art. Not many people can make a living that way, so you must be really talented. What subjects do you paint?"

"I paint mostly landscapes. A lot of them were of Texas. Not that I ever ventured outside Dallas. I just got on the internet and looked at places. Watched a lot of NatGeo and Rick Steves, my windows into the larger world." He paused, swallowing his pain. "When Miss Peggy passed, I had no ties to Dallas. I opted for a huge change and eventually moved to the mountains, which had always intrigued me."

"I've never seen mountains before in person. I'd love to go to them someday. I told you I had been thinking about doing some traveling with my job ending and the buyout. Where did you live? Would you recommend me seeing the area?"

"Jackson Hole. In Wyoming. The Grand Tetons are simply breathtaking. You would appreciate seeing them. I definitely went through a phase of painting my fair share of mountains."

"If it was such a beautiful place, why did you leave it to come to the Bay, where you knew absolutely no one?"

He didn't say anything, and Layne answered for him.

"You don't owe me any explanations, Keaton. You've already shared quite a bit of yourself with me now." She smiled. "Besides, we're going to be friends. The sharing of our stories will unfold a little at a time as we come to know one another and grow comfortable being around each other."

"Thanks," he said quietly. "I've shared more of myself with you in these last few minutes than I have with anyone. Ever. My upbringing caused me to be a loner. Not to trust others, Layne. Even though I've found a home here in Driftwood Bay, making friends with Carson, Mila, and Sullivan, I haven't opened up and talked about my past with anyone. They're getting to know the Keaton of Driftwood Bay—not the Keaton of my past."

"Do you want to leave that past behind? You can do that if you want to, Keaton. You've come to a new place. You can be anyone you want to be."

She reached and placed her hand over his. "I like this Keaton. The Driftwood Bay version. If he's the only one I ever get to know, I'll be happy with making that Keaton my friend."

Layne squeezed his hand and then removed hers, placing it in her lap again, leaving him with an emptiness. Somehow, this woman filled him with all the things he wanted. Needed. Yet he couldn't voice any of that, not when she was so broken. He told himself to bide his time and hoped she'd decide to stay in the Bay.

For good.

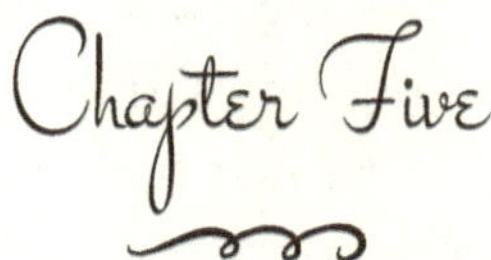

Chapter Five

After they finished their tea and rinsed their cups, Keaton offered to collect Layne's luggage from the car. She handed over the keys of the rental to him, telling that she had a suitcase and backpack in the trunk.

"Be right back," he told her, his tone sounding as if he were reluctant to leave her.

She had called herself a hot mess and couldn't imagine why he was sticking around. Yet there was a quiet air of strength about him that she found herself feeding off of. Layne dreaded him leaving her alone tonight. She had enjoyed his company over these last several hours and hoped that she would see him again while she was in the Bay, however long that might be.

She was torn about her future. A part of her wanted to bury her parents. Put the Bay Breeze up for sale, and travel the world without looking back. That would have been the old Layne, the successful Dallas professional. If she wrapped up things in the next week or so, she could go to far-flung places. Budapest. Tokyo. Iceland, to see the Northern Lights.

Yet the pull of home was proving to be stronger than she

had anticipated. Despite having left a dozen years ago with no intentions of ever living in her hometown again, Layne felt the magic of Driftwood Bay tempting her to stay. Mila was here, someone who was dearer to her than any sister could be. And now Keaton had made this appearance in her life. She would be a fool to entertain the notion of starting up something with this man, yet she had never had such a physical or emotional reaction to anyone of the opposite sex. Besides, why would he even be interested in her? She had shown him what a weak, pathetic person she was. Layne had cried more today in Keaton Maxwell's presence than she had her entire lifetime put together.

He came through the front door again. "Where would you like these to go?"

She wanted to shrug helplessly, but she needed some of the old Layne's confidence back.

"Let's go upstairs," she said brightly. "No one ever stays here during the holidays. Mom and Dad always took the last two weeks of December for themselves. Hardly anyone comes to the coast this time of year anyway, so it was their self-imposed vacation. Not that they ever traveled anywhere, but at least they didn't have sheets to wash and breakfasts to make for guests."

She led him up the wide staircase, and they stopped at the first room on the left. This had been her room growing up, but her parents long ago had turned it into another guestroom in order to generate more income.

Turning on the light, she gazed across it. Nothing of her remained. No trophies or awards she'd won placed on the dresser. No homecoming mums or posters of rock stars on the walls. It was simply another room she had no connection to.

Layne frowned. A shabby one, at that. The wallpaper looked old and sad. The carpet was worn, even threadbare in several places. The duvet looked as if had seen better days. Knowing this was the newest of the guestrooms to be updated, she dreaded seeing what the others one might look like.

Turning to Keaton, she asked, "How many other guests were staying here when you arrived?"

He answered without hesitation. "Only one. A woman named Lila."

She smiled at hearing the name, a picture of an older lady coming to mind. "Lila Carpenter. She and her husband Fred are from Corpus and honeymooned at the Bay Breeze decades ago. They always came back every spring to celebrate their wedding anniversary." She swallowed, realizing that Keaton hadn't mentioned Fred. "I assume if Lila stayed here by herself that Fred is no longer in the picture."

Keaton nodded. "I talked with her that first morning at breakfast. She did mention that she had lost her husband a few months back and that they had come to Driftwood Bay every year."

Frowning, Layne asked, "And no one else was here besides Lila?"

"No. Not in the three days in May when I stayed. I did think that was a little surprising, considering the location and time of year."

She hurried from her former bedroom, turning on lights as she moved down the hall, entering each guestroom. Every time, Layne found the same thing. Rooms which had a sad air about them. Paint which hadn't been freshened in years. Carpets which needed replacing. Bedding which had seen better days. At the last guestroom, she turned, finding Keaton had followed her.

"This place is dismal. I'm surprised anyone even stays here anymore." Her gaze met his. "What did you think of your time here?"

His face flushed with guilt, and Layne told herself to listen objectively and not be upset.

"I thought it was a little quaint. Worn out, to be honest. Your dad was friendly, though. The sheets were old but clean. Your mom cooked a mean breakfast, but she and I didn't interact much."

"I need to check the guest registry," she said, a sense of urgency filling her.

Layne raced from the bedroom and down the hall, noisily clattering down the stairs. She went behind the registration desk and flipped through the last several pages of the guest-book, noting the dates and how few people had stayed at the Bay Breeze, going back to the previous December. Then she opened a drawer and pulled the calendar for the next year. Her dad had always meticulously recorded future bookings in it. She opened it to January and saw no names listed. Turned to February. No names again. When she reached March and the time of spring break, she only saw a handful of bookings, a far cry from the full house which had been custom from spring break through late fall.

A line was drawn through each booking in March, and the word CANCELED was written out beside them. The same held true for the few scattered reservations in April and May, where she saw a dark line drawn through Lila's name. No pages after May—those critical summer months when her parents made most of their income—held names.

Nothing but empty pages.

Glancing up, she saw Keaton before her, concern on his face. "What did you find?" he asked.

"A few reservations," she said dully. "They've all been marked canceled, and high season is a total blank."

She shook her head sadly. "I feel as if I neglected my parents as much as they did the B&B. I hate myself now."

He stepped behind the registration desk and pulled her to him, his strong arms enveloping her. Layne wished she could make everything go away. Her parents' deaths. Her lack of interest in them and the Bay Breeze. All the times she called home, bragging about what she had accomplished at work. Her parents, especially her dad, had been supportive until the end, encouraging her to continue reaching for the stars.

Keaton released her but lightly clasped her elbows with his fingers.

"You're fragile now. Beaten up by everything that's happened. Don't let what you're finding now change your outlook on yourself or the relationship you had with your parents. You've mentioned how supportive of you they always were. *That's* what you hold on to, Layne. You had a loving, joyful relationship with them. They did their job as parents, letting you fly from the nest and spread your wings. You've soared—thanks to them. They taught you well, and you've carried those lessons throughout your life. I won't have you beat yourself up over something that wasn't under your control. They made the decisions they made for themselves together. You need to pick yourself up and keep making them proud of you."

She couldn't help it. Her hands framed his face and slowly pulled him down to her. She gave him ample time to pull away, but he didn't.

When their lips met, it was as if lightning struck. No slow period of exploration, only greedy need swept through her.

The electric kiss only increased in intensity as he thrust his tongue inside her mouth. Hot desire flooded her, causing her body to come alive. She kissed him with everything she had, a kiss so intense that she was afraid they would burn hotter than a funeral pyre.

She couldn't have begun to guess how long the kiss went

on until he broke it, and she clung to him, not wanting to part from him. Their gazes met, and she saw heat flickering in his eyes.

He whistled low. "That ... was some kiss. I've wanted to do that ever since I met you," he admitted. "Even that day of the wedding. When you mentioned you had a boyfriend. I felt something between us then." Keaton hesitated. "I don't know if this is going to go away, Layne. It's certainly not what you need now. Your life is already complicated enough."

"I know I asked for you to be my friend." She smiled ruefully at him. "I didn't think I was asking for a friend with benefits. But I don't want to be alone tonight, Keaton. Would you stay?"

She watched his face for a clue as to how he would respond to such declaration. He remained silent.

Embarrassed at her request, Layne tried to pull away. "Forget it. I'm sorry I asked."

His clasp tightened on her elbows. "It's not that I don't want to stay. I do. But I don't want to take advantage of you," he said, his voice low and rough. "I understand how vulnerable you are."

"I need someone tonight, Keaton. That someone is you," she said boldly. "I can't promise anything beyond this one night, but I'm hoping you would like to share it with me."

His boyish grin melted her heart, and his lips came crashing down on hers. The intensity of the kiss shouldn't have taken her by surprise—but it did.

Suddenly, they were tearing away one another's clothes in a frenzy, eager for skin to touch skin. He swept her from her feet and carried her up the stairs, to her childhood bedroom. Keaton set her on the bed. His hungry gaze roamed her body, telling her how much he wanted her. Then he raked his hands through his hair.

"I'm ... not prepared for this, Layne." He kissed her again, and she sensed the frustration in his kiss. "I don't have a condom with me."

Need driving her, she kissed him hard. "I have an IUD," she managed to get out. "We're good."

That was all it took. He climbed onto the bed, his body caging hers as he devoured her mouth. Desire poured from her, and her hands stroked the hard muscles of his chest.

His lips dropped to her throat, kissing and nipping at her pulse point, causing her core to throb in a sweet ache.

Slowly, he worked his way down her body, worshiping her breasts with teeth, tongue, and hands. His tongue dragged lower, gliding slowly down her flat belly, causing her abs to dance.

He moved from the bed, standing at its foot, his fingers taking her ankles and pulling her body until her legs hung from the bed. Then he knelt, his hands slipping beneath her ass and grasping it as his tongue danced along the seam of her sex. He pushed it inside her, and the orgasm began building as he thrust his tongue in and out of her. Then it hit her, full force, racing through her. Her body shuddered violently, wave after wave of pleasure releasing through her.

When it subsided, she felt as if every bone in her body had melted away, and she was merely a lump on the bed. He kissed his way back up her body, finally reaching her mouth. Tasting herself on him was an erotic thrill as he kissed her thoroughly.

He pushed himself from the bed and lifted her from it, setting her on her feet as he turned back the bedding. Then he picked her up again, placing her on the bed, and crawled in beside her. Layne lay on her right side, and Keaton draped a leg over hers, placing his arm possessively around her waist, pulling her so that she was flush against him. She felt his erection pressing against her. Still, he made no effort to enter her.

"We're ... through?" she asked sleepily, her eyes too heavy to remain open any longer.

She felt him kiss her hair. Then he whispered into her ear, "Sleep. You need it."

Too tired to protest, Layne drifted off into oblivion.

Chapter Six

Keaton listened to the even breathing coming from Layne and knew she had fallen asleep in seconds. Sleep would do her good. He had never met such a wounded soul. Then again, he hadn't been close to but a handful of others and wasn't in the habit of sharing his own problems.

That was what was different about tonight. The time he had spent in Layne's company had been exhilarating. Interesting. They had both unburdened to one another, something he was certain she never did and unthinkable for him. Yet every word had rung with truth. He wanted this woman to know all of him. The talent. The loneliness. The flaws. Just as she had things she needed to heal from, so did he.

He only wondered if they were meant to heal together.

It was time to stop thinking and merely enjoy lying next to her, the subtle scent of lavender wafting toward him from her. It had been a while since he'd had sex with a woman, much less slept overnight with her. Frankie was the last woman he'd had in his bed, and she was not one for cuddling after sex. Even though they had been in a serious relationship, she rarely stayed the night.

He had thought he had known Frankie, down to her poet's soul. She was brash. Lively. Even unfiltered. And so very talented. Whenever they had sex, though, she was always bursting with energy afterward, unlike the few other partners he had engaged with. Frankie had told him that sex made her restless. That she needed to go home and write. The few times she did stay at his place, he would awaken and feel for her in bed, the spot next to him cold and empty. He would get up on the pretext of needing a glass of water and find her at the kitchen table, scribbling manically. Back then, he had admired what he thought was her tremendous dedication to her craft.

The truth he had learned had been far darker.

Pushing aside all thoughts of Francesca Fairchild, Keaton concentrated on the feel of Layne against him. He matched his breathing to hers and soon tumbled into sleep himself.

When he awoke, he knew it was early. Warm woman nestled against him, filling Keaton with a sense of satisfaction, making him wish that he had a permanent arrangement with Layne Larson. Thoughts like this were insane, yet he wasn't quite willing to chase them away just yet. Yes, Layne was hurting and fragile right now, but he believed a resiliency lay within her. She would bounce back from this double tragedy and find her place in the world, becoming stronger for what she had survived. The question was whether or not this would occur in Driftwood Bay or some other far-flung place where she didn't have to think of her parents dying in the place she lived every single day.

He was in a quandary. He needed to get in his morning run, addicted to it as he was the air he breathed. Yet Keaton didn't want Layne to awaken and feel as if he had skipped out on her. Was she sleeping deeply enough for him to go for his run and make it back to the inn before she awakened?

She stirred, and he knew he wouldn't have to make that decision as she stretched her limbs. Then she laced her fingers through his, bringing their joined hands to her lips and brushing a soft kiss against his knuckles.

Though the room was dark still, he could feel the intensity of her moss green eyes upon him as she said, "I can't thank you enough for staying. For getting me through the first night under this roof. I'm only sorry that I feel asleep on you. You were so generous to me. Giving more than I could have asked for, Keaton. I'm sorry I didn't return the favor."

He brushed a kiss against her temple, smoothing her hair. "We were pretty darn good

together, weren't we? You have a lovely body, Layne. One I thoroughly enjoyed exploring. As for the rest?" He shrugged. "Maybe another time."

He sensed the intimacy which had been built between them in such a short time and hoped they wouldn't lose it. Keaton wanted to remain friends with her, no matter what her future held and where it took her.

"I need to get up," he reluctantly told her.

"I know. You're ready to get your morning run in. You mentioned it. I do tai chi first thing in the morning."

An image of people in a park in Jackson Hole came to him, and he chuckled.

"What's so funny about tai chi?" she asked, playfully punching him in the shoulder.

"The only time I've ever seen others do tai chi was in Wyoming. I lived in a cabin on the outskirts of town. When I would go in to pick up groceries, there was always a group doing tai chi in a local park. I think the youngest one might've been sixty. Maybe even seventy. I just can't picture you doing old people exercises. You're too vibrant."

She leaned over and kissed him, and he could feel her smile against his mouth.

"First of all, it's not just old people who practice tai chi. And second, it is the most disciplined form of exercise you can do. You should give it a try sometime."

"You're on," he said enthusiastically. "Wanna do some now?"

"Okay," she agreed. "I get out of bed every morning. Hydrate. And then I do tai chi. I prefer to do it outside, though. You game, Mr. Maxwell, to head outside?"

"I don't have any tai chi clothes with me," he quipped.

"You're close to my dad's height. We can find a pair of sweats for you to wear." She paused, smiling impishly. "Unless it creeps you out wearing a dead guy's clothing."

"Gallows humor. Good for you," he teased. Wanting to continue to be in her company, he added, "Let's go find them."

She told him to stay while she went to her parents' bedroom to hunt for the sweats. He took the opportunity to hit the bathroom and even splashed cold water on his face. Studying himself in the mirror, he wondered if he looked any different, thanks to his encounter with Layne.

She returned with the sweatpants.

"The bottoms should fit you. You're broader in the shoulders than Dad, so I brought back the largest long-sleeved T-shirt I could find. The sweatshirts all looked too small for you."

Layne handed the clothes over to him and said, "I need to go claim my workout gear from my suitcase. Meet you in the kitchen in five."

He knew there were two staircases from his stay at the Bay Breeze Inn, so Keaton took the back set to the kitchen. He opened the door to the fridge, surprised that it was almost totally empty. It seems Mr. Larson was meticulous in his planning, down to making certain there would be no spoiled milk for his daughter to dispose of. Since he didn't spy any bottled waters, he poured them tall glasses of cold water. He downed his, feeling parched, and refilled his glass.

Layne appeared, and he handed her a glass. She said, "I guess there were no bottled waters. Did the fridge stink? Mom always had all kinds of leftovers. I'm afraid to see what's still lurking there."

"No containers of leftovers. It was almost bare, save for a few jars of condiments."

He saw understanding dawn in her eyes. "Dad took care of even the little things," she said quietly. "Taking out the trash. Getting rid of leftovers. He was always thinking ahead."

Keaton stepped to her, enveloping her in his arms, no words necessary between them.

She pulled away, wiping her eyes. "I'm glad you didn't put on your boots. Tai chi is best done in bare feet. I like practicing it outside, though, where I have plenty of room. I just checked the weather. No wind and fifty-eight degrees. Not bad for Christmas Eve early morning. Are you willing to exercise on the porch?"

"You're the expert. Lead the way."

"First, we need to do some basic stretching. Limber up our bodies. Let's go to the foyer where we have some room to do that."

For the next ten minutes, Layne led him through a series of stretches. Some, he was familiar with. Others were new and really loosened up his muscles.

"I like this stretch," he told her, leaning hard into it, feeling the burn.

She grinned. "I stole some of these stretches from Piper years ago. She did them in drill team. I was captain of our soccer team, and so I got to lead everyone in exercises before we hit the field. This one was our favorite team stretch."

"Well, I'm adding it to my repertoire before I run every morning. My calves feel great now."

They finished warming up, and Layne told him, "In case you're wondering, tai chi is an ancient Chinese martial art inspired by the movement of birds and cheetahs. It brings your body to its natural state through a moving meditation. You let go of tension. All thoughts. Allow your *qi* to flow smoothly."

"Why does it look as if people doing it are in slow motion?" he questioned.

"The slow movements help you develop body awareness. The tempo improves your posture and helps your circulation. It aids in grounding you. You become more flexible and disciplined. The biggest thing is that you don't want to rush any of these poses."

"Similar to yoga," he commented. "I took a few classes of it in Wyoming at the local Y."

"Did you like it?" she asked.

"I liked the yoga. I didn't like being around a lot of people doing yoga."

"I hear you. Though I'm a people person, sometimes, I just have to turn off that spigot and have quiet time to myself. You ready to begin?"

They went out onto the wide porch. His body temperature had already warmed, thanks to the stretches they had done.

"I'm going to stand in front of you, my back to you," she told him. "Just do as I do and imitate my moves. And remember, form is key. No slouching. A slow pace is what'll make this effective."

For the next three-quarters of an hour, Layne led him through a set of what she called the Twenty-Four Form, telling him this was her standard training routine. She emphasized that he wouldn't pick up everything this first time. That tai chi was an art form you continued to grow in as you practiced. They did poses with crazy names such as Cloud Hands, White Crane Spreads its Wings, and Parting the Horse's Mane. He thought at first that the movements were incredibly simple, but that proved deceptive. As Keaton mimicked her moves, he saw the discipline required to perform the ancient art successfully. By the time the session ended, he had trembling muscles, yet a calm had descended upon him, unlike anything he'd ever known.

Turning to face him, she asked, "How do you feel?"

"This sounds crazy, but I pushed myself almost as much as I do during a run. I didn't move within a foot in any direction, yet I feel as if I've pounded the pavement for a few miles."

He took a deep breath. "Even better, I feel cleansed. As if I'm floating. Fresh. Alert. Ready to take on a new day."

"I'm glad you enjoyed it so much. It's something you can do anywhere. Believe me, I like to get outside and walk. Do Pilates. I even lift a few weights every now and then. But tai chi always centers me. I find the essence of me in doing it. It helps me to roll with my day more easily. An added bonus? I guarantee you'll sleep better tonight. At least, I do."

"You're preaching to the choir now, babe. I'm a tai chi convert. I'll have to get online and see if there are some YouTube videos I can watch."

"Oh, I have a great app for practicing the movements. I'll share it with you if you're truly interested and not just blowing smoke up my ass."

He stepped toward her, his hands reaching around to cradle her rounded bottom. "I would never do that to you, Layne. The foundation of our friendship is built on honesty." He squeezed her buttocks. "But you do have an incredible ass from doing tai chi."

She laughed, and Keaton leaned down and kissed her lightly. He stepped away, wanting to linger but knowing he needed to respect her boundaries. He didn't know if they would ever repeat the intimacies of last night. If they didn't, he would be disappointed, but he would understand. Right now, Layne needed the friendship he offered more than sex.

But he certainly could daydream about her hot body.

"Let's go inside," she said. "I need a water break. And I'm starved."

They hydrated again, and she rummaged through the fridge.

"You're right. There's not anything here." Opening the freezer, she said, "Bingo." Pulling out a loaf of frozen bread, she said, "Mom would always buy bread from Seaside Sweets, the local bakery, and freeze loaves. We can at least munch on some toast."

She defrosted several slices of bread in the microwave and then popped all four into the toaster. "Light, medium, or dark?"

"Medium light for me," he responded.

"Ah, we have that in common," she said, setting the controls on the toaster.

Layne retrieved two jars of jam from the fridge, one strawberry and one orange marmalade. For his part, Keaton fetched two plates and knives and refilled their glasses with water again.

She brought the toast to the table, and he smeared the strawberry on both his pieces, being partial to it. Biting into the toast, the deep, sweet rich flavor of strawberry exploded in his mouth.

"Wow, this is really good."

Smiling sadly, Layne said, "Mom made her own jams each year. Strawberry was always my favorite. I'm hoping there'll at least be a few more jars in the cupboard from the final batch she made. That'll be a nice reminder of her."

Keaton reached and took her hand. "Sadness is going to hit you every now and then. Out of the blue, someone will say something to trigger you. Or you might hear a song, causing a memory to arise. The hurt will be fresh at first. Painful. Jarring. Then it'll lessen with time. At least that's how it was after I lost Miss Peggy. It's been a four years now since she's been gone, and I can actually think of her now without choking up."

He raked a hand through his hair. "That woman loved her books. Sometimes, I pick up one of her favorite books she shared with me. I'll re-read a few chapters—even the entire book itself. I feel the essence of her still inside me. Guiding my choices. Inspiring me."

"I'm glad you had Miss Peggy in your life," Layne said quietly. "I realize now how I took my parents for granted all these years. They always loved me like crazy. If I had it to do over again, I would have come back to the Bay more often." She frowned. "I also would have cut ties with Jeremy a whole lot sooner. Yes, he was nice eye candy. He actually could be a lot of fun, but he had a lousy work ethic. No, no work ethic at all, which was too bad because I paid to put him through a master's program at SMU, and that wasn't cheap."

"*You* paid for that?"

She nodded. "I even told him not to work so he could concentrate on school. I'd completed my master's while working full-time, and I knew what a pain it was, being pulled in different directions. Jeremy quit job after job. Let met pay for just about everything. By then, I got so caught up in work that I really didn't notice he was bleeding me dry and how far apart we'd drifted. How often he went out with his friends and not me. I thought I was building a nest egg for our future— when we had no future."

Layne shook her head. "I let work blind me, Keaton. Possess me. I'm never going to let that happen again. While work will always be something I prioritize, I now understand that family and friends are what life is all about. It's an expensive lesson that I had to learn. I'm sorry Mom and Dad aren't around now so I could show them how much I really loved them. But I swear from this moment going forward, I will treasure those I keep close to me. I'll also take care of myself better."

She smiled at him. "And I will appreciate new friends, such as you and Carson."

"You know some of my story now. How I haven't had many friends. The Bay is changing me, Layne. Like you, I'm discovering that there's more to life than work."

A thought struck him. "I need to get to the grocery store!"

"Wow, that was random," she teased.

"No, I'm supposed to bring a potato casserole to Christmas dinner tomorrow. It's being held at the Perrys' house. With this being Christmas Eve day, the stores will close early."

He smiled at her. "You'll be invited to the Perrys' for Christmas dinner since you're in town."

Her mouth trembled. "I'm not sure if I'm up to being around a lot of people and faking being happy."

"Being alone and wallowing in self-pity is not going to make you feel any better, my friend. You need to go with me tomorrow. Period."

"But what if I bring everyone down with me?"

"If the need for a pity party strikes you, just excuse yourself. Go have a little cry in the powder room. Splash water on your face and then rejoin everyone." He looked at her sternly. "But you *are* coming to Christmas dinner tomorrow." He softened his tone. "I want you there, Layne."

Their gazes met. Something passed between them.
Then she gave him a faint smile. "I want that, too, Keaton."

83

Chapter Seven

After Keaton left, Layne unpacked the one suitcase she had brought. Besides her workout clothes, she had brought a dress for the eventual funeral, as well as two pairs of jeans and a few shirts. When she had left Dallas for her flight to Corpus, she had left Jeremy's things in boxes on the front porch. The last thing she had done was to stop at her next door neighbor's. Jenny had a key to Layne's house for emergencies, as well as the alarm code. Conveniently, Jenny's husband was a locksmith. Layne had asked Jenny to have her husband change the locks on the house immediately, explaining that Jeremy Riggs was no longer welcome on the property. With sympathy in her eyes, Jenny had assured her it would be taken care of immediately.

Even though Keaton had encouraged her not to make any big decisions regarding her future, Layne already had. Dallas was dead to her. Even though it was a large city with incredible business opportunities, she had a feeling if she remained that she would constantly run into Jeremy. She wanted to cut ties with him and get a fresh start. Whether that was in Driftwood Bay or somewhere else, it meant selling her house.

She showered and got dressed for the day, humming as she did so. Layne took that as a good sign. She'd always enjoyed singing in the shower or car, and she often hummed. Or she had until Jeremy told her it bothered him and she had curtailed the habit. Now, she belted out *Defying Gravity* as she made the bed, stopping to pick up the pillow and inhale the masculine scent left behind by Keaton. Clutching the pillow to her, she wondered at how out of character she had behaved with him, even blushing as she recalled the out of this world orgasm he had given her.

It would be wrong to pursue a relationship with him, especially coming out of a long-term one with Jeremy. Yet the handsome artist was the most appealing man Layne had ever met. She didn't think he would put any demands on her or try to put a label on what was going on between them. She told herself to take things one day at a time. Emotionally, she was as raw as she'd ever been. If the spark between them flamed into something, she would deal with it when that occurred.

Glancing at her watch, she decided she should call Piper, knowing her friend had no performances today or tomorrow because of it being Christmas. Layne went downstairs and settled into a favorite chair as she touched the screen to Face-Time with her friend.

Piper appeared, her face flushed. "Hey. I just finished a workout." She frowned. "Where are you? That looks like your parents' place. Wait. Don't tell me. You came home for Christmas! Oh, they are going to be so happy, Layne. You haven't been home for Christmas in ages." She paused. "But is Jeremy with you?"

Obviously, Piper's parents hadn't told their daughter what had happened. It would be up to Layne to break the awful news to her friend. She decided to start with the immediate question first.

"Jeremy is no longer a concern of mine."

"Hallelujah! He never was good enough for you, Layne. Oh, it's so nice to hear you've dumped him. I guess I can tell you now that Mila and I call him The Leech. He is more than a bloodsucker, honey. He took advantage of your generosity. I'm glad we've seen the last of his ass." Sympathy filled Piper's blue eyes. "How are you holding up? I know it's gotta be hard. You were together a long time."

"The Jeremy part stings. On top of everything, he was cheating on me. But I have more to tell you."

Briefly, Layne explained how she was out of a job and had received a generous exit package from the company which had bought out hers.

"That's terrific," Piper said brightly. "You poured heart and soul into that company. I'm glad to hear you received such a nice financial reward."

"There's more," she said quietly, her eyes welling with tears. "This is the hard part."

Layne took a deep breath, and the words came out in a torrent. How her mom had an inoperable brain tumor. How she suspected her dad was also ill. That they had decided to go out together, on their own terms.

Tears ran down Piper's face. "I am so, so sorry, Layne."

"Your dad flew up to Dallas to tell me. I can't tell you how much that meant to me."

"He did? He didn't tell me."

"I'm sure he thought it was best that you heard the news from me."

"Oh, this makes me even more homesick than I am," her friend wailed, brushing tears away as they fell down her cheeks.

"It's Christmas. I miss my family. I miss my friends. Dang it, I even miss the Bay."

Surprise filled her. "But I thought you enjoyed touring and performing. You've always talked about how exciting life on the road is. New cities, new adventures."

"I know. I still feel that way, and that's why I'm so torn. But do realize how long I've lived out of a suitcase? Almost a decade. I didn't finish college like you and Mila did. I let the lure of musical theater and the chance to perform and make money turn my head. I still love getting out on that stage, but Mila getting married and me not being there just about killed me."

"What are you saying, Piper?" Layne pressed.

"That I'm thinking about coming back home. I don't have anything worked out yet. I'm just toying with the idea. But hearing how your parents are gone and you'll never see them again makes me miss my parents so much. I've been this vagabond for years now, but honestly? I'm jealous of Mila. For coming back to the Bay and taking a job she loves. For finding a great guy like Carson and becoming a mom to Lily. And I know she'll turn up pregnant soon. I don't want to miss out on being an auntie."

Piper paused. "What are your plans, Layne? And what about the Bay Breeze?"

She shook her head. "I don't know. Before I learned about Mom and Dad, I'd decided I was going to take some time off before I began my job search. Maybe travel a little before I decide what my next chapter will be. I can tell you that Dallas is in my rear view mirror. I don't want to live or work there again. I'm not sure where I want to be or what I want to do. I also have the B&B to deal with. It's a mess, Piper. Remember how we read *The Picture of Dorian Gray* in high school? How his portrait kept fading? Well, that's what the Bay Breeze looks like to me. Old. Tired. Faded. It is crying to be updated."

"You'll need to decide whether it's worth your time to remodel and refresh it or sell it as it is." Piper paused. "Or you could stay in the Bay and run it."

"Me? Run the Bay Breeze?"

That hadn't occurred to her. She had thought either to sell it or hire someone to run it for her.

What would it be like to do that?

"You've got time to decide, especially with your sweet deal," her friend pointed out. "You aren't hurting for money anytime soon. That's a luxury, Layne. Be glad you don't have to rush and make a decision you might regret."

"That's what Keaton says. He's advised me to take my time."

"Who?" Piper asked, looking intrigued. "Wait, I've heard that name before. Mila's mentioned it."

"Keaton Maxwell. He lives across the street from Mila and Carson. He's an artist who moved to the Bay about six months ago. Runs an art gallery."

Piper leaned toward the screen, scrutinizing Layne.

"So, what's this Keaton Maxwell doing giving you advice? There's a story here."

"It's hard to explain. He's ... been a friend. Helped me out."

Piper studied her. "He's more than a friend. You *like* this guy."

"I do," she admitted. "And that's the absolutely last thing I need on my plate. Piper, I just broke up with Jeremy. We were together five years!"

Her friend smiled smugly. "And I'm betting Keaton is everything Jeremy wasn't. Am I right?"

Grudgingly, Layne nodded. "You are. He's different from

any man I've ever known. He's introspective. Kind. Smart." She hesitated. "I've never been so attracted to anyone in my life. It's almost frightening."

"Is he a good kisser?"

She sucked in a quick breath. "How do you know we've kissed?"

"There. What you said just tells me you already have. Layne, this is great."

"No, it's freaking confusing. That's what it is. Yes, we've kissed. His kisses are mind-blowing. I'm already addicted."

"So, you're staying in the Bay?"

"No. Yes. I don't know! Keaton says not to make any big decisions just yet. That I need time to grieve. To process things."

"I already like him a thousand, million, quadrillion times more than Jeremy. Whether you have a future with this guy or not, he's good for you now. Don't push him away. Promise me."

"I promise," she said begrudgingly. "Enough of me. What do you have going on?"

Piper explained how a few of her fellow actors were going to a Christmas luncheon buffet tomorrow at a fancy hotel. That she had another nine weeks of touring with this production before the tour ended at the beginning of March.

"That gives me a couple of months to figure out what I want to do. By then, you'll probably know where you're going to be." Piper paused. "If you stay in the Bay with Mila, then that'll make me want to come home even more."

"Don't let what I'm doing affect your own choice," Layne warned. "You need to do what's best for you."

"I know. I'll tell you, though, that I'm leaning heavily on coming home. For good." Piper grinned. "But don't let *my* decision influence yours."

"You are evil, Piper Roberts," she declared.

"And you love me for it."

They said their goodbyes, with Layne promising to call back tomorrow night, along with Mila.

After the conversation ended, she felt good having shared everything with her friend. It surprised her how homesick Piper was. She had lived for performing, and Layne had thought Piper would tour until she dropped dead decades from now. Yet it was easy to understand how life on the road could be lonely and monotonous. Piper had always been nurturing. Layne could picture her friend coming home and settling down, having a more normal life. She could also see Piper with babies. Lots of babies. Life on the road wasn't conducive to marriage or children.

Whatever Piper decided, Layne would have to make her own decision regarding where her future home would be, but with Mila already in the Bay and Piper also strongly considering a return home, Layne couldn't help but be influenced by that. As she was an only child, these two women were family to her, the three of them forming a sisterhood which had stood the test of time.

And whether she would admit it to herself or not, Keaton Maxwell would also factor into whatever decision she made.

Her phone rang, and she saw it was Laura Perry calling.

"Hi, Mrs. Perry."

"Hello, Layne, darling. I won't ask how you are because I know you're hurting. Bill and I are here for you. You're welcome to come stay with us instead of rattling around the Bay Breeze by yourself."

"Thank you for the invitation. I'm all right for now."

"Well, we're having people over for Christmas dinner, and you better agree to come. Two o'clock, as usual."

Her parents had spent many Christmas Days with the

Perrys, and Layne knew that while it would be difficult being around others, she needed to go.

"You can count me in, Mrs. Perry. What can I bring?"

Laura Perry laughed. "I don't suppose you've learned to cook by some miracle?"

"No," she admitted. "I'm happy to pick up something, though."

"We'll have plenty. Just bring yourself, dear."

"Okay, I'll see you tomorrow. Thanks again for thinking of me."

"You're family, Layne. We're here for whatever you need."

"I appreciate that."

Layne hung up, already feeling good about the decision to spend the holiday at the Perrys' house.

Then her cell rang again, and she saw it was Keaton calling.

"Hey. Get your groceries?" she asked.

"Yes, but it was a madhouse. I think everyone in the Bay decided to wait until today to do their shopping. How are you?"

"I called Piper. We had a good chat."

"Good. I'm glad you touched base with her."

"She's feeling a bit lonely, being on the road and away from the Bay and her parents. Laura Perry also called and invited me to lunch tomorrow."

"Good to hear. I'll pick you up."

"I can drive myself, Keaton."

"Can I see you before then?" he asked. "I know you're in limbo, waiting for the autopsies to be completed."

"I'd like you to come over. I'm going to warn you that if you do, I'll put you to work, though."

"Hmm, doing what?"

"The Bay Breeze is sorely in need of a makeover. You said you worked in construction for years. Would you be willing to walk through it with me and let me know everything that needs to be done in order to restore it to what it was before? I don't know if I'll keep it or sell it, but I figure any improvements I make will need to be done, regardless."

"I can do that," he said easily, and she could picture his smile.

"I'll pay you for your time," she told him.

"No payment necessary. Just one friend helping out another. Can I come now?"

"Now is good for me."

"See you soon."

Layne ended the call, and for the first time in days, she felt hopeful. About her future.

And whatever role Keaton Maxwell might play in it.

Chapter Eight

Keaton walked through the Bay Breeze with Layne, and she said, "You've been a guest here. I want you to think of your experience while you stayed here—plus using your critical eye—to help me decide what needs to be done in order to put the Bay Breeze back on the map. Don't think of the cost. Just tell me what you would do to make the inn inviting. Appealing. A place where guests want to return and recommend to their friends as a great place to stay."

"Okay. Complete honesty," he agreed.

She held a spiral notebook in one hand and a pen in her other, ready to take notes. Layne was all business now, commanding his attention. He knew she had been good at her job, and he was seeing a glimpse of the old Layne, who brimmed with confidence, beginning to return.

"Then we should start outside," he suggested. "Curb appeal is important. Your website will feature the outside prominently. That will be the first introduction people have to the Bay Breeze."

"Good idea."

They walked outside and down the porch steps, turning to face the front of the structure.

"Spruce up the landscaping," he began, giving her ideas for the types of plants and flowers. "Add a ramp so luggage can be rolled and not carried up the stairs." Moving up the steps, he added, "Replace all the furniture on the porch. Change it to better rockers. A few chairs with small rattan tables between a pair. I'm partial to Adirondack in both cases. They even make them with wine and cup holders now. They're durable. Colorful. Stylish. Or instead of rockers, go with swivel glider chairs." He glanced to the far side. "Maybe add a bistro table in the far corner."

He thought a moment and then pointed. "At the far end of the porch, you could place an additional set of stairs which lead to the ground. That space in front of the porch is open but not big enough for a car to be parked there. What if you added a fire pit and chairs? The weather never gets super cold here, but a fire pit would be fun to sit around during fall and winter nights."

Layne scribbled furiously. "Good. Keep going."

He mentioned checking the front columns on the porch for decay or damage, telling her how they could be repaired or even replaced. Keaton also recommended painting the entire outside, as well as placing a few ceiling fans on the porch.

"I'd also re-stain or even paint the porch. All those things should spruce up the outside and make it more inviting."

"Got it."

"I'd need to get on the roof to see if it's in good condition or if it needs replacing. That could be pricy, Layne."

"No talk of money," she reminded him. "This is a dream list of what can be done to make the Bay Breeze the best B&B around."

He had them walk around the entire outside of the inn,

recommending new gutters and drain pipes, as well as additional, low-maintenance landscaping.

Satisfied that they'd hit everything outside, he said, "Let's go inside."

They went through the bottom floor first. The entire house needed fresh paint inside, and he thought the wood floors should be refinished. The common room needed all new furniture, as everything there was worn out and dated.

"The fireplace is nice. I'd get a new TV. The biggest one you could find and mount it on that wall."

Keaton suggested both types of furniture and the layout, mentioning that the B&B hadn't provided free Wi-Fi during his stay, which had disappointed him.

"That's a must now, no matter where you stay." He glanced across the common area. "The puzzles and games are a nice touch, but a lot are missing pieces. I'd start from scratch. Same with the guidebooks on the bookrack. They're way out of date and should be replaced with newer versions."

Layne continued to write. "Move on."

They went into the dining room, which she said had been the place breakfast was served to guests for as long as she could remember. He remarked that since he and Lila had been the only ones staying at the Bay Breeze, that might have been why the morning meal had been served in the kitchen.

Keaton went to the table, running his hand along the polished cherrywood.

"This table is amazing. So are the chairs and sideboard. And that china cabinet should display not only china but glassware, along with a few local items to give it some local flavor. I'd serve breakfast in here instead of the kitchen, no matter how many guests are staying. This room is too nice to not be used. Plus, it frees up the kitchen for cooking."

"I agree, especially if there's a full house. Did Mom have a buffet in the kitchen, or was there a set menu?"

"She asked me what I wanted the days I was here. I asked for French toast and bacon one morning. That was pretty darn fabulous. Pancakes and sausage another. Eggs and bacon the last day. She added grits to my plate that morning.." He chuckled. "I wasn't too sure about them, but I really found I enjoyed the taste of them."

"Shrimp grits are the best. I have no idea how Mom made them, but they were a favorite of mine growing up."

"We'll find a recipe and make them together," he said, seeing his words caused color to flush her cheeks.

Keaton still had no idea where they were going. If this was meant to be a close friendship.

Or more.

"I'd probably do a buffet," she mused. "Or have a set menu each morning and serve it buffet-style. I'll pick your brain later about that."

They went to the kitchen and then the two restrooms on the first floor. One was for general use. The other was part of an ensuite, and this was the bedroom Layne's parents had used. He made his suggestions, from furniture to fixtures, and then they moved upstairs.

Six bedrooms were on the second floor. It seemed four had been in use for guests, with a fifth serving as an office and a sixth as a storage room for whatever the B&B used. Sheets and towels. Toiletries. Toilet paper. Cleaning supplies.

They agreed that all four bedrooms needed to be completely refurbished. The furniture wasn't antique. It was merely ancient. He revealed that his mattress had been less than desirable.

"If anything, we want guests to get a good night's sleep,"

Layne said. "That means first-class pillows, mattresses, and bed linens."

He noted she used the word *we*.

"Mom used to provide fresh flowers on the nightstand for each room. I like that practice."

"Yes, I had fresh flowers during my stay. They really made the room cheerful."

She thought a moment. "I'd like a more personal touch. Maybe add robes and slippers. Place a few books on the table by the bed."

"That would be nice."

"I stayed in a B&B once, and they had a tea and coffee bar set up in the guest lounge area. The owner also put out freshly-baked cookies mid-afternoon."

Keaton grinned. "Now you're talking my love language. I'm all about the cookie. Especially if there's chocolate involved."

"Do you have a sweet tooth, Mr. Maxwell?" she teased.

"Actually, I do. I never had sweets growing up. Miss Peggy baked a mean pie, though. Sweets were standard for her, not a luxury. I was the beneficiary of her baking."

Layne glanced around. "So, new furniture, linens, carpets, and curtains. New paint. What about the wallpaper?"

"It's too faded. Either layer another choice over it, or we paint over it."

Now, he was also using *we*.

"I think wallpaper can be charming," she said. "It can give a room an identity. I think I'd like each room to have a color or a theme. Piper was always reading Regency romance books when we were teens. She talked about how in the rich people's houses, guests were shown to the blue room or the gold room."

"That's not a bad idea, working around a color palette to define each guestroom. I can help you there, picking out colors that go well together or varying shades. You could have a main color, using several lighter hues in the same family, and then possibly an accent color."

"Ooh, I like that idea, Keaton. I've never been into color or design, but I think it'll be fun to bring each of these rooms to life."

"Do you want to keep it at four bedrooms to rent?"

She tucked a lock of hair behind her ear. "Maybe. I think we definitely need to keep one bedroom upstairs for storage and the cleaning equipment and supplies. Though I think we could go all IKEA and have shelving to organize and store things better than the hodgepodge that's present now. The one being used as an office, though, might be a guestroom. Then again, the other rooms are all ensuite, and that one wouldn't be."

"You could still turn it into a bedroom. We could reconfigure things and cut a door so that it led into the bathroom next door to it. Then it would be a suite. Two bedrooms with the bath in the middle. Or even a bedroom, sitting room, and bath."

"Yes, I like that idea. A lot," she said, enthusiasm brimming from her.

"Let me draw it up both ways, and you can decide which would be a better use of the space."

"You're on." Layne smiled at him. "You're a real big help, Keaton. You have a good eye. And I really like your idea about redoing all the closets. We've made an excellent start today." She paused. "I mean, this is a good start for me. For what I need to do."

"You know my background, Layne. I can handle most of the work for you. Paint. Build the shelves in the closets. Resand the floors."

"No, I can't ask you to put your own painting on hold to do menial labor for me."

He stepped toward her, clasping one elbow lightly. "I'd like to do this. I just finished a series of paintings, and I always take a break after that. I don't like to be idle, though. I enjoy using my hands." Keaton grinned. "And I'd be a lot cheaper than anyone else you'd hire."

She looked as if she might be wavering, so he sweetened the pot. "You can help me with everything. I'll teach you. It'll give you time to think about the future of the Bay Breeze. Whether you want to sell it or keep it. You don't have a job to rush back to. This way, you'll be a part of the renovation. Pick up a few new skills. You won't be rushed to make any kind of decision."

He lifted her chin with a finger. "And we could get to spend time together. I'd like that. Would you?"

Her eyes widened at his bold declaration. "I would," she said firmly, pleasing him.

"Good. It's settled. We can start Monday. I'll map out a plan for us. Make a list of the supplies we need. Most we can buy in the Bay, but for things such as the furniture and curtains, that'll most likely mean a trip into Corpus."

"I'm fine with that. I can work on a budget on my end."

"I may hire a few day laborers for the painting outside and inside. That can be time consuming. All the rest, though, I can handle."

"We can handle," she corrected.

"We," he agreed.

Keaton wanted to kiss her. Instead, he took a step back, disengaging from her. For a moment, he saw disappoint flash in her eyes.

And that gave him hope.

"Wait. I just thought about something. One thing I can't do is assess the HVAC system. Do you know how old it is?"

"I have no idea. Dad never mentioned things like that to me."

"We'll need to have someone come in and look at the system then. I think we're done here for now. Have any plans for Christmas Eve, Miss Larson?"

For a moment, she looked startled. "Oh, it is Christmas Eve. I shouldn't have taken up so much of your time, Keaton."

"Don't apologize. I wanted to be here with you. But it's almost five o'clock, and I'm getting hungry. Want to come back to my place and put together some dinner? In fact, I think you should stay over. I've got a second bedroom," he added quickly. "That way, you could help me make my contributions to Christmas dinner tomorrow, and we could go straight from my place to the Perry house. What do you say, Layne?"

More than anything, Keaton wanted to be with this woman. He knew it was already hard enough for her to be alone in this rambling inn, and he wanted to smooth the way for her.

She nibbled on her full, bottom lip, making him want to jerk her to him and sink his teeth into her. Quickly, he tamped down that thought.

"Okay. Let me pack a few things. Give me ten minutes."

"Will do." He pulled out his phone. "I'll start making a list of supplies we need."

Good to her word, Layne was back in under ten minutes. He took her suitcase out to his truck and placed it in the cab.

"Leave your car here," he advised. Not that he cared if his neighbors knew she was staying over, but Layne might. He'd already learned during the months he'd spent in the Bay that the gossip mill churned twenty-four/seven in a small town.

They returned to his house, and he pulled into the garage, closing the door before they got out of the car. He retrieved her suitcase and carried it into the spare bedroom he'd never used.

"It'll be Mexican food for dinner tonight," he told her. "Miss Peggy's next-door neighbor always brought us home-made tamales on Christmas Eve. That's what I make every year. I like honoring that tradition."

"Is that very complicated to make?" she asked, looking worried.

"It's more time-consuming than anything," he told her. "You have to cook the pork and make the sauce. Soak the husks and make the dough. Combine everything and then steam the tamales. Usually, it takes about three-and-a-half hours or so from start to finish."

Layne giggled. "Then by the time you're done, we can invite Santa Claus to sit down and have some tamales with us because it's going to be late."

"I've already done everything but the steaming yesterday. It'll take about an hour for that. While they're steaming, we can make some guac. Toss a salad. Heat some refried beans. That is, if you're game for that."

Her radiant smile warmed him down to his toes. "It sounds wonderful, Keaton. I haven't had tamales in forever, much less had a man cook for me. In fact, I don't ever think I went out with a guy who made a meal for me."

He flashed a devilish grin. "Then you've been going out with the wrong kind of men, Miss Larson. Come follow my lead."

Removing the prepared tamales from the fridge, Keaton put them on to steam. He halved several avocados and scooped out the fruit, teaching Layne how to mash the avocados with a fork while he diced tomatoes and minced onions and garlic.

"I don't have a recipe for guac. It's a bit of taste and test," he explained, tossing in what he'd chopped and having her stir everything together.

Taking out salt, pepper, and lime juice, he added all three to the mixture, and then she stirred it thoroughly.

Keaton lifted the spoon with a bit of the guacamole and held it to her lips. She tasted it.

"Mmm. Very good. Maybe a touch more salt, though."

He did as she requested, sprinkling a dash of salt, and allowed her to sample it again.

"Perfect," she complimented. "And you were right. That wasn't hard at all. Even I could do that."

"I think you'll see most cooking is pretty easy. It's just getting familiar with things."

"No, calling for takeout is easy, but I do like how fresh this guac tastes."

He covered it with foil and placed the dip in the fridge to chill a bit, removing the makings for a salad. They prepared it together, and then he blended margaritas for them.

Layne took a small sip of hers. "Wow. If this art thing doesn't work out for you, you definitely have a future in bartending. This is the best margarita I've ever tasted."

She watched as he opened a can of refried beans and grated fresh cheese atop it.

"Microwaving this. Some cooks look at using a microwave as cheating, but it's a real convenience to me."

Ten minutes later, they were seated at his kitchen table, a feast before them.

Layne held up her margarita glass, now half-empty. "A toast. To my new friend, Keaton. Thank you for opening your home and heart to me."

She tapped her glass against his, and they both drank.

Digging into the tamales, Layne sighed after chewing her first bite. "These are amazing. Forget the bartending. You could be a chef."

"I'm pretty decent in the kitchen. I can teach you how to be, too."

Her eyes softened. "I'd really like that, Keaton. I think you have a lot to teach me. And I have a lot I need to discover—and rediscover—about myself."

This time, he was the one to hold his glass up. "To new discoveries," he said, and she echoed his toast.

They finished their meal, and Layne insisted she clean up the kitchen.

"You're my guest," he protested

"No. I'm a friend. That's different."

"My house, my rules. I'll help you," he insisted.

They moved to the sofa after the kitchen was spotless. He turned on a channel where an orchestra played Christmas carols, and they talked idly about things in the Bay. He caught her up on gossip, while she gave him background on people and places which helped him put several things into perspective.

Then Layne yawned. "Sorry. You're not boring me. I'm just tired. And the margarita made me a little sleepy."

"Hope you don't mind having to share a bathroom," he said. "This rental is small. Only one bath with the two bedrooms."

"Are you thinking about settling down in the Bay?" she asked. "I would think you would need more room if you do."

"As a matter of fact, I bought a house yesterday. That's why I stopped by Pelican Porch. I wanted a celebratory drink to mark the occasion of purchasing my first home."

"Oh, that's wonderful, Keaton. You'll have to tell me all about it." She yawned again. "Tomorrow. When I can stay awake and actually remember what you share about it."

"You can have the bathroom first," he said, trying to be a generous host.

He remained on the couch as Layne retreated from the room. She was only in the bathroom a few minutes, and then he took his turn before stripping off his clothes and climbing into bed.

Sleep wouldn't come, though. A thousand thoughts swirled in his head.

Most of them concerned Layne.

Then he heard a soft tap on his door. For a moment, he held his breath, then he called out, "Come in."

In the moonlight, he saw her silhouette enter the room.

"I couldn't sleep," she said, coming across the room, causing his heart to pound against his ribs.

"Neither could I." He held up the covers. "Climb in."

"Thanks. I promise I won't make a habit of this."

Hell, he'd take Layne Larson in his bed any night.

She turned on her side, facing away from him. Automatically, he rolled to spoon with her, his arm going around her waist, the familiar scent of lavender tickling his nose.

"Goodnight, Keaton," she said sleepily.

"Goodnight, Layne," he responded.

He wanted to stay awake, just to enjoy the feel of her against him. She was all soft curves to his male hardness. But the curtain of sleep quickly fell.

Keaton went to sleep with a smile on his face.

Chapter Nine

Layne awoke, enveloped by Keaton. The cocoon she found herself in made her feel safe.

And desired ...

She told herself it was wrong to have such strong feelings for him after having known him such a short time. It was also crazy that she already was considering him living in the Bay as she debated where her future would be. She would stay in her hometown for at least as long as it took for the renovations to the Bay Breeze to occur. While she didn't think she had the temperament to run the B&B herself, surely she could find someone competent who would be able to manage it in her stead.

If she did remain on the Gulf Coast permanently, though, what would she do for a living? Layne had been driven her entire life, whether it was on the soccer field or at work, making a name for herself. Whatever career she decided to pursue, she didn't think it would be viable to do so in the Bay. Plus, she didn't see herself as the kind who would have a fling with anyone, especially Keaton Maxwell. It would be disingenuous to do so.

She couldn't believe she had asked to crawl into his bed last night. She wasn't looking for a pity fuck. No, she wanted more from him.

And that frightened her more than any obstacle she'd ever faced.

His breathing changed, and Layne knew he was stirring to consciousness. She savored these last few moments, cradled against his hard body.

"Good morning," he said in a low rumble.

"Good morning," she replied. "I'm sorry, Keaton. I'm embarrassed that I asked to sleep with you last night. I hope you don't think I'm a tease."

He stroked her hair gently, making her feel more secure than she ever had with Jeremy.

"I was happy to have your company. I figured you needed me. Or at least a warm body."

"I don't know if it was being in a strange place." She chuckled. "Or the lumpy mattress and flat pillow, which sucked, but I couldn't fall asleep. And as much as I would like a repeat of two nights ago, adding more into the mix, I don't think I'm quite ready for sex yet."

"I get that." He leaned in and kissed her softly. "I get you, Layne. I would never rush you or push you into something which made you uncomfortable."

She smiled wistfully. "Why did you have to leave Dallas? Why couldn't our paths have crossed there?"

"I've become a believer in fate," he told her, the back of his fingers stroking her cheek. "We wouldn't have been ready for one another then. I doubt you would have given a blue-collar laborer the time of day. Not that I think you're a snob, but I just didn't have much to offer to any woman during my Dallas days."

"I admire you more than I can ever convey, Keaton," she said. "You are a true, self-made Renaissance man. You took the proverbial lemons and made lemonade. You learned various construction jobs, and you had to be excellent at them to be in demand as you were. All the while, you kept reading, discussing things with Miss Peggy and improving your mind and broadening your perspective. More importantly, you were dedicated and painted all those years. You honed your craft. When the time was right—and fate stepped in—you sold your work. You're talented. Accomplished. And I assume you must be doing pretty well since you bought a house."

"Not just any house," he said, and she heard pride in his tone. "Do you know John and Anna Smith from your days of living in the Bay?"

"The dating app guy? Sure. Hey, I even used his app a few times. Wait. You mean you bought his house." Excitement filled her. "I know exactly which one it is. It's probably three or four acres and sits right on the water. Good for you."

"I had a list of things required in order for me to purchase a house. Then I had a secret wish list of items which would be nice, but I never thought I could find all of them. The Smith house checked every box and added more than I ever imagined having. I can't wait to show it to you."

"When do you close?"

"My realtor says sooner than usual. They're going to do inspections, probably tomorrow or Tuesday. She's already sent the paperwork to the Smiths' attorney, who'll be handling the sale. They still have all their furniture in the house, though. They'll need to clear it out and move everything to their new house in Houston. Or Galveston. I gather they've purchased more than one house. I wasn't in any rush. I have this rental until the end of January. Mrs. Smith promised they'd be out before then. I do need to notify my landlord and inform him that I'll be vacating the premises in a little over a month."

He nuzzled her neck, causing tingles to ripple through Layne.

"As soon as I have the keys, I'll take you by. I want you to see it. They're even throwing in their boat as a bonus. I've rented a boat several times, going out and catching dinner in the bay, but now I'll have one at my disposal all the time. It's as if I'm living someone else's life, Layne."

"I'm proud of you," she praised. "Excited for you to have your own place. But I'm keeping you from your run."

"I do want to get that in. You can do your tai chi while I'm out. Then we can have a light breakfast together, and you can help me make the two dishes I'm bringing to lunch today. I told Laura I'd bring one, but there's another one with pineapple in it that I decided to bring, as well."

"Oh, right. I was so much help last night in the kitchen."

"You're a confident woman. Cooking is more of a science, and that will appeal to your practical nature. Following directions for the most part, and sometimes adding a little twist as you taste, like we did with the guac last night. Now baking? That's a blend of science and artistry."

He kissed the tip of her nose and then threw back the covers. Although the room was somewhat dark, she could tell by his silhouette that he was naked. She had been in bed with a naked Keaton—and he hadn't taken advantage of her.

He was not just a gentleman.

He was a keeper.

Layne suddenly realized that she could put all kinds of arbitrary timelines on whether or not she wanted to pursue a physical relationship with him. The attraction would be there in a week. A month. Even a year.

But why wait?

She was over Jeremy. Done with him and that part of her life. It was time to move ahead. Put the past behind her.

"Keaton?"

He was stepping into a pair of shorts and pulled them up before turning to face her.

Boldly, Layne said, "There are other ways to get exercise, you know."

He slipped back into the bed, and she placed a palm against his muscular chest. Beneath her fingertips, his heart beat wildly.

"Much as I appreciate the invitation to burn calories with you, I'm going to pass."

Hurt filled her. She started to pull her hand away, but he caught her wrist, keeping her palm flat against him.

"It's not that I don't want to make love to you, Layne. Hell, it's all I've been thinking about every waking moment since I met you. I don't think we should go there right now, though. I want to be your friend now. I hope to be your lover in the future. In the meantime, I don't want you as a fuck buddy. I think more of you—and our friendship—than that."

Her respect for this man grew exponentially. "I understand. And thank you for that."

He released her wrist, capturing and cradling her nape in his large, warm hand. "I hope you do. I see a future with you. Whether it's as close friends or more, I'm not sure. I want us both on the same page. At the same time. If and when we do make love together, it's going to be something that will join us in a way neither of us have ever been with anyone before. Okay?"

"Okay," she whispered.

Keaton brushed his lips lightly against hers and left the bed again. She watched him finish dressing, and then he came around to her side of the bed.

Tossing the covers back, he pulled her from the bed and to her feet. "Go tai chi it, Miss Larson. And Merry Christmas."

He kissed her again, softly, lingering a bit, causing a warmth to spread through her. Then he broke the kiss and winked at her.

While he was gone, Layne ran through her form. Usually, she was able to push aside everything and mindlessly meditate as she performed each pose. Today, however, her thoughts were disjointed, disrupting her practice. Things didn't flow smoothly. Frustrated, she ended her session early and decided to shower. She pinned her hair atop her head and was disappointed by the weak flow of water coming from the showerhead. She made a mental note to discuss water flow with Keaton. Guests would want a steady stream and not this pathetic trickle, and she wanted all showerheads to have more than adequate water pressure.

Toweling off, she dressed for the day before applying a light touch of makeup and brushing her hair.

When she entered the kitchen, Keaton had already returned. He stood at the stove, pushing around scrambled eggs in a pan. Another frying pan contained four pieces of sizzling bacon. The smell caused her stomach to gurgle noisily.

"Good, you're here. I was about to go hunt you down. It's almost time to eat. Would you turn on the coffeemaker? I've got some juice if you'd like it."

"Coffee will be fine," she said. "I thought you said a light breakfast."

He laughed easily. "This is light. For me. Besides we aren't eating until two this afternoon. I can't let you starve, can I?"

She prepared the coffee while he plated their meal. They talked throughout their leisurely breakfast, and Layne was relaxed in his company. It was as if they had known each other for years. She wasn't a believer in past lives, but if she had been, she decided Keaton and she had known one another very well. She also respected the fact that he had turned down her offer of having sex. She couldn't think of a single guy who would've done so, but he knew how raw she was emotionally and was giving her time to heal. That spoke volumes about his character. He may have had a rough upbringing, but somewhere along the way, Keaton had molded himself into a man of principle.

"I'll let you clean this up while I jump in the shower. Then it'll be time for your cooking lesson."

Thoughts of him naked in the shower danced in her head, and Layne forced them aside. "Okay."

"I'll meet you back here in twenty minutes. And don't put those iron skillets in the dishwasher."

"I may not know how to cook, but I do know that iron skillets are seasoned and never see the inside of a dishwasher. Go, Keaton. You can trust me."

Their gazes met. "I already do," he said.

Layne cleaned the kitchen and then sat at the table, scrolling through her phone and seeing what little email she had. During her working days, she received well over a hundred emails each day, even on weekends. She no longer had that account, though, and merely checked her personal one. Most of it were things she immediately deleted.

One email bore Jeremy's address, however.

She had blocked him on her phone and social media accounts, but she hadn't thought to do so with email. Layne decided that she wasn't up to reading any diatribe he had sent. She didn't delete it, though, thinking she might open it at some point and see what he had written. Creating a new folder, she named it BREAKUP and slid the email into it.

Keaton returned, smelling wonderful and appearing freshly-shaved. Though he was handsome clean-shaven, he was also appealing with a bit of stubble.

"Let me tell you about the two dishes we'll make, and then we'll get out all the ingredients," he said.

The first one he called Miss Peggy's Potatoes, saying, "This is something Miss Peggy only made twice a year, at Easter and Christmas. I swear I could have eaten nothing at those holiday dinners but these potatoes and been totally happy."

He listed the ingredients, which included shredded hash browns, cream of chicken soup, sour cream, butter, and cheese. *Lots* of cheese and butter. He got out everything they would need and greased a 9x13 glass pan, opening the thawed hash browns and scattering them in the pan. Then he dumped each ingredient, one at a time, into a giant bowl, and Layne stirred everything well. Keaton had her spread the potato mixture over the potatoes.

"Run the back of the spoon up and down until everything is nice and even."

She did as instructed, smoothly the mixture, and he sprinkled more sharp, shredded cheese atop it. Then he took out a box of cereal, which totally confused her.

"The secret ingredient," he announced, grinning broadly.

He tossed a few handfuls of cornflakes into a Ziplock bag. After sealing it, he placed it on the counter.

"Take the heel of your hand and mash it against the cornflakes," he told her. "Not too much. Just rock enough to break it up some."

When he was satisfied with her effort, he had Layne sprinkle the crunchy mix atop the casserole.

"The cornflakes don't actually add any taste to the casserole because they're so bland, but the crunch they provide is a nice surprise and balances the creaminess of the potatoes."

Keaton picked up a plastic lid and popped it into place atop the casserole dish. Sliding it into the fridge, he said, "On to round two. Pineapple Stuff."

"Wow, that's an original name," she said sarcastically.

"It's something Miss Peggy's mom made. She could never remember the actual name of it, so she nicknamed it Pineapple Stuff. Let me grab everything that goes into it."

Once again, he set out all the ingredients they would need in an organized fashion before greasing a round, porcelain dish. This time around, she blended beaten eggs with crushed pineapple, sugar, and whipping cream gently, per his orders. Then Keaton had them tear up several dinner rolls into small, bite-sized pieces, which they added to the mixing bowl. Layne stirred in the bread and then transferred everything in the bowl to the casserole dish.

Keaton placed it in the fridge, as well, saying, "We'll bake these in a couple of hours before we head over to Mr. and Mrs. Perry's house. I've got a warming tray I'll take with us. I didn't want to be presumptuous and assume there would be room in the oven for me to bake both dishes over there."

They went into the small living room and sat on the couch.

"I spent my fair share of Christmases at their house. Mrs. Perry always said Mom and Dad were on vacation at Christmastime and wouldn't let them bring anything to eat. Piper's family would also join us. It was my blood family and my chosen family coming together to celebrate Christmas, my favorite day of the year."

Her throat swelled with emotion, and Keaton slipped his hand around hers. He took her mind off her sadness, telling her about the series of paintings he had just completed.

"I'll keep one to hang in my new house. Maybe another one to sell at the gallery. The rest I'll drive up to the Clifford

Gallery in Dallas. They've represented me from the beginning."

"You personally deliver the paintings you create each time?"

He shrugged. "It's easier for me to transport them than pack them. I worry about them being damaged if I ship them. That happened once when I sent some from Wyoming. One canvas was beyond repair. I swore then that I'd never ship any of my work again. I've only had to make one trip north since I moved to the Bay. This'll be my second time to make the trip."

"Were you thinking about doing that anytime soon?" she asked.

"Probably sometime this week. Why?"

"Could I go with you? I need to pack up the rest of my clothes and some personal items and bring them back to the Bay. I also want to talk to a realtor about putting my house on the market."

He eyed her with interest. "So, are you considering a permanent move to Driftwood Bay?"

"I don't know if the Bay will be a temporary stop or a permanent move at this point," she said, not ready to make a commitment just yet. "I'll definitely stay during the renovation. By then, I'll have had time to think about what I want to pursue next and go from there."

Keaton nodded thoughtfully. "Good plan."

"I know I don't want to be in Dallas. I might as well bring my things here for now." She hesitated. "If it's not convenient for you, though, I'll simply fly back and handle everything."

"No, let's drive together. I'd like that."

"We'll make it a real road trip. I'll buy snacks. And we must stop at Buc-ees. That's a given."

"I got gas at one once. They had a ton of pumps."

"Oh, it's so much more than gas pumps. The cleanest

restrooms you'll ever find on a road trip. Beaver nuggets. Piña Colada Icees. Terrific BBQ sandwiches."

"It sounds as if you have road tripping down to a science."

"I went on vacation with both the Perrys and the Roberts every summer since Mom and Dad were tied up with their busy season. Believe me, I know how to organize a good car trip."

"When would you like to leave?"

Layne thought a moment. "Let me talk with Chief Roberts at lunch today. He may have an update on when the bodies will be released and the funeral can be held. Before, he seemed to think it would be late this coming week. If so, we could drive up in the next day or two." She paused. "Are you sure you don't mind me inviting myself along?"

"Not at all," Keaton assured her. "Road trips help friends bond."

The way he looked at her, though, heat in his eyes, Layne wondered just how long either of them would be able to hold out and simply remain friends.

Chapter Ten

Though Layne had been reluctant to attend Christmas at the Perry household, afraid it would remind her of other, happier celebrations she had experienced there, her warm welcome quickly dispelled any feelings of gloom.

Bill Perry answered the door, pulling Layne to him, saying, "We are so glad you decided to come today, honey. It wouldn't be Christmas without you."

"Thanks, Dr. Perry."

"Hello to you, too, Keaton," the educator greeted, offering Keaton his hand. "Glad you could make it."

Keaton shook it and held up a large, insulated bag containing the dishes they'd made. "Our contributions to the merriment."

"Take them in the kitchen," Dr. Perry said. "Laura will tell you what to do with them."

Layne followed Keaton there since she had the warming tray. Mrs. Perry flitted about the kitchen but took time to embrace her warmly.

"Thank you for coming, Layne. I know today will be difficult for you, but you've got family here to get you through it."

"I appreciate being here. More than ever before," she admitted.

"Thank you for bringing some food," Mrs. Perry told Keaton. "Mila has said she's sampled your potato casserole before and declares it is out of this world."

Mila, who was tossing a salad, looked up and grinned. "When I first heard him talk about it, I begged Keaton to make it. He said it was only for holidays."

"And you made up some holiday on the spot, if I recall," Keaton said, laughing. "Some only celebrated in the Bay holiday if I recall correctly."

Mila laughed merrily. "I'd lie my way from here to China for potatoes. Mom, you'll love these. They have everything bad for you in them, and that's why they taste so good."

"Did I hear potatoes?" asked Cecily Perry, entering the kitchen with a pie in hand and her two preschoolers trailing behind her. "You know I could eat my weight in potatoes."

"Right?" Mila agreed. "Hey, Gina. Bobby. Lily is upstairs watching Paw Patrol."

Both kids turned and ran from the kitchen, causing the adults to laugh. Cecily set down the pie and gave Layne a hug. Michael, her husband and Mila's brother, appeared and did the same.

"It's good to see you, Layne," Michael said. "Been a while."

"It sure has," she agreed.

Keaton had plugged in the warmer and placed his hot dishes on top of it. He and Michael greeted one another, and Michael led them from the kitchen.

"Are the Roberts coming?" she asked.

"They are," Mrs. Perry said. "But not Don."

Don was Piper's brother. He was a decade older and was a travel writer, rarely venturing back to the Bay.

Just then, Mrs. Roberts came into the kitchen and made a beeline for Layne. She wrapped her arms around her, hugging her tightly.

"Oh, sweetheart. It's so good to see you," Mrs. Roberts said.

Chief Roberts arrived, carrying a large canvas bag. "The green bean casserole and sweet potatoes have arrived," he announced.

"More potatoes, more fun," Mila quipped.

"Anything I can do to help?" Layne asked. "Set the table? Make some iced tea?"

"We've got everything covered," Mrs. Perry said. "I'm just doing a few last-minute things. Everyone out. We'll eat in ten minutes. Cecily, wait five minutes and then round up the kids. They'll be eating in the kitchen this year, and they're old enough to allow their parents to all be at the big table."

Mila slipped her arm through Layne's, leading her from the kitchen to the den. The men had gathered around the TV, and she saw that some basketball game was on.

"I'm really glad you came," her friend said. "I worried you'd stay at the inn and wander around all the empty rooms, but Keaton told Carson that he was bringing you." Mila arched a brow. "So, how is that going?"

Glancing around, she leaned in and quietly said, "I like him. He's kind. Open. Honest. A really good listener. He's been a good friend. In fact, we're driving up to Dallas together, probably this week. I just need to check with Chief Roberts about when my parents will be released from the morgue."

"Dallas is six or more hours away without stops for food or gas," Mila pointed out. "That's a long time to be in the car with someone."

"It won't be a problem. We seem to have a lot to talk about."

Mila nodded in satisfaction. "I'm glad to hear it. I like Keaton. A lot. I think you two could be good for each other. Why are you going?"

"He's finished up a series of paintings and wants to hand-deliver them to the gallery which represents him. I need to get the rest of my clothing and belongings and bring them back to the Bay." She paused. "I'm going to see a realtor while we're there and put my house on the market. Of course, this isn't a great time of year to be doing so, but I don't want to live and work in Dallas anymore."

Mila smiled hopefully. "Does that mean you're staying in the Bay?"

She shrugged. "For now. Keaton is going to help with some renovations I want to do to the B&B. I'll hang around at least until those are completed. It'll give me time to figure out what I want to do and where I want to be doing it. Hey, has Piper mentioned anything to you about quitting the road?"

"No! Seriously?"

"She mentioned it to me when we talked yesterday. I think ten years of traveling nonstop has worn her down. That—and you getting married. Of the three of us, Piper was always the most nurturing. I always saw her with babies."

"Yup. That was definitely Piper. Did she say if she would come back here?"

"She indicated that she's thinking about it. Of course, she has no idea what she'd do to earn a living."

"We're supposed to FaceTime around five today. We can talk about it then."

"If you'll excuse me a minute, I need to talk to Chief Roberts before we eat."

"Sure," Mila said, giving her another hug. "It's so good to have you here."

Layne went to where the police chief was sitting. "I wanted to ask you if you had an update about the autopsies."

Chief Roberts nodded. "I do. Unfortunately, there's a backlog. With the holiday—and the chief coroner taking off the week between Christmas and New Year's—they're backed up at the morgue. It looks like Friday is the earliest the autopsies could be performed. That means the bodies wouldn't be released before Saturday. My best guess is next Monday or later. I wish I had better news, Layne. I know you're eager to have the funeral and put this tragedy behind you."

"If that's the case, I may head up to Dallas this week. I need to get the rest of my things. I'm going to be doing quite a few updates to the Bay Breeze, so I'll be around for a few months."

"Feel free to go," he encouraged. "If anything changes here, I'll be in touch."

Mrs. Perry swept into the room, and Cecily brought the children in.

"Bill, will you say the prayer for us?" Mrs. Perry asked her husband.

They gathered in a circle, holding hands. Keaton had come up beside her on her right. She had Mila on her left. She glanced at her friend, who held Lily's hand, and saw how happy Mila looked. A sense of peace washed over Layne, being with people she loved and who loved her.

And Keaton.

She looked up at him, and he smiled at her.

"Let's bow our heads," Mr. Perry said. "Father, we want to thank you for everyone who's gathered here today to celebrate your birth. While we're missing Jack and Lark like crazy, we know they're with you and watching over all of us, especially Layne."

Keaton squeezed her hand on one side. Mila did the same on the other.

"Bless this food we'll eat today and thanks to those who prepared it for us, Father. And thank you for all the blessings, both big and small, which you've given us this year. In Jesus' name we pray, amen."

The group echoed, "Amen."

Mrs. Perry got the children situated at the kitchen table as everyone else went to the dining room. They filled ten of the twelve seats, the empty ones belonging to her parents. In a way, Layne felt as if they were seated at this table today, and she took comfort in that.

Michael shared that he'd just received the results from the dive rescue testing he had undergone two weeks, and he had passed at the top of the class of those involved in the training.

"I already had certification in rope rescue and advance extrication. Adding the dive rescue piece—especially living on the coast—will really help my résumé, as well as make me a more valuable member of the Driftwood Bay Fire Department."

Congratulations were offered to him, and Mila beamed at her big brother, saying, "You're going to be the battalion chief someday, Michael. I just know it."

Cecily also had good news, having recently received a promotion to charge nurse at the hospital she worked at in Corpus. She said the hours would be better and allow her to handle patients part of the time and administrative duties regarding the nursing staff the rest of the time.

"I've always loved caring for others, but I'm looking forward to doing something new," she explained.

"I'm ready for something new, as well," Dr. Perry said, looking at his wife. "Laura and I have decided this will be my last year to serve as the Bay's school superintendent."

The table erupted, with everyone firing questions at him.

Dr. Perry held up a hand. "No, I don't know what I'm going to do, other than get in more fishing and maybe take up golf. I feel that it's time to pass the torch to a younger man. I'll announce my retirement at the school board meeting come January, so keep the news under your hats for a bit."

Chief Roberts cleared his throat. "Funny you say that, Bill, because I'm going to do the same. I turn sixty-five in January. Though Texas doesn't have a mandatory retirement age, like New York or California, I've qualified for retirement for a few years now."

He looked to his wife and took her hand. "Ellen and I have talked it over, and we think we're going to go out together."

Mrs. Roberts nodded. "I'll talk to George Crumby once we go back to school in January. He told me once to give him plenty of notice when I was ready to leave since it's hard to find someone who is crazy enough to take on both drama and choir."

Dr. Perry chuckled. "Mae Williams is going to have her hands full, interviewing candidates for both our jobs. I'm glad I'm not in HR."

"Everyone is full of news this holiday," Mila said. "Anyone else have anything going on?"

Layne looked to Keaton, nudging him under the table with her foot.

He spoke up. "I bought a house from John and Anna Smith."

"The one right on the water?" Carson asked. "Boy, that is a sweet piece of property."

"Hillary Horton is setting up inspections for early this coming week," Keaton continued. "The Smiths are moving to the Houston area to be closer to their grandkids. It's perfect timing."

"Anna Smith had a tea for the women's club a few years ago," Mrs. Perry said. "It's a lovely house, Keaton. It's certainly large enough to turn one of the rooms into an art studio."

"Actually, there's a small cottage which is separate from the main house," he shared. "It gets excellent light. Has a small kitchen area, so I can clean my brushes, along with a large storage area where I can keep paints and canvases. I plan to work from there and keep work and home life separate."

Lily appeared in the doorway. "Is it time for dessert?"

"Sure, honey," Carson said, rising and placing his napkin on his chair. "Laura and I can go tackle that and get the kids situated."

The pair excused themselves, and Cecily said, "Your potatoes are fantastic, Keaton. I am going to need the recipe."

"Me, too," chimed in Mila. "I forgot to ask for it when you made them for us before."

"It's easy," he told them. "Layne helped me make them and the pineapple side dish."

"Layne helped?" Mila asked in mock surprise. "Our Layne as in Layne who can't boil water Layne?"

She laughed. "I deserve that."

"Especially when you set the oven on fire that time we were making cookies for the school bake sale," Mila said. "I thought your mom was going to kill us."

She glanced at Keaton. "See? I have a history in the kitchen. Short and disastrous."

It surprised her when he took her hand—and she knew it did others who were seated at the table.

"Yet you helped with both dishes we brought. I'll bet after making them once, you could easily create them yourself. Besides, how old were you when you almost burned your house down?"

"Seven," she said, laughter bubbling up from her.

Then Layne looked around the table, seeing that Carson and Mrs. Perry had rejoined them, placing the pie and cake on the table.

"I dreaded today," she began. "No Mom and Dad here. But I have felt embraced. Loved. And I've laughed today, really laughed. I want to thank everyone at this table for making this holiday a good one for me. Mom and Dad made the decision that they thought was best for them, but they also knew they left me in good hands. Everyone seated here is family to me."

She turned to Keaton. "I especially want to thank Keaton for keeping my spirits up. For listening and letting me cry when I needed to. I'm expecting it to be rough the day of the funeral and for days after that, but I know I have the support and love of everyone at this table. For that, I am so grateful."

Mrs. Perry smiled at her. "You are a daughter to us, sweetheart. We will always be here for you." She glanced around the table. "It looks like everyone is ready for some dessert. Now who wants cake and who wants pie?"

"I say you need to ask who wants both," Keaton said, causing everyone to laugh.

As Mrs. Perry sliced the pie and Carson took care of the requests for cake, Layne kept her hand in Keaton's.

Today could have been a depressing one, spent alone as she wandered through the Bay Breeze. Instead, being here let Layne see she could miss her parents and still keep on living with those she loved surrounding her.

Mila grinned from across the table. "I've opted for more potatoes as my dessert. I can't wait for Layne to show me how to make them."

"I'll do that once we get back from Dallas," she said.

As everyone dug into their desserts, Layne's heart whispered that her decision had been made. She would be staying in Driftwood Bay.

Because she wanted to see if she had a future with Keaton.

Chapter Eleven

For the first time in three days, Keaton awoke with no company in his bed. A poignant ache filled him, wishing Layne were here beside him.

The only people he'd ever become close to were Miss Peggy and Frankie. Even then, it had taken him a while to warm up to both women. After Frankie's betrayal, he didn't think he would ever let down his guard again as far as a woman was concerned. But Driftwood Bay was slowly changing him. The residents of the Bay had a warmth about them. A friendliness. It seeped into his soul. He had already made friends with Carson and Sullivan and expected the bonds of their friendship to grow over time.

Layne had thrown him for a loop, though. He had never bared his soul to anyone as he had her. It had thrilled him when she had said she would be staying in town, at least for a little while.

Keaton planned to make the most of that time with her.

He rolled out of bed, stretching his muscles, and then set out for his daily run. He wasn't sure what today would bring.

He'd told Layne that he needed to check in with Hillary before they made plans to take off to Dallas. If the realtor had been able to set up the house inspections, he wanted to be present for those. Miss Peggy had drilled into him that home ownership was a responsibility, and he wanted to be aware of every aspect of his new home from the beginning.

Once he arrived home from his run, he showered and got ready for the day. As he was brewing coffee, a text came in from Hillary, asking him to call her at his earliest convenience. He did so, and she answered on the first ring.

"I thought you were an early bird, Keaton," she said. "I wanted you to know that both inspections are on for this afternoon. The Smiths' attorney has already agreed to everything in the paperwork I drew up. That means once the inspections are completed, we've got smooth sailing ahead of us, especially since you aren't having to finance a mortgage. Do you still want to be present this afternoon while the inspections take place?"

"Absolutely. Can I bring someone with me?"

"Of course. I don't think any red flags will appear in these inspections and throw a kink into the sale. The Smiths have lived there for years and have maintained the property well, as you saw. Be there at one this afternoon. It'll probably take two to three hours."

"Will you be there, too?" he asked, having come to trust his realtor and knowing she had both the knowledge and experience to help him through this process.

"No. I have a showing at one-thirty. Besides, the reports will be texted to me right after the inspections are completed. Let me look at my calendar." She paused a moment. "Would you like to stop by the office about four-thirty? We can look things over together and decide if you're ready to proceed."

He couldn't think of anything that would cause him to

back out of the deal at this point and agreed to be at her office later this afternoon.

Knowing now that he and Layne wouldn't be able to leave for Dallas today, he texted her, asking her to call him when she had a chance.

Immediately, his phone rang, causing him to grin like a schoolboy when he saw her name light up his screen.

"Hey. I just heard from Hillary. She was able to get the inspections scheduled for this afternoon, so we can leave for Dallas early tomorrow morning if that's all right with you."

"I'm glad that'll be taken care of. You'll be one step closer to home ownership once those are out of the way."

"Are you free this morning? While I want to patronize local businesses as much as possible regarding the renovation, the hardware store's selections of paints is pretty limited. If you're up for it, we can go into Corpus this morning and choose the paints for the interiors and exteriors of the inn."

"That would be fantastic. What time? I'm ready now."

"Let me head over and show you what I've drawn up so far. We should also talk about color choices before we hit the store. It would better to have solid ideas in mind before we get there."

She chuckled. "You're telling me I would be overwhelmed by the choices available? I get it. I'm all about having a game plan going into this. See you in a few."

His step light, he went to his truck and drove to the Bay Breeze. The structure had good bones. It just needed a facelift to become more appealing and highlight its beauty.

Layne was sitting on the porch steps when he arrived and rose to greet him as he came up them. Keaton brushed a quick kiss on her cheek, fighting the urge to devour her. He told himself she wasn't going anywhere anytime soon and that these sparks would not fizzle and die out.

"Come on in," she told him. "I'll make us a cup of tea, and we can look over what you've come up with."

He sat at the kitchen table while she bustled about, preparing their tea. Soon, she placed two mugs on the table and joined him. The smell of orange spice floated up to greet him.

Dunking her teabag a few times, she asked, "What do you think about the idea of each bedroom having a different color? Remember, we talked about that possibility before. I got online, studying about forty or fifty B&B's up and down the Texas coast. A lot of people have themes for their rooms. They might pick the name of classic authors, such as the Shakespeare or Jane Austen room. One place chose the four seasons as their theme. I know living near the water, I could go with an all-coastal look in each room, but that wouldn't distinguish the guestrooms."

"I like the idea of using color to identify a room. Are you partial to any?"

He picked up his pen and opened his notebook, ready to take notes.

"I've always loved flowers," Layne said. "I would enjoy naming each room after a particular flower and working within that palette of colors. The Daffodil Room. The Hydrangea Room. That kind of thing."

"Okay, the four rooms. What colors do you want to run with?"

"Definitely daffodil. I can see pale yellows with accents of slate blue or soft grays."

Keaton made a note. "That sounds appealing. Go on."

"I mentioned hydrangeas. I'd like to maybe have shades of blue in another room."

"We can work with that," noting her choice. "That's two. Number three?"

"Roses might sound clichéd, but I still think that would be a good choice. Maybe tea roses on the wallpaper."

"What about a rose gold?" he suggested.

When she frowned, he pulled out his phone and brought up a few images using that color.

"Oh, that's lovely. I'm definitely on board with rose gold. Rose. Blue. Yellow. Maybe something in the purple family. Lilacs?"

Writing down her final choice, he said, "I like that. It'll give each guestroom a distinct flavor and identity. You mentioned wallpaper. Would you like to see that in all the guestrooms?"

"Only if we can find something suitable, running with that flower theme. If not, we can just focus on the color scheme. What about the rest of the house, though?"

"That's where you can draw in some elements of the coast. Incorporate things related to the beach. The surf."

Once more, he tapped his phone and brought up a series of images he had saved to a folder. One had light gray walls, with furniture and accents in white and sandstone. Another layered blue tones, from sky to sea. One example leaned into nautical themes, using anchors and sails, while another focused on starfish and seashells. They discussed each photo, and Layne liked the idea of the light gray walls and mixing whites and sandstone shades with a few pops of color on accent pillows. She really liked the idea of using seashells and starfish.

"Bringing elements of surf and sand into the neutral palette appeals to me," she said.

"Not that I'm pushing the artists represented at my gallery, but I want to stop by there and show you some of the pieces available. I think if you had paintings of the coast and various art objects scattered in the public rooms, playing up the coastal design theme, it would unify the place. Make it light and airy and still homey at the same time."

"This is where I'm going to really lean on you, Keaton. I don't have your vision or sense of style. I'm going to turn over the colors and furniture choices downstairs to you. The public room. The kitchen and dining room, minus the table there, which we have to keep. Let your vision flow. I know I'll be fine with whatever you come up with."

Then she bit her lip. "I need to also redo Mom and Dad's room, as well. I don't think I would be happy running an inn. I'll hire someone to do that for me. They would be given that room, in addition to their salary."

"Then definitely neutrals for it," he said, his heart beating quickly. "You want it suitable to a man or woman." Casually, he added, "Where would you stay?"

Her gaze met his. "I have gotten that far yet. Because I'll need to stay in the Bay for a few months—just to get the inn up and running—I could rent something for myself. Maybe even the house you're in now when you move out. That would be ideal, being so close to Mila."

He relaxed a little, hoping she would consider remaining in the Bay permanently.

They spent a few minutes talking about the kind of furniture to purchase for the common rooms, and then he pitched ideas for paint choices regarding the exterior. She narrowed her choices down to two after seeing his photos he'd saved, and Keaton told her they could make a final decision based upon the paint selection available in Corpus.

"Let's leave now. The store I have in mind will be open by the time we get there," he said. "We can choose all the paints and then even look at items such as light fixtures. Faucets for the bathrooms. Handles for kitchen and bathroom cabinets. That kind of thing."

As they drove into Corpus, he told Layne his plan to redo each of the bathrooms, as well as sprucing up the kitchen, and she followed along, looking at the sketches he had made of each.

"The kitchen appliances are dated. No, outdated. As long as we're putting in new countertops, backsplash, and flooring, we might as well buy new appliances to match instead of having something go out a month from now. Just start brand-new with everything."

"You know more about this than I do. I'll bow to your judgment."

They parked and went inside the store, heading straight for the paint section. She was amazed at the myriad of choices.

"I always thought white paint was white paint. There must be two dozen variations on white alone. Alabaster. Pearl. Super White. Snow White. Milk White. I'm glad you prepped me before and we arrived at the hues we wanted to use. This is mind-boggling. You can make the paint decisions, Keaton. You know the colors and look I'm going for."

She placed a hand on his forearm, causing his heart to beat faster. "And I'm paying you for this job, both your time and labor involved. Don't even think about protesting," Layne warned. "This is going to take away from your painting, which is your livelihood. I want you to be well compensated for the work you're doing for me."

Rather than arguing with her, he simply nodded. "I'm good at what I do. After all my years in construction, I know how to be efficient with my time and not cut corners."

"How long do you think this renovation is going to take?"

"As I mentioned, we'll contract out the exterior and interior painting," he said. "If done right, with a large crew, that'll take a solid week, if both inside and outside are being painted at the same time. If they're painted separately, with a smaller crew, then ten to twelve days is my best estimate. I run a tight ship, Layne, and I'll be supervising whatever crew we hire. It'll get done in less than two weeks. I guarantee that.

"As far as all the other work goes, I think that can all happen within two months."

"So, we're looking at the end of February," she mused. "That would be good, with spring break and then the high season around the corner."

"You'll need to find someone to take professional photographs once the work is complete. I'm a decent photographer, but a pro will know more about how to light each room and maximize the size of the space. They'll make it look good for online. If I were you, I'd take down all the pictures on the current website immediately. Just have a disclaimer that the inn is undergoing renovations and will be open for reservations soon. Say, March first. That'll give me incentive to get my rear in gear and get this job done."

"That means I'll also have to act quickly and find someone to manage the Bay Breeze." She smiled, her face lighting up. "I can't wait to restore the B&B to its former glory. I have you to thank for that, Keaton."

She squeezed his forearm and then dropped her hand.

They spent the next two hours making their final choices, first with the help of a clerk, who then summoned the paint department's manager to assist them when he saw how big a job this would be. Joe Jordan fetched a clipboard and made notes of every color and the number of gallons which would be needed.

"If you'll start pulling the order now, Joe, Layne and I are going to peruse other things in the store."

As they moved away from the customer desk, she said, "That is a heckuva lot of paint. I'm glad you knew how to estimate the amount we needed. I wouldn't have had a clue where to start."

"We're just going to look at some things today. I wanted to expose you to what's available. We can spend more time online, looking at inventory and then narrowing down what you want for each bathroom and the rooms downstairs."

They spent half an hour inspecting bathroom faucets. Toilets. Showerheads. Lighting fixtures. He could tell she was becoming more than overwhelmed and said, "We'll stop the fact-finding mission now since your head is swimming."

"That's one way of putting it," she joked. "I do need a breather. There are so many decisions to be made."

They stopped by the paint desk again, and the clerk walked them to the front, where Joe stood next to three large, flatbed handcarts stacked high with gallon paint cans.

The paint manager gave Keaton his card. "If you need anything else, give me a call."

"As a matter of fact, I'm going to need a crew to put this paint to good use if you know of any reliable ones," he replied. "The job is in Driftwood Bay."

Joe broke out in a smile. "My son lives the next town over from the Bay. He has a painting and remodeling business. Even though I'm his dad, I would hire him. Joey's got a great work ethic. A small, dedicated crew."

Keaton handed the card back. "Put Joey's number on the back for me. I'll give him a call today."

"Thanks, Keaton. I appreciate your business here and for considering Joey, as well."

The clerk finished ringing up their purchases, and store staff helped roll the handcarts out to his truck, loading dozens of cans into the bed.

On the way home, he asked, "Would you mind going with this Joey fellow, or do you have someone in the Bay in mind?"

"I've been gone too long. Besides, I like having a personal recommendation. Let's call Joey now."

Keaton did so, putting it on speakerphone. Joey already knew the call was coming because his dad had given him a heads up. Keaton explained that the interior and exterior of the Bay Breeze Inn would need to be painted, and the owner wanted it done as soon as possible.

"I've given my crew the week off between Christmas and New Year's," Joey said. "Business is slow this time of year, but we could start next Monday, the second of January, if that's good for you, Keaton."

"That'll be fine. I'm going to be doing the inside remodeling myself. If I need some help, I may call upon you and your crew for some assistance. We'll be working for Layne Larson. She's the owner of the B&B."

"I suppose she's related to the Larsons who owned the inn ten years ago. My wife and I stayed there for our honeymoon, and the couple who ran it were really kind to us."

"That would be Layne's parents. They've recently passed on, and she's inherited the inn. She's giving it a makeover before she'll start taking reservations again."

Spontaneously, Layne said, "Once all the work is done, Joey, maybe you and your wife would like to have a room for the weekend, free of charge."

"Wow! That would be terrific, Miss Larson," Joey said enthusiastically.

"Layne," she told him. "And thank you for putting us on your schedule."

"Thank you for giving us the work. I think you'll like what we'll do for you, Layne. Looking forward to meeting you and Keaton."

They decided that work would begin at seven on the day after New Year's and ended the conversation.

"I'm glad we're using Joey," she said. "I think it's one of those circular things, him having stayed at the Bay Breeze in the past and now getting to be a part of restoring it for future guests."

He glanced at his watch. "We have time for a quick lunch before we need to be at the Smiths' place. That is, if you'd like to go see the house while the inspections are being conducted."

"Oh, absolutely. I can't wait to see the interior."

"What sounds good to eat?"

"How about Coastal Catch Café?" she suggested. "I love their fried catfish sandwich, and they have wonderful steak fries."

"I've never been to it."

"You haven't? Well, you're in for a treat."

Keaton headed to the café, thinking the best treat was being in Layne Larson's company.

Chapter Twelve

Layne sat in the passenger seat of Keaton's truck, feeling more content than she had in a long time. Her life had changed radically in the past week. Returning to the Bay had led to a slower pace of life, allowing her to catch her breath. She was beginning to remember to appreciate the small things around her. The song of a bird chirping. The satisfaction of sipping a cup of hot tea without hurrying.

And the man sitting next to her.

It seemed impossible that they had only known each other for such a short length of time because she felt she knew Keaton better than she had any other man, and that included her five years with Jeremy. Keaton also had glimpsed deeply into her. Thank goodness he hadn't tucked tail and run, especially with the mess her life was at the moment.

Yet she was more grounded now that they had firm plans for the Bay Breeze. Layne liked how Keaton had a vision for the inn and would help bring it back to life. It was in a wonderful location and once the renovation had been completed, she believed it would reflect the charm of the B&B.

They had left the Bay at six o'clock this morning for their long trek to Dallas, stopping at a Buc-ees for gas and a stretch break. Once inside, Keaton had marveled at all the merchandise available, as well as the spotless restrooms. He had gobbled down a BBQ sandwich and sugared pecans, joking that he had fallen under the spell of Buc-ees. She teased him about needing to join a Facebook group dedicated to fans of the place.

It was half-past noon when they reached the outskirts of Dallas, and he glanced to her.

"Mind if we go to the gallery first? I want to get my paintings into Sidney's hands."

"I have yet to see any of your work. You'll have to take me to your gallery once we return to the Bay. I assume you have a few examples of your own work on display there."

"I can do that. If you like, we can stay and watch as they unwrap a few canvases at the Clifford Gallery now."

"Do they know you're coming?"

He nodded. "I texted Sidney yesterday and told him to expect us early afternoon."

Dallas traffic was heavy. Layne didn't miss that aspect of living in a big city. She could reach anywhere in the Bay within ten to twelve minutes and liked that part of small-town life. While the renovation was in progress, she needed to figure out a job she could do remotely—so she could stay in her hometown—and see if anything permanent could occur between Keaton and her. Part of her was afraid to explore a relationship with him because of the heat already between them. She was afraid it would burn brightly for a short while and then fizzle out. If it did, so be it. She had a feeling they would remain friends, regardless of whatever physical happened between them.

They wound up in the Knox-Henderson area, and Keaton pulled into an alley and then a parking lot behind a building which she assumed was the Clifford Gallery. Cutting the engine, he picked up his phone from the cup holder and sent a quick text.

"Someone will unlock the back door and meet us now," he told her.

The door swung open, and a man in a navy, double-breasted suit stepped through it. He looked to be in his late forties, with a dash of silver at his temples. He was followed by two younger men who hurried toward them as they got out of the truck.

"Everything is under the tarp, guys," Keaton told the pair. He offered his hand to the older man.

Layne went around the front of the truck and joined them.

"Sidney McAlister, I'd like you to meet Layne Larson. She recently moved back to Driftwood Bay from Dallas."

Sidney greeted her. "A pleasure to meet you, Miss Larson."

"Layne, please. I'm eager to see the art you have on display at your gallery, especially if you have something of Keaton's on display."

"I only have one Keaton Maxwell hanging on the walls, and it is already spoken for." Sidney glanced to Keaton. "*Stormy Night*. Monica bought it, but she's been in Paris since before Thanksgiving. She'll be back after New Year's and claim it. Please, come inside."

Sidney turned and led them into the building. Keaton threaded his fingers through hers, saying, "Monica is a lady from Highland Park. I did a lot of work for her back in the day. She was an early purchaser of my work and introduced me to Sidney. I wouldn't be where I am today without Monica's support."

They made their way through a storeroom and then moved into the gallery itself. She had never stepped foot inside an art gallery before. The only thing she knew about art was from a freshman-level art appreciation class she had taken in college to fulfill a fine arts requirement for her business degree. All she remembered was that she had liked Impressionism. Nothing else had stuck with her.

Glancing about now, though, she could tell the quality of art in this gallery was at the highest level. She caught sight of the placard beside a painting, listing its price, and did a quick intake of breath. If Keaton commanded these kinds of prices, he must be extremely well off.

Sidney stopped and indicated a canvas on the wall. They joined him, and her eyes moved to the painting hanging before them. It depicted a storm rolling in, and she easily recognized Driftwood Bay as its subject. The colors were bold. Beautiful. Angry. She could feel the tremendous power of the approaching storm as the scene generated both awe and fear within her.

"It's breathtaking," she declared, blown away by Keaton's talent. "I can't look away from it."

"Thank you," he said. "I had been struggling as to what my next subject would be, and then one night a storm just like this blew into the Bay. I went out and experienced it as it moved toward me. Feeling the turbulence. Watching it move across the water. Then I was hit by the powerful blow of the wind. The driving rain. Immediately, I knew I had to capture on canvas the moment in time I had been a part of."

"You certainly did. I know great art evokes strong emotions, and I feel the turbulence inside me that this brings."

His eyes shined brightly. "That is a terrific compliment."

"You didn't say how many paintings you were bringing to me, Keaton," Sidney said.

"I'll text you a doc with the numbers and titles. The series has fifteen paintings altogether. I kept two of them. One for myself and one which is hanging in Gulf Coastal Gallery now."

"Will you sell either of them?" Sidney inquired.

"I'm not certain at this point. I just purchased a house in Driftwood Bay, and I have an idea where I would like to hang one of them once I move in. The painting in the gallery is for display now, just so browsers can get an idea of the art behind the gallery's owner. I may sell it at some point, or I might bring it up here with me the next time I deliver canvases to you. I have taken pictures of both, though. I'll text those to you. Even though they won't be available to your clients, you can at least include them in the series."

"Please do so," the gallery manager said.

"Let's go back to the storeroom," Keaton suggested. "We can watch as a few of the canvases are unwrapped."

They returned the way they came, and Layne saw the two men had finished bringing in the paintings from the truck. They now unwrapped the first one carefully, cutting through a thick layer of bubble wrap. Keaton had done a thorough job of securing the safety of his work on their trip north. Anticipation built inside her as the first painting was finally unveiled.

She gasped upon seeing it.

The painting was of sunset over the Bay, a myriad of colors streaking the sky, taking her breath away.

Turning to Keaton, she quietly said, "I knew you were talented, but this is insane."

A satisfied smile turned up the corners of his mouth. "I'm glad you like it. When is your birthday?"

The random question threw her. "March fifteenth. Why?"

He smiled enigmatically. "Just asking."

"Are you saying you would paint a picture for me?"

"I'd like for you to have something of mine, Layne."

Happiness bubbled through her. "I would be honored to own a Keaton Maxwell landscape. Especially if it reflected Driftwood Bay. I took an art appreciation course in college.

Just think, there may be freshmen out there right now, studying your work." She grinned and quietly added, "And if they knew how handsome the artist was, they would be in love with him, as well as his art."

That caused him to burst out laughing. The two men stopped what they were doing and stared. Keaton ignored them and said to Sidney, "My work here is done. You can send me the price list once you've assessed the work."

"How long will you be in town?" Sidney asked.

"Just a day or two. Layne has some business to handle, and then we'll drive back to the coast. Text if you need anything."

"Will do," Sidney replied. "Thanks for delivering these to me, Keaton."

They returned to his truck, and Keaton said, "I'm famished. That sandwich was hours ago." He glanced at his watch. "It's only two-thirty, but I don't think I can hold out for dinner."

"I know the perfect place to grab a late lunch," she told him. "It's not too far from here. Once we eat, it'll be time to meet with Liza."

Liza Franklin had sold a house last summer to a friend of Layne's from work. She had met the realtor at the open house her friend held upon moving in and saved the card Liza had given her. Layne had texted the realtor on their way to Dallas this morning, and they had a four o'clock appointment with her at her office in Lakewood.

"Tell me where to go. I'm hoping it'll be Mexican food."

Layne laughed. "As a matter of fact, it is."

Ten minutes later, they pulled into the parking lot of El Perro Perezoso.

"The Lazy Dog," he translated.

"You speak Spanish?"

"I picked up a lot during my construction years. I'm not fluent, but I can get by."

Only two other cars were there. As Keaton helped her from the truck, he commented, "Either very late lunch goers—or early for happy hour people."

They went inside the familiar restaurant, and the hostess seated them.

"What's good here?" he asked, looking over the menu.

"I've never had a bad meal here. The enchiladas are fabulous. The fajitas are even better. It's possible that their guacamole just might rival yours," she teased.

"Want to split some fajitas?" he asked.

She set aside her menu. "As long as we get some queso to go along with them."

They placed their order and nibbled on chips and salsa until the queso arrived. It was even better than she remembered, and Keaton raved about it.

"What is your next series of paintings going to be about?" she asked.

"I haven't a clue," he admitted. "Usually, I take a few weeks off after finishing a group. Just to cleanse my mind. Recharge my batteries. Stir the well of creativity a bit. This reno is coming at the perfect time. I enjoy working with my hands. Letting my mind drift. A theme will come to me, whatever is next for me to paint."

"I saw how much some of that art cost. If you're pulling even half of the prices I spotted, I'll feel super-guilty taking you away from your craft and your earning potential."

He shrugged. "I wouldn't be painting anyway. I would be loafing. Trying to hit on the next series." He grinned. "Probably getting in a lot of fishing. This way, I'm keeping my construction skills at my fingertips. I'd rather do something productive while I'm waiting for the muse to strike me again."

Their fajitas arrived, a sizzling mixture of steak and chicken, accompanied by grilled onions and peppers, shredded cheese, guacamole, sour cream, pico de gallo, and piping hot flour tortillas.

After a few bites, Keaton told her, "These might be the best fajitas I've ever eaten. You're also right about their guac. It's outstanding."

They talked some about Carson's basketball team, and he promised to accompany Layne to a game. They also discussed a few details about the funeral she would hold for her parents, and she was glad she had Keaton as a sounding board.

He paid for their meal, and they headed to Liza's office, which was only a few minutes away from the restaurant.

"It's nice to see you again, Layne," the realtor said upon them entering the office.

"Thanks for taking the time to meet with us," she replied. "This is Keaton Maxwell, a good friend of mine."

Putting the friend label on Keaton would suffice for now, but Layne knew he was much more to her than that.

"He's in charge of renovating the inn I recently inherited, and he's also an artist."

Liza's eyes went wide. "You're *that* Keaton Maxwell? Oh, I've seen your art hanging on walls of homes I've sold in High-land Park. I'm an admirer of your work."

"Thank you," he said humbly.

"Let's have a seat," Liza suggested. "I'm familiar with your neighborhood and recently sold a house a few blocks from where you live. I've pulled comps for the area, as well as the records from when you bought the house. It's darling, Layne. It has great curb appeal. I think we'll make a killing on it. I can't wait to see the inside."

For the next half-hour, they went over the particulars of her house, with Liza typing into her laptop specifics about the property. Then they studied the comps, which showed the sales of houses which had sold during the last few months in her neighborhood. Liza focused on three in particular, since they had similar square footage to hers. One was right down the street from her. Another two blocks over. The third had just gone on the market and was only three doors down from her.

"If you have time now, we can go over and look at the inside," Liza said. "Once I see it, I'll have a better idea about how to price it. That is, if you're ready to commit to me."

"Definitely," Layne said. "Let me sign whatever I need to make that official. I'll be leaving Dallas, so I'll need to clear out the house. Do you think I should leave the furniture in it for now, or would it do better if it were empty?"

"It depends upon how things look. If the furniture makes the rooms look overcrowded, I'll have you clear it out. I have a person I use to stage houses. We can work with her on dressing up a few rooms if necessary."

Layne stood. "Then let's go see it and get your opinion."

She and Keaton returned to his truck, with Liza following in her sedan. When they turned on her street, a wave of nostalgia rippled through her. This had been the first house she had bought, and she was so proud of it and the neighborhood.

"It'll be the second one on the end. On the right," she told him.

They reached the house, and Keaton wheeled into the driveway. Layne went numb inside. Splashed across the garage in angry red paint was one word in capital letters ten feet tall.

BITCH

Chapter Thirteen

They met with the police. Keaton had insisted they remain outside the house, not knowing whether or not Layne's ex had broken in and caused damage there. Liza patiently waited with them, telling Layne that this wouldn't affect her decision to represent Layne in selling the house.

That had caused Layne to cry, and he had wrapped her in his arms, murmuring comforting nonsense to her. He wasn't a violent man—but if he ever came face-to-face with the asshole who had done this to Layne, there wouldn't be much left of him when Keaton was done.

Two patrol officers arrived on the scene, and one called for a detective to meet them. The cops entered the house, using Layne's key, and reported back that the interior seemed intact. Because of that, they waited for the detective inside. Layne had encouraged Liza to go ahead and look around. The realtor did so, telling them that the furniture was well suited for the house and would photograph well.

"I'm sorry this has happened," Liza said. "But you can file

your report. Ask for a restraining order regarding your ex. I'll call someone and have the garage repainted first thing tomorrow, and then we'll photograph the inside and outside. I'll have the listing up by late afternoon if that's all right with you."

"The sooner you can sell it, the better," Layne said, sounding defeated. "Frankly, I don't want any of the furniture. Either include it in the sale or help me find a place to donate it to. I want my clothes and photographs. That's it. I can't even stay here anymore."

She fished Jeremy's keys out of a bowl on an end table and handed them over. "It's in your hands now, Liza. Thank you for handling the garage."

The realtor hugged Layne. "I'm going to get you top dollar. The house is in great condition. The updates to it will really help in selling it."

Layne blew her nose. "The previous owners did those. I just tried to take care of things once I moved in."

Liza said goodbye. As she left, the police detective showed up.

"Detective Jeff Robinson," he said, introducing himself. "I assume you're Layne Larson."

"Yes. This is Keaton Maxwell, a friend of mine from Driftwood Bay, near Corpus. It's my hometown. Please have a seat, Detective."

He took out a pen and opened a small notebook. "I saw the vandalism on the garage door. I've already taken several pictures of it for my report. I noticed you don't have a Ring camera on your front door."

She shrugged. "I never have much company. I also don't have an Amazon habit, so I don't receive many packages. I just never thought I needed one."

"I'd advise you to rethink that, Miss Larson. These cameras

aren't expensive and offer a measure of safety and comfort. Do you have any idea who might have a grudge against you?"

"Although I don't have any proof, I know it had to be Jeremy Riggs. We dated for the last five years. He lived here until a week ago, when I asked him to move out."

Robinson made a note. "I assume it wasn't an amicable breakup."

"No, it wasn't. I own the house, however. My name is on the deed, so when I told him we were through, I asked him to leave. He was angry. I informed him I would have his things packed and in boxes waiting for him on the porch the next morning."

"Did Mr. Riggs ring the doorbell when he returned? Confront you in any way?"

"I was gone by then," she said softly.

Keaton wrapped his hand around hers and looked at the detective. "Miss Larson learned her parents had died that evening. Chief Roberts from Driftwood Bay, a family friend, flew up to give her the news. She flew to Corpus and rented a car there in order to drive to Driftwood Bay and has been there the past week."

"I see," Robinson said, scribbling furiously on his pad.

"I'm putting the house up for sale," Layne informed him. "I only returned to Dallas to pick up the rest of my things. You passed my realtor leaving as you arrived."

"You'll be moving to Driftwood Bay?" the detective asked.

"Yes. My parents left me a bed and breakfast. Mr. Maxwell is helping me with renovating it. I'm leaving Dallas for good."

Robinson asked for some background information about her and Jeremy. Layne explained how her company had been bought, and she had received a generous severance package and would be looking for work.

"I miss my hometown, Detective. I needed a change of pace, ending my relationship with Jeremy and leaving my job. Driftwood Bay is going to be home again to me." She hesitated. "Do you think I should file a restraining order against Jeremy?"

"No," he advised. "First, you have no proof that Mr. Riggs is responsible for the graffiti on your garage door. Of course, I'll talk to your neighbors. See if anyone spotted him or if they have a security camera which shows who might be responsible for the vandalism. To receive a restraining order in the State of Texas, you need an abundance of proof, such as printouts of fifty unwanted emails or a series of text messages. That kind of thing. While I agree that it's likely your ex is responsible for the damage to your house, that one act alone wouldn't warrant receiving the restraining order. I assume you have no contact with him?"

"None" she said firmly. "I've blocked him everywhere."

"Then he won't even know where you are living, Miss Larson. I'll need your contact information." He handed over his card. "I'll keep in touch with you regarding the investigation."

"My agent wants to put the house on the market tomorrow. She said she has someone who can repaint the garage immediately. Is that okay?"

"Yes. I have what I need. I'll be contacting Mr. Riggs now and scheduling an interview with him. Since you've provided his work address, I'll head there now."

She snorted. "Let's just hope he's there. Jeremy doesn't have the most reliable work record. I'm sorry I wasn't able to tell you where he's moved. Frankly, I don't want to know. I don't care to have anything to do with him."

"But you do want to press charges for the vandalism if I can find proof he was involved?" Robinson asked.

"Definitely."

Keaton was glad she said that as firmly as she did.

"I'll be in touch after I've spoken with Mr. Riggs," the detective promised.

"I'll see you out," Keaton said, accompanying the detective to the door. He passed Robinson a card with his own information on it. "In case you can't get a hold of Layne, you can always contact me. I'll see she gets in touch with you. We'll probably drive back to the coast tomorrow since my business is concluded and she's turned over the sale of her house to a realtor."

"Thank you." Robinson pocketed the card. "I think it's smart to get her out of Dallas as soon as possible. I'm not saying that she's in imminent danger, but her ex seems to be pretty angry with her. If she's gone from town and he has no idea where she is, it's better for her. I'll make a note to have a patrol car swing by the house for the next week or so. When Riggs sees the sign in the yard and learns it's for sale, he could either back off—or it'll push him to act out even worse. Best Miss Larson isn't around."

"Thank you, Detective."

He returned to Layne, who looked totally wiped out. Sitting beside her, he slid an arm around her waist. "You look like you need some sleep."

"Not here," she said, shaking her head vigorously. "Pulling up and seeing the garage door that way, I felt so ... violated." Her eyes welled with unshed tears. "I wouldn't feel safe here, Keaton. What if Jeremy broke in?"

"I think if he has the balls to come by again, he'll see you've got the house on the market. Liza will have a lockbox on the front door. You know I'm handy. I can go get a camera and install one on the front porch and the back door right now if that'll give you peace of mind."

"No, don't go to that trouble. I agree that once Jeremy sees

I'm gone, he'll let things go. He's not that confrontational. It surprises me he did what he did as it is."

"Where do you want to go tonight? We can stay anywhere you want. My treat."

"I need to pack up some things. Not a lot. Just my clothes and a few miscellaneous items. I also need to make a list of things to do. Cancel the streaming services and the lawn maintenance. They aren't due to start back until March. Hopefully, the house will have sold by then. And I have a maid that comes every other week. She was my one luxury. I didn't want to waste any free time I had having to mop and vacuum and swish toilets."

He leaned in and kissed her brow. "You can make the list in the morning. Go pack now. We can stay somewhere tonight and then swing by tomorrow and load anything you have in the back of the truck. Throw the tarp over it for protection on the way home."

"Okay." Layne stood. "I don't think I'll need twenty minutes. Why don't you see what's close by? Nothing fancy. I just want to sleep and get up in the morning and go home."

He liked that she was thinking of the Bay as home again.

ONCE HER THINGS WERE PACKED, Layne was ready to leave her house and never set foot inside it again. With electronic signings these days, she wouldn't need to return to Dallas for the closing. She trusted Liza Franklin implicitly and knew the go-getter would obtain the best price for her home. The sale would be a nice nest egg. She could use some of it to go toward the inn's renovations.

Layne didn't know what she would've done if Keaton

hadn't been here with her. Already, she was dependent upon him. No, not just dependent. She needed him in her life.

And tonight would be the time to show him that.

Leaving her bedroom, she found him scrolling through his phone. He looked up.

"Just booked us double beds at a chain motel near SMU. They even serve breakfast starting at six in the morning. I figure we can eat, stop by here for your things, and then be on the road no later than seven."

"Ugh. That means sitting in morning traffic. Maybe we could sleep in and then grab breakfast. Somewhere better than the hotel."

He nodded thoughtfully. "Okay. I know a greasy spoon not far from the SMU campus. It's got the best bacon ever. French toast that would make you cry."

She laughed. "I have cried enough this past week to last a lifetime. My crying days are behind me, Mr. Maxwell. I suppose that means I'll order the pancakes or maybe eggs Benedict."

"You're a sassy little thing," he teased.

"My dad would tell you I have spunk."

"Well, come on, Spunky. Let's go."

She looked at him in mock horror. "What have I done? Giving you an absolutely dreadful nickname for me."

Grinning, he said, "It's okay, Spunky. I'm sure you'll come up with some equally obnoxious nickname for me."

They went to his truck, and she steeled herself, looking at her house for the last time. She hated that her final glimpse had that hateful word scrawled across the garage. Layne decided she would get online after Liza posted the listing and pull some of the photographs from the site in order to have a better way to remember her first home.

No, it had never really been a home. It had been the house

she had purchased and lived in, but she and Jeremy had never made it into a true home. She hadn't decorated for the holidays. Made friends with the neighbors and asked them to barbeques in the backyard. It hadn't been important to her to put out knickknacks or hang art on the wall. Her next house would be different. It would be a home.

One she hoped she might share with Keaton.

Layne knew she was getting far ahead of herself. She was coming off a long—and bad—relationship. She had a lot of work to do on herself, but if he were willing, she thought fate had stepped in and placed Keaton in her life now for a reason. Tonight, she would begin to show him how she felt about him.

They checked into their hotel. She carried her backpack, which she'd brought with her from the Bay. It had PJs, a change of clothes, and a few toiletries. He had a duffle bag. The clerk at the registration desk handed over their room keys and reminded them that breakfast was served from six to nine tomorrow morning.

"When is checkout?" she asked.

"Eleven."

She hoped by eleven tomorrow morning that she would have made love with Keaton at least twice.

They headed to the elevator and rode to the fifth floor. They were the last room at the end of the hall, which was quiet. He unlocked the door and allowed her to go inside first. She dropped her backpack on the first bed. He passed her and placed his duffle bag on the other one. Layne walked over, picked it up, and set it beside her backpack, causing him to frown.

"Why did you do that?"

Layne stepped to him, entwining her arms around his neck. "Because we're going to need every inch of that bed. I plan to have my way with you, Mr. Maxwell."

His eyes lit in surprise, and then they darkened with heat. His arms went about her.

"Are you absolutely certain, Miss Larson?"

"Positively," she said, her gut telling her this was the smartest move she had ever made.

Then before she could say anything else, his mouth came crashing down on hers.

Chapter Fourteen

Keaton Maxwell certainly knew how to kiss.

Layne was consumed by the passionate, hungry kiss. The attraction which had been building between them suddenly exploded with this kiss, and she felt rocked to her core. Her arms went about his waist, even as his enveloped her, yanking her flush against him. Already, she could feel his hard erection pressing against her. A thrill shot through her, knowing he would soon be inside her.

This was a man who was thorough, though. He wasn't going to race to any conclusion. Keaton was going to take his time with her.

And Layne would revel in every touch.

Hungrily, he kissed her, his tongue thrusting deeply inside her mouth, searching every crevice. Molten heat ran through her, heating her body and melting her bones. Her nails dug into his back as he consumed her.

Then he broke the kiss, his gaze searching her face. "Are you sure ... this is what you want?" he asked huskily. "I can wait. We can wait."

"We've waited long enough. If I've learned anything since Chief Roberts appeared on my doorstep and told me about my parents being gone, it's that I don't want to miss out on any opportunity. I don't want to lose any more time with you, Keaton. Logic would compel me to step back. Wait. But why punish both of us, letting some arbitrary timetable rule our lives?"

She touched her palm to his cheek. "I was in a dead-end relationship for way too long. I'm not going to push you away now, not when I'm feeling what I am in my heart."

His brows knitted. "What are you saying, Layne?"

A boldness she had never known compelled her to reply, "Everything is right with you. I want to be with you—for as long as you want to be with me."

He was a handsome man, albeit usually a solemn one, but the rare smile which now graced his face turned him into the most handsome guy on the planet. Her heart told her that he was now hers.

Forever and always …

"I'm going to love you like no man ever has," he promised.

Layne knew he wasn't saying that he loved her, only that he was going to thoroughly worship her body. She didn't need any declaration of love from him now. She merely needed his healing touch.

His lips returned to hers, the smoldering heat still lying just beneath the surface, but he slowed things down now. His kiss was still intense. Passionate. But he was definitely taking his time, giving her ample opportunity to step away. That was the last thing she would choose to do. If anything, this man had become her rock, and she would cling to him through thick and thin.

She wound her arms about his neck, pressing her body

against his, hearing his low groan. Immense satisfaction filled her, hearing that sound.

Ever so slowly, he began undressing her, kissing her deeply as each button of her blouse was undone. He peeled the shirt away from her and slid it down her arms, letting it float to the floor. His fingers moved to her back, undoing the clasp of her bra and ridding her of it, as well.

He cupped her breasts, murmuring, "So perfect," fondling them as his lips trailed along her jaw and to her neck. As he kissed and nipped at her throat, her breasts swelled in his hands. He brushed the pad of his thumbs against her nipples, back and forth, causing them to pebble in need.

She began working the buttons on his shirt now, folding it back and pressing her lips against his bare chest. Her palms grazed that magnificent expanse of muscle as he continued to play with her breasts, tweaking the nipples playfully.

He nudged her back a few steps, and she bumped into the mattress. He moved her to it and then knelt, removing her shoes and socks. Rising, he took her hands and brought her to her feet again before undoing her jeans and working them down her hips. She stepped out of them with his help, only wearing her black thong now. His large hands caressed her buttocks as he kissed her deeply. Then his fingers slid beneath the thong, moving along her slit, pushing a finger into her. She gasped at the intimate caress.

His lips moved to her ear. "You are so ready for me. So wet. I'm going to make you come, hard and fast."

His words thrilled her.

Easing her back on the bed again, his mouth sought out one breast. Using tongue and teeth, he had her writhing beneath him, even as his finger moved within her, stroking her into a frenzy.

"Yes!" she cried, her orgasm slamming through her, her

hips rising to meet his hand even as he sucked hard on her breast.

The orgasm rocked her entire body, energizing her, and she found herself starved for him.

She pushed him from her until he was flat on his back, and then she worked his jeans over his hips, stopping at his knees to remove his socks and shoes before pulling the worn denim from him. He had incredible legs, sculpted by his daily run, and she drank him in, her hands running over them.

Their gazes met, and he casually asked, "Like what you see?"

"So far," she teased, causing a smile to play about his lips.

She slipped her fingers beneath the band of his boxer-briefs and pulled them down, discarding them over her shoulder.

His cock was fully erect now, long and thick. She bent, licking its tip. His groan brought her satisfaction.

She took him into her mouth, marveling at his size and velvet smoothness. He made noises of pleasure, and she was happy she could make him feel so good. He touched her hair, gasping, "Stop."

Lifting her head, she asked, "Why?"

Heat glazed his eyes. "Because when I come, I want to be inside you."

He pulled her up until she was draped atop him. Their mouths fused together, greedily taking from one another. Their hands roamed each other's body, getting to know the flesh and curves.

"I can't wait any longer. I need to be inside you. Now."

Out of habit, she moved to lay on her back, next to him, but he ordered, "Get back on top."

Jeremy had been a strict, missionary position only kind of guy, so the idea that she would be in complete control brought a new wave of desire sizzling through her.

She straddled him, her palms moving up and down his chest, their gazes locked.

"Take me into you," he said roughly. "You set the pace,"

Her fingers encircled his cock, guiding him inside her until her body had completely taken him in. She sat a moment, looking down at him, admiring in the rock-hard body which was now hers. A possessive wave filled her, and she rocked against him, hearing his grunt of satisfaction as his hands latched on to her hips. Slowly, she moved, finding her way. He took her hands and threaded their fingers together, helping to give her even more leverage as she leaned into him. She began moving with abandon, freer than she had ever been, his hips rising to meet her, each thrust going more deeply.

The dance of love was in full force now, and Layne felt the flush of heat sweep through her body, engulfing her. The orgasm built within her, and she now moved frenetically against him, riding him hard. They cried out at the same moment as the wave of pleasure struck her. She rode it, thoroughly absorbing everything in this precious moment. Then she collapsed against him, her ear against his heart, which beat wildly. Her fingers rested against his shoulders, kneading him like a kitten.

His hand swept along the length of her back, stroking it up and down, calming her. Centering her. His other hand found her hair, touching it lightly.

"That was something," she said, having no words to describe what had just passed between them.

"That was everything," he corrected.

She lifted her head, pillowing her hands beneath her chin and resting it atop them. "You are a very skilled lover, Keaton. I've never been more satisfied in my life."

"Making love to you feels like coming home," he told her. "To a place I always knew was there, but I didn't know how to find my way to it. You *are* my way, Layne. The light which brightens my path."

Tears stung her eyes. "No one has ever understood me as you have. I grow stronger and more confident with every caress —every kiss—from you."

"I worried that we were doing this too soon," he confessed. "I hope I haven't chased you away."

"If anything, you've bonded us together," she assured him. "I'm not going anywhere, Keaton. Not now. Not ever."

His eyes lit with hope. "Are you saying that you'll be staying in the Bay for good?"

"How can I go anywhere when my heart would be lost without you near me?"

He clasped her elbows, pulling her up to him. Their lips met in a tender kiss.

"I want you in my life, Layne." He paused. "I love you."

If she would have been told that she would hear such a declaration from Keaton—or any man—so soon after kicking Jeremy to the curb and learning of her parents' deaths, she would have laughed, thinking it some grand fiction. But Layne was right when she told him that she wasn't going to put off living. Their love was a part of living. A part of her healing. Growing. Maturing.

She brushed her fingers against his cheek. "I love you, too. It's almost frightening, the depth of this love. If it feels like this now? What will it be like tomorrow? Next week? A year from now?"

"Love has no limits," he told her. "Our love will flourish because we will nurse it along, every single day of our lives. Move in with me, Layne," he urged. "I want you in my house. No, our house. Our home. Everything I have is yours. *I* am yours."

Love for him swept through her, and she touched her mouth to his, the kiss sealing the promises between them.

Chapter Fifteen

Keaton was glad Layne had mentioned not getting up at the crack of dawn and rushing back to Driftwood Bay. It allowed him to make love to her leisurely, knowing no deadlines were hovering over them. His tongue followed every curve of her body, his hands caressing every bit of her flesh. He was quickly learning what brought delicious shivers to her. The inside of her elbow was sensitive, as was the place behind her ear.

As they lay entwined, he ran his fingers through the silky strands of her caramel hair, wondering at how he had become so lucky.

"Fate," she said, almost as if she had heard his thoughts spoken aloud. "Fate led us to one another." Her fingers trailed along his jaw. "I like you with stubble. It's so sexy."

He grinned wolfishly. "Well, I like you without clothes." He dragged his thumb across her nipple, seeing it spring to life.

She laughed. "You are incorrigible."

"But I'm your incorrigible."

Her fingers brushed the hair from his brow. "You most certainly are."

Layne kissed him, a soft, sweet kiss which had him ready for another round of sex. He held off, though, liking the sheer pleasure of intimately lying together.

"Are you ready to go home today?" he asked.

Her gaze met his. "Home is wherever you are."

Keaton made love to her again. Slowly. Tenderly. A satisfaction filled him, and he realized it was contentment, something he'd never truly experienced during his lifetime.

"Let's take our time on the way back to the Bay," he suggested.

"You have a stop or two in mind? Besides Buc-ees?" she teased.

"Oh, that's a definite. I'm thinking we might spend a few hours in Salado. They have several art galleries there. Some antique shops."

"If you have the time, I'd like that."

"Babe, we have all the time in the world."

They showered together and then dressed. Keaton had them stop at a place she enjoyed for breakfast. She ordered the Texan special, which came with eggs, bacon, hash browns, and biscuits and gravy, while he went with pancakes and sausage. They wound up feeding one another bites of their own breakfast, something he had thought was hokey when he'd seen others in public restaurants do so, but with Layne?

It seemed perfectly natural.

He stopped by her house, and they made a few trips, bringing out what she would take with her to the Bay and covering it with the heavy tarp which had protected his paintings on their trip north. The painter Liza had hired had already come and gone, and the garage door looked pristine again. Keaton sensed Layne's relief at that.

They drove to Salado with a quick stop at Buc-ees for gas, a restroom break, and drinks, arriving in Salado two-and-a-half hours after they had cleared the Dallas city limits. He parked the truck, and they set out on foot, hand-in-hand. They stopped at two art galleries and a glassblowing shop, and Keaton bought Layne a pitcher in hues of greens and blues which she had admired.

After stopping for a snack at a café, they visited two antique stores and another art gallery. He had never been a browser, instead entering stores and going straight to whatever he wished to purchase. Having Layne with him changed everything. He was seeing the world through new eyes.

The eyes of love ...

"Oh, we have to go in here," she declared, pulling him into a candy store. "I am a fudge fiend."

"Ah, now I know how to have my wicked way with you. Regular? Dark? Blond?" he asked, naming some of the different kinds of fudges he saw on display. "Wait." His eyes continued skimming. "Red velvet fudge? Rocky road? German chocolate? This place is amazing!"

They asked to sample a few of the choices, including butterscotch and peanut butter fudge, purchasing both of those and three other kinds. He also picked up bottled water for them, and they went to sit in his truck, savoring their sweets.

"I think you should open a fudge shop in the Bay," he told her, biting into a piece of dark chocolate fudge. "It would be a big hit."

"Hmm. I've never thought about opening a business, much less something food-related. You know I can't cook."

"I've shown you it's easy. We're going to practice lots. Soon, it'll become second nature to you."

She frowned. "Maybe cooking meals, but I'm thinking

fudge is an art. Still, it's a good idea, bringing fudge to the Bay. Or I might come up with another shop. Mila's mom owns Coastal Charm Boutique. I could pick her brain. She's got her pulse on the community and might be able to steer me in the right direction."

He leaned over and kissed her, tasting red velvet. "There's no rush. You should focus on the inn's reno first." He slipped his hand around her nape, drawing her closer for a lingering kiss. "Besides, you'll be living with me."

Layne shook her head. "I'm going to pull my weight. I had enough of Jeremy freeloading off me. You're not going to be my sugar daddy, Keaton. I'm smart. I'll figure things out and bring in money."

"You will. How about finding some cute B&B here in Salado and staying for the night? We can call it research. You can see how it's decorated. What amenities they include." He smiled. "And we could test out a new bed. What do you say, Spunky?"

"Ugh. I'd hoped you'd forgotten about that nickname. Promise me you'll never use it again, and we can find a B&B and have wild sex all night."

"You're on."

Instead of pulling out his cell and finding somewhere to stay, Keaton simply drove around, the Driftwood Bay way. They spotted several B&Bs and decided on one with a gingerbread look about it. It wasn't hard to book a room. The clerk told them they were wide open.

"People are gone, seeing relatives for Christmas. I'm glad you two are checking in."

She told them what time breakfast was served in the morning. Keaton asked if anywhere nearby delivered, and the clerk named a pizza place.

"Thanks. We'll be eating in tonight," he said, taking Layne's hand and leading her upstairs to their room.

His appetite for her was insatiable, and she was the same about him. It was as if they had both been starved for affection. That, combined with the connection they experienced, made for a very entertaining night.

Once they dressed the next morning, Layne said, "It's about two hours until we reach San Antonio. You want to keep playing hooky today?"

"Why not?" he agreed. "Joey's crew won't come until early next week. You haven't heard anything from Chief Roberts yet, so the funeral is still on hold. I've driven through San Antonio but never stopped."

She looked shocked. "Seriously? The Riverwalk is inviting. Romantic."

"Sold!" he proclaimed.

They went downstairs for the B&B's breakfast, and Keaton could tell Layne was observing everything with a critical eye. Once they had paid the bill and were inside his truck, heading south, he asked if she had seen anything she would want to implement at the Bay Breeze.

"I liked the fresh flowers in our room. Even though they weren't booked up, the room was ready for anyone to step into and feel welcomed. What I really liked were the freshly-baked croissants that came with breakfast. I wonder if they contract out to a bakery for those. Guests would go wild over them."

"Who could do that in the Bay?"

"Seaside Sweets Bakery," she replied. "Don't tell me you haven't been there. You've lived in town over six months."

He shrugged. "Though I enjoy them, I just don't think about buying sweets."

"Says the man who polished off his fair share of fudge yesterday."

"I can't remember the last time I had fudge. Maybe never. Sweets just weren't on my radar." He didn't remind her that growing up in foster care, sweets were a luxury that most orphans never tasted.

"While you were settling the bill, I did wander over to the beverage stand. It had a coffeemaker, with a basket of pods. There was also a tea caddy with a great variety, both regular and decaf herbal teas, so you could simply run hot water through the coffeemaker and make a cup of tea. I think guests would find that convenient for a mid-afternoon pickup or maybe an after dinner beverage to sip on."

"You could put a table in the alcove just off the foyer," he suggested.

"That would be perfect." She took out her phone and tapped a note to remind her later.

They arrived in San Antonio at a quarter before noon, and Layne directed him where to park. She led him down a set of stairs, and it was as if they entered another world. Wide side-walks shaded by huge trees lined a narrow river. They began walking beside it, passing shops, hotels, and restaurants. Every so often, a stone bridge appeared, allowing pedestrians to cross from one side of the river to the other.

"I wish we were here at night," she said. "It's lit up for the Christmas season."

"We can stay over if you want."

"No, maybe some other time." She glanced around. "It's crowded because of the holidays. School is out. People are in town, visiting relatives. I'd rather come back at a quieter time of year."

He made a mental note to bring her back. Maybe when they finished the reno at the B&B, they could steal away for a couple of days and return here. Stay on the river. Eat. Take in a Spurs game.

"Want to stop for some lunch?" she asked. "Plenty of Mexican food places along the way. Also pizza. Barbeque."

"You choose."

Layne laughed. "If you leave it up to me, then it'll be Mexican every time. Come on. I have a place in mind."

They walked for almost ten minutes, arriving at a restaurant which had a good two dozen tables lining the water. The day was cool but not cold, with plenty of sunshine, and so they opted to eat outdoors.

Keaton went with brisket tacos and a pork tamale, while Layne ordered tacos al carbon. She insisted he take a bite of the tender steak, and he enjoyed such a simple gesture of her sharing with him. They split an order of flan for dessert, the creamy custard topped with a rich caramel sauce.

"I'm stuffed," she proclaimed. "You may have to carry me back to the truck."

He indicated a passing boat filled with tourists. "Nah. I'll just buy you a ticket on one of those and meet you down river."

Playfully, she punched him in the arm. He caught her hand and brought it to his lips, kissing her knuckles tenderly. Layne sighed at the romantic gesture.

"You certainly know how to treat a lady." She hesitated. "You haven't mentioned any of your exes. I'm not prying. I promise. But I am a little curious about who came before me."

His gut tightened. "You know I'm a loner. *Was* a loner," he corrected. "Living in the Bay is changing me for the better."

She pursed her lips. "You didn't just figure out how to kiss when I came to town, Keaton. Forget I said anything. I don't need to know about your past love life." She squeezed his fingers. "As long as I'm the only one in the picture now."

He told himself he didn't owe it to Layne to spill his guts, but he found himself wanting to share more with her about his past.

"Let's go home."

Keaton signaled the server and paid the bill, leading Layne back to the truck. Once they were on the outskirts of San Antonio and he was able to speed up and set the cruise control, he cleared his throat.

"I meant what I said before. I have kept to myself pretty much. Except in Jackson Hole. I had a girlfriend."

"Keaton, stop. I was being nosy. I really don't want to hear about an old flame. Whoever she was, she's your past, the same as Jeremy is history with me."

"No, I need to tell you about Frankie."

He kept one hand on the steering wheel and captured her hand with his free one, drawing warmth from the contact.

"Frankie Fairchild—Francesca—was my same age. Barista by day, poet by night."

"Was she published?"

"In a few obscure literary journals."

"Was she any good?"

"I thought so. Frankie had a unique perspective. She looked at the world differently from most people. As a poet, she captured that point of view through imagery. Similes. Some of her stuff could get pretty dark, but I suppose that was her tortured poet's soul."

"I'm sure you were drawn to her because of her talent," Layne said quietly.

He squeezed her hand. "In part. Frankie wasn't what you would consider pretty. Instead, she was striking, though. Large eyes. A nose which was a little too big for her face. Flawless skin. A wide mouth. Somehow, it all worked together. She knew art. Literature. Foreign films were her passion. I never could get past the subtitles, but she gobbled them up."

"What happened between the two of you? Is she the reason you left Wyoming?"

"You could say that."

They rode in silence for a few minutes before he spoke again.

"We met the first week I moved there. I patronized the coffeehouse she worked at. I would take my sketchbook there. Sit and drink coffee, idly drawing, mulling over ideas. We got to talking. I learned she wrote poetry, and art seemed to give us something in common. Other than that, we were really different people."

"How so?"

"She was outgoing. Yet fragile. She bruised easily. By that, I mean her feelings. I was quieter. Tougher, because of the way I grew up. She was vegan, and I love my meat. Frankie wouldn't touch alcohol, while I enjoy a cold beer. Yet she was easy to talk to. We struck up a friendship. It turned into something more."

"Did you love her?"

"Maybe. I'm not sure now because of how things ended between us. I'd never been in love before. Never really dated much. The only person I had loved was Miss Peggy, and that was more a fierce devotion because I was so grateful to her for rescuing me. So yeah, maybe I loved her."

Keaton glanced to Layne. "But it was nothing like what I feel for you."

She swallowed. "This isn't a competition."

He looked back to the road. "I know. I just want you to know that even though I was with her about eighteen months—and the sex was great—I didn't have the connection with her that I instantly had with you. Yes, I think I loved her. But she poisoned the well of trust. Trust is everything to me, Layne. There was no coming back from what she did."

Again, silence fell between them, with Layne finally breaking it several miles later.

"Did she cheat on you?"

"Yes and no. Not with a guy. With drugs."

Keaton released her hand, raking his hand through his hair, needing to tell her about this part of his past without being swallowed up by it again.

"I've told you that my parents were drug addicts. Drugs were their god and drove everything they did. They brought a wedge between us. They were so absorbed in where their next fix was coming from that they severely neglected me. I won't go into any horror stories. Just know my life was no bed of roses. They voluntarily gave up their parental rights—me, their own flesh and blood—because they couldn't give up the high drugs brought. Because of that, I knew I would never touch any drug. Hell, I hate to even take a Tylenol if I get a headache. I never wanted anything to be so powerful that it rendered me helpless. I like being in control. I don't want anything, especially drugs, to have control over me."

He paused. "I shared some about my childhood with Frankie. She seemed to be this straighter than an arrow person. Didn't even touch wine. She was sympathetic. Said all the right things. She *knew* how anti-drugs I was."

When he hesitated, Layne filled in the blanks. "She was an addict herself. A functioning one who hid her addiction well."

Keaton nodded. "She was. I never knew it the entire time we were together and believe me, I was more than familiar with the signs. I never saw any needle marks. No constricted pupils or reddened eyes. Never had mood swings. Those were all things I knew. But there were more subtle signs which I just didn't put together at the time. She was thin as a rail. Never had much of an appetite. She never seem to sleep much.

Frankie was forgetful, but I chalked that up to her living in her head, thinking about her poetry."

"How did you find out?" she asked quietly.

"She told me she quit her job, but I ran into one of her co-workers. He asked me how Frankie was handling things after being fired. That's when I became suspicious, but I held back from asking her about it. Then she wanted for me to loan her some money. By then, we were practically living together. She still had a room in town she rented, but she spent all day and most every night at my place. She'd spend time in town, writing. I'd wake up, and she'd be gone. She'd leave me a note, telling me she'd gone for a walk or headed back to do some writing. My suspicions grew.

"And then I caught her in another lie. A big one."

Keaton kept looking straight ahead. "I won't go into particulars. I caught her getting high. She lied about that, saying it wasn't something she ever did. That she was just low on creativity and was trying it to boost herself. But I knew. I began tearing her room apart. I found drugs. Lots of them." He shook his head. "I felt like such a fool. The one thing I had wanted from her was honesty. Well, two. That—and no drug use."

"Did you leave Jackson Hole when you found out about her using?"

"Not at first. I was hardheaded. Why should I leave? I hadn't done anything wrong. Of course, she came around a few times. Begged me to take her back. Pleaded with me, saying she'd stopped cold turkey and was going to meetings. I offered to pay for her to go to rehab. She refused. Said she'd been to it twice, and more drug use occurred in a rehab clinic than out on the streets. That's when I told her not to come around again. I wanted to cut all ties with her. I went into a deep depression. It affected my art."

Layne reached for his hand. "I'm sorry your relationship ended on such a bad note."

"What ended it permanently was that she OD'd," he said, bitterness seeping into his tone.

She gasped. "She ... died?"

"Yes. She left a note for me. The police contacted me, informing me of her death and asking about our relationship. I explained how I'd discovered she was an addict and that I didn't want to have anything to do with her. That we'd broken up months ago. Or rather I'd cut all ties. The police chief said Frankie had left a note, which they'd read. He said he didn't think it would be good for me to read it, especially since we weren't even together anymore. I took him at his word and told him to burn it. I'm sure Frankie wrote something about how it was all my fault. I didn't need to carry that burden. I was already hurting bad enough as it was."

Keaton glanced to her. "That's when I left Jackson Hole." He looked back ahead of him. "I'd loved the mountains, but everywhere I went—everything I saw—reminded me of Frankie and how she'd abused not only drugs but my trust in her. In what we had. I wanted to get as far away as possible. Have a completely different lifestyle. I'd never seen an ocean. Never been to the Gulf Coast. I did know water had a soothing effect on me, though, because I'd sketched and painted on the banks of a nearby creek and a lake not far from my cabin. I brought up a map of Texas on my tablet, closed my eyes, and touched the screen. My finger had landed on Driftwood Bay."

"That's why you came to the Bay? Oh, Keaton, what a leap of faith for you."

"Sounds pretty crazy, now that I think about it. I packed up my truck. Told the landlord I was breaking my lease. The news about Frankie's death was out by then, so he got it. He only had me pay until the end of that month. I drove to Dallas and dropped off what I'd been working on with Sidney, then drove straight to Driftwood Bay. I'd found Hillary Horton online and had emailed her about finding me a house to rent."

He laughed. "I wasn't totally crazy. I decided I'd rent for a few months and see if I liked living in Driftwood Bay. If I did, I'd think about buying a place, preferably on the water. And that's the story, Layne. How I came to the Bay. Living here, it felt like where I should have always been. I picked up running again. I rented a boat and starting going out on the water. My painting is getting better. Being close to the water has a soothing effect on me. I've made some friends."

Keaton smiled at her. "I've found a woman to love. We're going to live in a house on the bay." He swallowed. "Hopefully, happily ever after."

She brought their joined hands to her cheek, nuzzling his hand against her face.

"That had to hurt like hell, sharing all that with me. Thank you for doing so, Keaton. It helps me understand you better. I promise I will never give you any reason to doubt me or my love for you. Trust is also important to me.

"And you're the man I would trust with my life."

"Same."

They drove two more hours in silence, not a strained silence, but one which was good. Comfortable. Things were solid between them. They both had suffered in different ways, but they had found one another. Even though he'd ripped open the old scab by talking about Frankie, Keaton knew doing so had been important.

Now, it was time to help each other heal.

Chapter Sixteen

Layne stood under the hot shower spray, allowing it to wash away not only the sweat from her workout but the aftermath of yesterday's funeral. The service had been bittersweet, and the reception held after at the First Baptist Church had been difficult to get through. The ladies of her parents' church had prepared a virtual feast for after the graveside burial, and the citizens of Driftwood Bay had come to honor Jack and Lark Larson. She had known her parents were respected members of the Bay's community, but she didn't realize how many lives they had touched. Countless people had told her wonderful stories of how Jack and Lark had made a difference in their lives. The day had been an emotional one for her, but she knew she could now shut the door on some of her hurt, the funeral giving her some closure. She might not have agreed with the choices her dad made, but she had come to terms with his decision.

She dressed for the day in jeans and a long-sleeved T-shirt and drove to the Bay Breeze, where Joey and his crew were already hard at work. They had finished painting the exterior of the inn and would begin on the interior this morning. She had hired them for an additional task, and they had moved every stick of furniture from the inside of the B&B to the outside. Layne had contacted a place in Corpus and donated everything inside the inn, from furniture to bedding, as well as her parents' clothes. She had kept one flannel shirt of her dad's, and she wore her mom's pearl earrings every day. Everything else had been carted away.

The interior painting would go much easier without having to place drop cloths protecting furniture and rugs which had seen better days. She would get online once the painting was completed and choose new furniture for the entire inn with Keaton's help. She trusted his artist's eye far more than she did her own. While she was a whiz with numbers and computers, Layne knew she would second guess her interior design choices without his input.

Today, she was tackling the attic. Most likely, there would be more items to give away up there, as well, but she could always have the donation truck come by again if there proved to be more things than would fit in the back of Keaton's pickup. She hadn't ever set foot in the attic and had no idea what her parents stored in it.

She found Joey and his crew upstairs. The crew consisted of two men in their mid-twenties who had been best friends since third grade. They were painting one guestroom, while Joey was tackling another one on his own. She stopped and exchanged brief pleasantries with everyone and then told Joey she was headed up to the attic.

Layne pulled the cord in the hallway, lowering the stairs to the attic, glad that she was investigating in January and not the heat of July. She found a few odd pieces of furniture. A wonderful, full-length antique mirror which she would defi-nitely put to good use. She came across two trunks and decided to ask Joey to bring those downstairs for her. It would be easier to go through their contents where she had better light.

He willingly obliged, and she walked the attic's length to make sure she hadn't missed anything. She actually had, finding a tarp in the far corner. Pulling it up, she saw several frames stacked together, leaning against the wall, and thought it might be artwork which had once graced the walls of the inn, paintings her parents hadn't favored and merely tucked away in the attic. She and Keaton could explore those together after she investigated the contents of the trunks. Layne replaced the tarp, heading down the stairs and to the common room, where she'd asked Joey to move both trunks.

Layne decided to brew herself a cup of tea before she looked at what the trunks held. Once she made it, she brought it back to where the trunks sat.

The first one she opened had clothes from decades ago. They outdated even her parents' youth, and she supposed the trunk had been something from the previous owners. She decided to give the contents of the trunk to Piper's mom. Perhaps her drama students could use some of items as costumes in one of their plays.

She thought of how Mrs. Roberts and the chief would be retiring soon, along with Dr. Perry. Mrs. Perry had said she would keep Coastal Charms Boutique but step away from going in on a daily basis once her husband retired. Layne's gut told her that Mrs. Perry would sell the shop sooner rather than later. The two couples were in their mid-sixties, just as her parents had been, and all four seemed in excellent health. She wondered if her parents hadn't received the medical diagnoses they had if they would have sold the inn and retired. Something told her they wouldn't have. The inn was more than their livelihood. It had been a way of life for them.

She had discovered that her dad had been diagnosed with

Parkinson's, as Keaton had suspected. In going through bills a few days ago, Layne had found not only ones regarding her mom's medical treatments but a separate folder for her dad. Even though her dad was deceased, she figured with HIPAA laws, his doctor would not be forthcoming. She googled the medical practice and found it was run by a neurological doctor who specialized in movement disorder. He exclusively treated patients with Parkinson's disease. Though there was printout in the folder with future appointments scheduled, Jack Larson had drawn a line through each, with the notation *CANCELED* next to each one. She had to give it to her dad. He had been thorough in his plan on how to leave this world.

Folding the last shirt and closing the trunk, Layne texted Mrs. Roberts, who was back in school now for the spring semester. She explained that she had found some old clothes in the attic that might be suitable for the drama productions at the high school. Mrs. Roberts texted back, thanking her and saying that she would stop by the inn today after school to claim the trunk if that were convenient. Layne merely texted back a thumbs up, knowing she would still be here.

Going to the second trunk now, she saw the initials *JLL* embossed on it and knew it belonged to her dad, Jackson Lemuel Larson. Excitement filled her, wondering what the trunk might hold. It would be great to have a piece of her dad, something more personal than his clothes or books on the shelves in the common room, which she knew he had chosen since he was a voracious reader.

She opened it, anticipation filling her, and saw a bundle of letters on top, tied with twine. She set those beside her, deciding to go through the trunk's contents first before sitting back and reading through the correspondence.

The first item she found was an artist's sketchbook. She was familiar with it because she had seen one at Keaton's house. Layne had moved in with him once they returned from their trip to Dallas. It only made sense for her to be gone while the inn was undergoing extensive renovations. The fact that she was also crazy in love with Keaton and wanting to spend every waking moment she could in his presence had made it an easy decision.

Curious, she opened the sketchbook, having never seen her dad sketch anything. Slowly, she turned the pages. It contained mostly drawings of landscapes, and she recognized places in and around the Bay. In the corner of each sketch she saw *JLL*, proving they had been drawn by her dad. As she continued perusing the sketchbook, Layne also found drawings of animals. Even fish. Then she recognized one which had to be her mother. She had seen a few photographs of Mom when she was younger, but these leapt off the page, capturing the essence of her mom and bringing Lark Larson to life. The laughing eyes. The carefree, natural beauty. An ache filled Layne, seeing her mom at such a young age, so vibrant.

She found a few other sketches of her mom and then one self-portrait her dad had drawn of himself. Tears stung her eyes as she saw the mischief in his eyes. He had always been such a fun, happy man, one larger than life.

Why hadn't she known he could draw like this? He'd never spoken of his artistic talent before.

Immediately, she thought of the canvases in the attic. Her gut told her they had been painted by her dad, and Layne hurried back upstairs. She removed the drop cloth and counted a dozen framed canvases. Picking up the first one, which faced the wall, she turned it toward her and saw Driftwood Bay's largest cove. Layne dropped to her knees, resting the painting on the ground before her, studying it carefully.

It depicted a tranquil day in Driftwood Bay, the water calm and the skies blue, not a cloud in sight. She knew very little about art, but she admired the subtle shading of the water as it changed from a light green to varying and deeper shades of blue. The way the light struck the water gave her chills.

"Dad was talented," she said aloud, stunned by this discovery.

Her eyes dropped to the right corner of the painting, where she saw *JL Larson*.

Why were these paintings hidden away in the attic? Better yet, why hadn't Dad pursued a career in art when he had such an obvious talent?

Instead of trying to carry the canvases downstairs herself, Layne returned to the common room, hoping the answers to her questions might lie within the pages of bundled correspondence he had saved.

She untied the twine binding the envelopes into a single stack. They were of varying sizes. Using the return address in the top left corner of each envelope, she divided them by sender and then date, placing them in a chronological manner. It left her with three stacks. The largest of those were letters Mom had written to her future husband, based upon the dates. A smaller stack contained half a dozen letters from her grandmother. The final pile only held a single envelope from her grandfather. She had fond memories of Grandma, but Grandpa had been a tall, stern, angry man. He had died when Layne was only six, so she had never really gotten to know him.

She decided to read her grandmother's letters to Dad first, and they turned out to be as warm and loving as the woman she recalled. Apparently, her father had spent some time in Chicago because they were all addressed to him on a street in Chicago. Layne hadn't known that he'd lived there for any length of time.

Opening the first, she began to read. They sounded just like Grandma spoke and were full of events happening in the

Bay. People that her dad would have known. Each letter ended with how much Grandma loved and missed her only child. The tone and content of the final letter was different, however. No fun bits of gossip. Only a single page. As Layne read it, her throat swelled with emotion.

My dearest Jack –

Thank you for your call last night. It was so good to hear your voice after months of not hearing you. I understand your decision to come home. I know how much your father has nagged you to do so. I'm sorry about that, honey. I know you left the Bay with big dreams.

You may not live the life you dreamed of by coming home, but at least you have the love of a sweet girl. Lark is a wonderful person and will support you in whatever you choose to do.

I'll see you in two weeks. I'll even make my special pot roast for you since you've written how you've missed the taste of it.

All my love,
Mama

Layne didn't know what Dad had been doing in Chicago, but she suspected it was tied to his art—and that Grandpa hadn't approved.

She turned to his letter, opening it with trepidation.

Jack –

It's time for you to quit playing artist and come back to the Bay. Art doesn't put food on the table. You need to be practical and grow up. Put your foolish notions behind you. Lark isn't going to wait forever for you. In fact, I saw her with that Gilmore boy the other day, and they looked as if they were having a fine time together.

If you don't want to lose your girl—and lose my respect —you'll come home and get a real job. You know I've refused to put a dime toward this art school you enrolled in. I never intend to. It's your responsibility to come home and find a solid way to make a living. You're good with your hands, I'll give you that. That will be a start. Maybe you can go to a trade school in Corpus. Learn to put up sheetrock or lay flooring.

The point is, you need to get your ass back to the Bay. You've had your head in the clouds too long. Your mama and Lark encouraged you to pursue art, and they were plain wrong. It's time to stop being Peter Pan and earn a living.

A sick feeling washed over Layne, a memory she had forgotten about suddenly flooding her.

She had always enjoyed drawing when she was young, her crayons a constant companion as she drew pictures and made up stories about what she had drawn. In second grade, she'd won an award for a painting she had done in her art class, and she had proudly brought home both the painting and the blue ribbon signifying her win. Mom had hugged her, telling Layne how proud she was of her, but Dad had been unusually quiet, his usual praise of her absent. She remembered thinking she had done something wrong.

After dinner that night, he had stopped to visit her in her bedroom while she did her homework. Layne had forgotten that conversation until now. She couldn't remember everything Dad had said, only that there wasn't any money to be made in art. That it would be impossible to earn a living at it. He had encouraged her to abandon drawing, saying she was a whiz at numbers and told her that was the path she should follow. He stressed how she could make good money if she went into business. Because she idolized him, she had immediately set aside art, believing him when he told her that art would never amount to anything.

Everything she pursued after that, from sports to debate, Dad had praised her efforts. He was her biggest cheerleader, and she was always proud to share her latest accomplishments with him. She had forgotten all about her love of drawing.

Until now.

It hurt her that Dad had given in to the demands of his own father and abandoned art school. Grandpa had been a stern disciplinarian, and she could only imagine the pressure her dad had felt, being under his thumb, as well as the financial burden since Grandpa didn't provide any money. The thought of losing Mom to another guy probably was another factor influencing him. A part of her wondered if Grandpa had even made that up, simply to convince his son to return to Texas.

It was hard to learn that Dad had artistic talent and yet had never pursued it. She would honor his memory by hanging this painting in a prominent spot at the Bay Breeze.

Layne came to her feet and took the painting downstairs with her. In the better light, she could see the fine brushstrokes of each wave, and she hoped the remaining framed works upstairs were all painted by her dad.

Over the next hour, she read the letters Mom had written to Dad before their marriage. It was obvious how much Mom loved and missed her boyfriend, but she never pressured him to come back to Texas. In fact, Mom had a plan to join him in Chicago. She had found a secretarial school and been accepted to it, writing with joy how she would go through the program it offered and then find a job so Jack could finish art school and have plenty of time to paint.

Obviously, that had never come to pass. Jack Larson had

returned to his hometown and married Lark the next summer. She knew her dad had been a carpenter during the early years of his marriage, and then he and Mom had bought the Bay Breeze. Dad was the inn's handyman and handled all the books, while Mom did the cooking and cleaning for guests. She truly believed her parents had a happy marriage, but she couldn't help but wonder what might have happened if Dad hadn't listened to his father's demands to return to the Bay and instead continued with his art.

Now, she would never be able to ask him and learn those answers.

"Hey, what're you up to?"

Layne looked up, seeing Keaton had arrived.

"My dad was an artist," she told him, seeing him frown. "I've been cleaning out the attic. I found letters. This painting."

She indicated the framed art, and Keaton came and raised it, studying it carefully.

"Your dad painted this? Layne, it's amazing."

"I know. I never knew he could paint. In fact, he discouraged me from doing so because his own father said Dad couldn't earn a living pursuing art. I didn't even remember him nudging me in the direction of math until I discovered all this."

"Are there more paintings of his?" Keaton asked.

"Yes. In the attic."

"Let's bring them down."

They went upstairs, making a couple of trips, until all dozen paintings were in the common room. Keaton scattered them across the room, and they went from one to the next, marveling at Jack Larson's skill.

Eight of the paintings were landscapes, done in and around the Driftwood Bay area. Two were portraits of her mother, one as a bride and one while she was pregnant with Layne. One painting was of Layne when she was perhaps three or so. She didn't recall sitting for it and realized her dad had known her well enough not to need her to pose for him.

The final one must have been completed a dozen years ago, and she ached that he had never shared it with her. It was a family portrait, with Layne in her high school graduation gown, Mom and Dad on either side of her. She remembered Dr. Perry had taken a picture of the three of them, and Dad must have used it as his guide. Her mom had kept it on the bureau in the bedroom. It was one of the few things Layne had held on to when she cleaned everything out.

"He had remarkable talent," Keaton said. "Most people who do landscapes can't paint portraits, and vice-versa. Jack Larson did both with ease." He shook his head. "I'm sorry he was discouraged from making art his profession."

"My grandfather was a difficult man. I can see where he beat Dad down. Not physically, but emotionally. Dad was the kind of guy who liked to please others, and he would've been that way about his own parents. It just hurts so much to see how these were put away for so long."

Keaton rubbed her back. "He might have had a hard time looking at them. It probably was painful for him to have set aside what he wanted to do. Displaying these paintings would have been a reminder of the dreams he'd had to set aside."

"Well, I plan to hang these throughout the Bay Breeze. At least the landscapes. I want to keep the portraits."

"You should," he encouraged.

"I turned my back on art years ago because I was a daddy's girl. I wonder if I still have any artistic ability? I told you I didn't have an eye for anything. It might be a case of use it or lose it."

"Possibly, but you're welcome to use any of my sketchbooks or paints. I can teach you a little about oil paints. How to blend them. How to create shadow and light. Even how to clean the brushes.”

“I’ll have to think about it, Keaton. This is a lot to absorb. I need some time to process things.”

He wrapped his arms around her. “Take all the time you need. We can have one artist in the family—or two. No rush.”

His words warmed her. “Thanks for being so supportive.”

“You’ll find what you’re meant to do. You may stick with business. You may investigate art. Whatever, I’m here for you, Layne.”

Keaton kissed her, and her world was right again.

Chapter Seventeen

Keaton felt contentment wash over him at the simple, domestic routine he and Layne had fallen into. He stirred the linguini again and told her she could begin tossing the salad, while he moved to the skillet where garlic, onions, wine, and spices simmered. Tossing in the clams, he stirred and then covered the pan with a lid. As Layne prepared an oil and vinegar salad dressing and drizzled it atop their salads, Keaton opened a bottle of white wine and poured a glass for them both, setting the glasses on the kitchen table.

After a few minutes, he removed the pan from the heat, adding butter, lemon zest, lemon juice, and parsley, along with a dash of salt.

Although they went out occasionally for dinner, most nights they enjoyed cooking together. She had caught on quickly, and her confidence in the kitchen was growing.

The renovations at the inn would be completed in the next two to three days, almost three weeks sooner than his original estimate. Then again, the work had moved quickly along because they had hired Joey's crew to help with tasks beyond painting. They had proved efficient and professional in tackling the interior and exterior of the B&B. After the painting was completed, he turned over all the plumbing to them, while he worked on things such as restoring the floors and wallpapering, something Layne had assisted him with. Remembering she had once enjoyed artistic endeavors as a child, she had helped choose items from curtains to cabinet hardware, learning to trust her gut. He thought the inn would not only be restored to its former glory, but it would shine more brightly than ever before.

Stacy had offered to take the pictures to be used on the Bay Breeze's website and had already completed the exterior photos, highlighting both the porch's new furniture and the landscaping, which had been refreshened. His gallery manager would then move to take all the interior photographs once work had been completed. With Layne's computer skills, she would place the photos on the website. Already, she had written new copy for the site, including not only things about the Bayside Breeze but spotlighting activities and events around Driftwood Bay. Those tabs would go up once Stacy finished up. Even with the website being practically empty, several reservations had come in, most from longtime guests who were eager to see the new and improved Bay Breeze Inn.

She handed him two, large bowls, and he placed a generous portion of linguini and clams in them. Keaton took the bowls to the kitchen table and removed the bread from the oven, the final touch to their meal, and they took a seat, with Layne topping off their glasses of chardonnay.

"It's Monday. Do you have your FaceTime with Mila and Piper tonight?"

He had learned the trio communicated this way a few times a month, often on a Monday night because the theater was dark and no performances were scheduled.

She nodded. "Piper will finish the run of this musical in two weeks."

"Where does it conclude?" he asked.

"I think Kansas City, but don't quote me on that."

"Would you like to go and see her last performance?"

Layne's face lit up. "Could we? That would be fantastic. Should we tell her—or surprise her?"

"You know her best. I'd ask Mila and Carson to join us, but he's right in the heart of his basketball season. Do you think Piper is going to return to the Bay?"

The last time Layne had spoken with Piper, her friend had mentioned returning to Driftwood Bay after her current tour ended.

"She's definitely leaning that way."

A thought occurred to him, and Keaton asked, "How is the hunt coming for someone to manage the Bay Breeze?"

Layne frowned. "It's not. I may wind up taking over, at least for this first tourist season."

"What if you asked Piper to do it?" he suggested, gauging her reaction. "It wouldn't have to last beyond this first season. It would give you more time to find a permanent manager and give her a source of income while she decides what she wants to do."

She smiled. "That's a brilliant idea. Let me hit her up with it when we talk in a few minutes. Changing subjects, have you thought anymore about offering art classes at the gallery?"

Layne had been sketching for the last few weeks, mostly animals and flowers. She had raw talent and had asked Keaton to give her lessons. He had been reluctant to do so, not wanting to infringe upon their personal relationship. That's when she had hit him up to open Gulf Coastal Gallery for lessons. While he didn't have any desire, much less the time, to devote to people making art a hobby, he had come up with an idea which he thought would please her.

"As a matter of fact, I'm meeting with Collin Barton the day after tomorrow about that very thing."

"He's the one we saw at Bayside Brewery the other night, right?"

"The very one. Collin is one of the most promising artists in the area, and his paintings are starting to sell at the gallery. He works at a gas station days and paints at night and on weekends, but I think he'd be willing to devote a couple of nights a week to teaching art classes. The thing is, you know the gallery doesn't really have room for something like this. We'd need another space."

"I might have a solution to that problem. Mila told me that the tenant next to her mom's shop is going to be leaving soon when his lease ends. He and his wife are retiring. They've just bought an RV, and they're going to spend the next few years seeing America."

"Good to know. The square would be a great location to hold classes. I'll stop by and visit with him. Check out the space and see if it might work. What's his name?"

Layne told him and said that all the tenants on the square rented their space from a management company.

"I believe Hillary handles transactions for them. You might also want to check in with her tomorrow regarding the rent."

"Will do."

Keaton told her he would clean the kitchen so that she could get on her FaceTime call. By the time he finished and joined her on the sofa, he saw Mila and Carson in one frame and Piper in the other.

"Hey, everyone," he said, sliding an arm about Layne's shoulders.

They greeted him, and the five of them spoke for a few minutes until Lily arrived.

"What are you doing out of bed, honey?" Carson asked as Lily climbed into his lap and looked at the screen, saying hello to all of them.

Then she leaned forward, wiggling her tooth, which barely hung by a thread. Looking at her dad, she said, "I'm afraid it'll fall out, Daddy. If I swallow it, the Tooth Fairy won't come because it'll be in my tummy and not under the pillow."

Mila spoke up. "I think it's time to pull it, Lily. That way you can put it under your pillow tonight, and the Tooth Fairy will leave you something." She looked to the screen. "We're going to go handle pulling this first tooth. Talk with you later."

The Andrews signed off, leaving just the three of them.

"How is the house sale going?" Piper asked.

"You know it sold after only eight days on the market. I'm happy to report that the closing was finalized last week," Layne said.

"I'm sure that additional cash will help pay for the renovations at the Bay Breeze," Piper said.

"Speaking of that, you know I'm looking for someone to manage the inn for me." Layne paused. "Keaton suggested that you be the one to do so."

"Me?" squeaked Piper.

"Are you coming back to the Bay or not?" Keaton asked. "If you are, you'll need a place to stay, and the manager gets the owner's suite downstairs as part of the job."

"That's a really generous offer," Piper said. "I know I could handle the business end of everything, as well as the cleaning. I remember your mom used to make wonderful, big breakfasts, though, Layne. I'm not much of a cook, and I know people would expect a hot breakfast if they stayed there."

"We can figure that out," Layne said. "Even if it means

Keaton and me coming over and making breakfast until we find someone permanent."

"You? Cook?"

"Keaton's been teaching me how to cook. I've actually gotten pretty good, especially with breakfast. This guy is an excellent teacher." She flashed him a smile.

Piper nibbled on her bottom lip. "Part of me wants to tell you that I'm going to think it over, but the biggest part of me is screaming yes."

"It's a yes?" Layne asked.

Piper nodded. "A temporary yes. I don't know if managing the inn is something I want to do full-time or not, but I'm definitely willing to move in and give it a go during the spring and summer seasons. By then, I should have a good idea if it's something I want to continue doing or let you know you should find someone else."

"That's fabulous!" Layne exclaimed.

"I can't thank you enough for thinking of this, Keaton," Piper told him. "I know with Mom and Dad retiring at the beginning of summer that they sure don't want a thirty-year-old child moving back in with them, cramping their style. Staying at the inn and being employed by you will keep me from having to move home. You need to make a list for me, Layne. Everything that I'll be responsible for doing. I had worried if I came back to the Bay, especially without a college degree, that I would have trouble finding work. This will give me time to regroup and help you out at the same time."

"I'll get started on the list and email it to you," Layne promised. "Will you go to New York after your show closes to get your things?"

"I don't need to. I gave up my share in the apartment before this current tour began because I was never there. I had one of my roommates who was in town at the time ship me the few clothes that I'd left behind, so I can rent something and drive back to Texas once the show is done."

He nudged Layne. She looked at him, and he nodded.

Turning back to the screen, she said, "We were going to surprise you and come to your final performance, but we can drive up in Keaton's truck. It would have plenty of room for whatever you want to bring back to the Bay."

"You guys would do that? Really?"

"I'd love to see you perform before you put your touring days behind you," he said. "We're happy to have you ride back to the Bay with us. Just let us know what theater the performance is in so we can get tickets and a hotel room."

"The tickets are on me. I promise you'll have the best seats in the house. The hotel we just arrived at is nearby. Modest and affordable. If you'd like, I can book you a room here, and we can leave the Monday morning after the Sunday matinee."

"Sounds good," he said. "Just text us any details we need to know."

"You two are lifesavers," Piper declared. "And while I'm not certain my future is in B&B management, taking care of the Bay Breeze for you will give me time to figure out what I want to do with my life."

They said their goodbyes, and Layne wrapped her arms around him, kissing him enthusiastically.

"You are brilliant, Mr. Maxwell. I don't think Piper is the final solution, but it'll definitely give me more time to get things settled with the B&B."

"Remember, you don't have to maintain ownership of it. You can always sell it."

"I'm sentimentally attached to it, though. It would be hard to let go of it, especially seeing how it's coming back to life. I'll think long and hard on it, though."

He saw her eyes light with mischief.

"Right now, I believe we need to make love a final time in this house since this time tomorrow night, we'll be in the new one."

The Smiths had vacated the premises, and the sale of their house to him had gone through without a hitch. Layne didn't know it, but Keaton had Hillary include Layne's name on the deed. Along with shopping for furniture for the inn, they had also picked out numerous pieces for the new house. The furniture would be delivered tomorrow to both the B&B and their new house, which is why they had waited to move in. While not every room would be furnished from the start, they had furniture for most of the great room, the kitchen, and the primary suite.

He had taken a break from the reno and spent a majority of today moving art supplies to the caretaker's cottage and getting everything set up exactly as he liked. He'd set up shelves and bins in the storage area to house everything from tubes of paints and brush holders to cleaning solvents. He had adequate room for easels, as well as storing paintings once they had dried. The small fridge was stocked with bottled waters, and he had bought snacks, such as cashews and protein bars, things he enjoyed nibbling on as he sketched or paused during painting, thinking about which direction he wished to head. Keaton was itching to begin the next series he had been mulling over during the renovation, and his new studio was calling out to him.

Keaton stood and leaned down, scooping up Layne. She entwined her arms about his neck and gave him a lingering kiss.

"To the bedroom, Mr. Maxwell," she commanded.

He laughed. "At your service, Miss Larson."

In the bedroom, he slowly undressed her. Already, he had her every curve memorized, he ran his hands along her body, reveling in the feel of her smooth skin. Heat filled him as she pulled him down for a passionate kiss. His appetite for her had proved insatiable, and he made love to her with urgency, shouting her name as he came and collapsing atop her, driving her into the mattress.

She kissed him hungrily. "I love you so much, Keaton. I can't wait for the reno to be completed so that you can get back to painting. It's what you're meant to do."

"That—and love you," he said huskily, seizing her mouth again.

This first chapter of their romance was now closing. They had met. Fallen in love. Moved in together. Now, they would leave this house tomorrow and head to their forever home.

Keaton decided that once they did, he would ask Layne to marry him.

Chapter Eighteen

They were both out of bed earlier than usual the next morning, with Keaton getting his run in and Layne opting for yoga. She mixed her tai chi training with both yoga and walking, preferring to add variety to her workout routine. Today would be busy, with the furniture delivery coming from Corpus. The truck would stop at the Bay Breeze first before heading to the new house.

Keaton had already left for the inn. His part of the renovation would wrap up today. All that he had left to do was to hang the paintings she had found in the attic, and Sullivan had offered to help with that. Layne liked Keaton's friend, who was the architect of the new resort being built just off the coast of Driftwood Bay. Sullivan was really smart and quite funny. She was glad both he and Carson had formed a friendship with Keaton. Layne didn't know how long Sullivan would be in the Bay, though.

Her cell rang, and she saw it was Detective Robinson calling. She answered, a knot forming in her belly.

"Good morning, Detective. Any news?"

"I wish I had some, Layne," he apologized. "But the case has gone nowhere."

Robinson had kept them posted over the last several weeks. He had interviewed her neighbors, but no one had seen Jeremy at her house—and no one had caught whoever vandalized her garage on video. Jeremy had voluntarily sat for an interview with the police, but Robinson said he denied having anything to do with the graffiti. He'd told the detective that he had been home that night, and his phone would prove it. Of course, Jeremy could have simply left his cell at his new apartment while he defaced her property.

"I'm sorry to hear that, but it doesn't surprise me. Wait. Something just occurred to me. I got an email from him right after the breakup. I was too raw and angry to open it."

"See what it says," Robinson encouraged. "You never know. It might be important."

Layne changed to speakerphone and switched to her email, finding the folder she'd slid Jeremy's message into. Opening it, she quickly read its contents.

> *Layne –*
> *I'm sorry. That's the biggest thing I can say. I took you for granted. You're such a loving, giving person. I took a lot more than I ever gave back. For that, I'm ashamed. You're smart. Creative. You work hard. I know you were just trying to do what was best for us as a couple.*
> *I was an ignorant ass. I hope you'll forgive me.*
> *Love, Jeremy*

"No. It's not going to help," she told Detective Robinson. "It's an apology. The only reason he sent it was to test the waters and see if I would take him back."

"I'm betting since you didn't reply, it ticked him off. He

probably stewed over it, and that's when he bought the spray paint and decided to teach you a lesson. I'm sorry, Layne. I wish I could've done more for you, but I'm going to have to put the case aside. I'll revisit it occasionally, but it was always a long shot tying your ex to the vandalism."

"I completely understand. To be honest, I'm ready to move on. It's in my past. The house sold. I've moved to Driftwood Bay permanently. I won't ever see Jeremy again. Thanks for touching base with me and letting me know the case will go from active to inactive."

"I wish you the best," Robinson said.

"If you're ever near Corpus, stop by the Bay Breeze Inn," she said cheerfully. "I'll even give you a discount on a room."

"How's the fishing?"

"Pretty spectacular. At least according to the people I know who do fish here. I'm more of a ride in the boat or water ski person. I love to eat fish. I just don't have the patience to sit and catch them. Much less clean them."

He laughed. "You sound like my wife. Who knows? Maybe we will come and stay at your inn."

"I'll text you the website. It's been going through a makeover the last few weeks. Once I get the new pictures up, I'll send it to you."

They said their goodbyes, and though disappointed, Layne was glad she could close the door to that chapter of her life. Leaving Dallas on a sour note, thanks to Jeremy, had colored her memories of her time in the city. She needed to remember the good times. The friends she'd made. The products she'd worked on. The professional reputation she'd built. That should be her focus and not the failed relationship with an immature man-child. After all, if things had worked out between Jeremy and her, she wouldn't be with Keaton now. He was the silver lining to any cloud on her horizon.

Layne left and drove to the Bay Breeze. She would need to think about buying or renting a car soon. The rental she had booked in Corpus when she first returned to the Bay was small and cramped. She would prefer something larger, maybe even an SUV. It would be nice if she and Mila could make a day of it and go into Corpus, finding her a car and having lunch.

She arrived at the inn and went inside, wandering downstairs and finding some of her father's landscapes on the walls. A lump formed in her throat, seeing the paintings adorn the walls. She was glad she had found them and that others who stayed at the Bay Breeze would be able to enjoy his art.

Not finding Keaton and Sullivan, she headed upstairs, locating them in the last guestroom at the end of the hall.

"Hey," she said brightly. "I saw the paintings hanging downstairs. They look wonderful."

Sullivan said, "They're incredible, Layne. Your dad had real talent." He indicated Keaton. "He would've blown this guy out of the water."

Keaton gave as good as he got. "And this guy's only talent is to stand around and tell me to lower the right corner a millimeter. No, wait. Move it back up."

Both men laughed, and it warmed her heart to see Keaton so happy. With his friend. With her. With the work he had accomplished at the inn and the art he had yet to create.

Sullivan said, "I've seen all the downstairs. Keaton walked me through the projects he completed there. We've looked at each the guestrooms as we've placed your dad's landscapes. I like the color scheme you hit on. It's an easy way to identify each room."

"We'll have a better idea of any adjustments to make once the furniture arrives," she told him.

"Do you mind if I stick around for that?" Sullivan asked. "This is the last painting to hang."

"We'd be happy to have your help placing things," she said.

The doorbell rang.

"Must be the movers," Keaton said.

The three of them went downstairs, and soon a team of three men were placing furniture in various rooms. Most every piece went where they had pictured it, but Sullivan made a couple of suggestions, having them switch a few things. He was spot on each time.

"I know you're an architect, but you have a great idea for placement," she said. "Maybe your next career can be as an interior designer. You could turn the inside of Tidewater into something spectacular, just as I'm sure the outside will be."

"I am sticking around a while for this project," Sullivan shared. "Usually, I only draw up the plans and then meet with the construction manager onsite before I leave town and move on to my next assignment. This time, I told my bosses I needed a break. I'll be staying in town as Tidewater is being built, contributing if I can to the final outcome. In the meantime, I'll work remotely from the Bay."

"Already calling it the Bay?" she teased. "Then I would say you're meant to stay."

His face grew contemplative. "I'm actually considering that." Then he brightened. "We can talk about that another time. You need to focus on what's at hand."

The last of the furniture was brought in, and Stacy arrived as the movers were leaving.

"I know you and Keaton need to head to your house now with the movers so that you can see everything goes where you want it," she said. "I thought I'd come by and help get the little things done at the B&B. Make the beds. Put towels in the bathrooms. See what I have to work with because I know you want the photos up as soon as possible on the website."

"I can help with all that," Sullivan volunteered. "I tuck a

mean hospital corner. Learned that at my military boarding school."

"That would be terrific," Layne said, leading them to the storage room. "I've marked where each set of bedsheets, comforters, and throw pillows go. Each room is color-coordinated, and all the bed linens and bath towels match. The Daffodil Room. The Rose Gold Room."

"Leave it to us," Sullivan said. "Stacy and I will have every guestroom looking like *House Beautiful* in no time."

Keaton added, "Joey said they'll be done with the final touches before noon. They're installing the last of the towel racks and sink fixtures. That means you can hang towels in each bathroom. Shower curtains. Place bathmats."

She pointed to a shelf. "All the complimentary toiletries are here. Bath gel. Shampoo and conditioner. Hand soaps."

"We've got you covered," Stacy said. "Go. You don't want the movers to beat you there."

Keaton grinned. "I already know to bribe Sullivan with all the craft beer he can drink for helping out. You'll need to let me know how we can repay you."

Stacy shook her head. "You've already done so much for me, Keaton. Plus, Layne is paying me to take the photos for the website."

"We'll have you both over for dinner then," Layne said. "Whatever you want, we'll serve."

"Surf and turf," Stacy said. "Grilled shrimp and steaks."

"You're on," Keaton said, taking Layne's hand and pulling her from the room.

They went to their separate vehicles and drove home, arriving just as the movers were getting out of their van. Layne unlocked the house, a small thrill running through her. The place was so light and airy, and the views of the water from many of the rooms spectacular. It would be a privilege living here.

Especially with the man she loved.

She met the movers in the foyer, directing them to the great room with the sofa they carried. They placed it where she wanted and left for the next item. Soon, the great room took shape, with two sofas, a loveseat, and a reclining rocker. A coffee table and end tables followed, then two club chairs, which would sit by a window. An oversized leather chair which reclined was placed in what would be a reading nook.

More furniture came through the door, including the table and chairs for the kitchen. They would eat all their meals there for now since they had yet to choose anything for the dining room.

While the movers returned with all the pieces for their primary suite, another delivery truck arrived with a washer and dryer. The Smiths had left all their kitchen appliances, as well as those in the outdoor kitchen, but Anna Smith had wanted to take her washer and dryer. Layne was glad they would have one of their own since Keaton's rental hadn't had a set. She had gone to the Perry household a few times and then Roberts' place to do laundry. Both couples had been welcoming, but she didn't like disturbing people's routines.

The washer and dryer connection didn't take long, and that duo left, accepting a tip from Keaton. Once the remainder of the furniture was placed where they wanted, he also tipped the movers for the wonderful job they had done.

"They were really careful with every item," he said. "It's not always like that."

"Did you receive tips from the clients you worked for?"

He nodded. "Sometimes. I always took pride in the work I did and thought my boss paid me a fair wage. My salary increased the longer I stayed with his crew. He knew I was bringing in lots of business for him, thanks to the word-of-mouth of women who liked the work that I did. But when I received a tip, it made such a difference. It allowed me to buy new tubes of paint. A better quality frame for a painting. I was in the same boat as those movers not that long ago. I'll never forget my humble beginnings." He looked around. "Living here seems like a dream."

Layne came and entwined her arms around his neck. "The best dreams do come true. Even the dreams we don't know about." She kissed him softly. "I never knew I'd be back in the Bay, much less living with a man I love. My life is pretty darn perfect the way it is, Keaton. Mostly, because of you."

He kissed her, fanning the ever-constant flame that blazed between them. She hoisted herself up, wrapping her legs around him, kissing him back.

Breaking the kiss, she said, "Want to go try out our new bed?"

"I can't wait that long," he told her. "Too much time to put on the new sheets we bought."

Keaton carried Layne into the kitchen and placed her on the island.

"We're having sex ... *here*?" she asked.

He smiled lazily at her. "Babe, we're going to have sex in every inch of this house. Even in places you hadn't thought about."

She couldn't help but laugh. "Something tells me I may never look at a kitchen island the same way again."

Chapter Nineteen

Keaton delayed his morning run, making slow, sweet love to Layne, and then cuddling in bed with her for a few minutes. They had definitely christened the house last night, first making inventive use of the kitchen island and then later making love again in front of the fireplace of the great room. Afterward, they had gone for a stroll along the beach behind the house, and he still had to pinch himself, not believing he had this wonderful woman in his life and now lived in a large, sprawling house on the water in Driftwood Bay.

He kissed her again and rose, dressing for his run. He ran through the neighborhood, knowing in the next days and weeks he would become familiar with aspects of every house. Who placed hanging baskets on their porch. Who parked cars in their driveways. Even the few who still subscribed to a newspaper and had one lying on the sidewalk leading up to their doorway.

When he returned home, Keaton downed the bottle of water Layne offered to him.

"We'll need to go out to breakfast. We ate our way down until hardly anything was left. The only food items we had to move yesterday—besides your bottles of spices—were a jar of peanut butter, my mom's jams, and half a dozen bottles of water."

"Let me grab a quick shower, then I'll take you to the diner for breakfast," he told her, heading to their bathroom.

The shower stall was large enough to hold a party, with multiple heads. Keaton thought it would be very easy to get used to this luxury, especially after the pathetic water flow he'd put up with in the rental.

Layne said she would drive separately to the diner and stop by the grocery store after they ate in order to stock the pantry, freezer, and fridge.

Nellie greeted them, leading them to a table and handing them menus. "I hear yesterday was moving day. How are you liking the Smith place?"

He met Layne's eyes. "It's a dream come true, Nellie," he told the diner owner. "One coffee and an English breakfast tea for now, please."

"Coming right up," she replied.

After their meals arrived, Keaton said, "Don't forget that we're meeting Joey at noon today at the Bay Breeze. All the work should be completed, and he wants us to do a walk-through with him before he presents us with the final invoice."

"He's been a lifesaver. We finished all the remodeling so much faster, thanks to him and his workers."

"I know Stacy was going to come over and take photographs of the interior this morning."

"She already texted me a few sample shots she took yesterday after she and Sullivan put together a couple of the guest rooms. She wanted to see if they had set up everything the way I wanted. It was so nice of them to help out. They did a great job. We need to see when we can have them over for dinner."

"We can ask her when we get to the inn. What's on your agenda before we meet with Joey?"

"I texted Hillary yesterday, and she said I could stop by this morning. I want to ask her about the space that's about to be vacated next to Laura's store. If the rent sounds reasonable, I'll drop by and look it over. I also need to head over and talk with Collin Barton about teaching the art lessons."

They finished their breakfasts, and he walked Layne to her car, giving her a swift kiss.

"See you at the B&B."

Keaton decided to walk to his realtor's office since it was just a block off the square. Hillary greeted him, asking if he wanted some coffee.

"No, I just came from the diner. I think Nellie refilled my cup three different times. I have enough caffeine in me to last through tomorrow."

She led him into her office. "What's on your mind? I hope there's not anything wrong with your new house. I hope you and Layne will hold a big open house once you have things like you want. Everyone is dying to see it.

He wasn't keen on dozens of people traipsing through his private domain and simply changed topics. "What I'm here about today is looking for some extra space. Layne has come up with an idea that I should hold art lessons for those in the community who might have an interest in drawing or painting, and there's no room for that at the gallery.'"

"You have time for something like that?" Hillary asked.

He shook his head. "Oh, I'm not the one giving the lessons. I don't have the time or patience for something like that. I'm hoping it'll be Collin Barton doing the teaching."

She frowned, looking as if she were trying to place him. "Collin from the gas station? He paints?"

Keaton chuckled. "Obviously, you haven't been in Gulf Coastal Gallery for a while. Collin is a talented painter and has a couple of watercolors for sale. He could use the extra income right now, though, and I think it would be a nice opportunity for the citizens of the Bay. Layne heard that the souvenir shop on the square is closing. I wondered about the rent there, It would be centrally located, so a convenient location for people who sign up for lessons."

"I'm afraid that space won't be available. The owner and his wife are retiring, but he's already sold his entire inventory to someone else. In a town this size, with all the tourists we get come good weather, a shop filled with T-shirts, shells, and floaties is practically a legal requirement."

She thought a moment. "No other openings are available on the square, but I do have an idea which might work. Want to go see it?"

"Sure," he said, and she locked the office.

"It's only a block from here. Would you mind walking?"

"Fine by me."

He was surprised when she turned north, knowing that area was residential from his many runs. They stopped at a house on the corner, and Hillary looked at him.

"What do you think?"

"A house?"

"You don't need too large a space if you were considering the shop on the square. This is about fourteen hundred square feet. Just come inside and see what you think."

She punched the code of the lock box and removed the key. After she opened the door, he followed her inside.

They stepped into a fairly large room, which had most likely served as a living room and dining room combination.

The wood floors had seen better days. The inside could definitely stand a coat of paint to brighten it up a bit.

"This is definitely large enough to hold lessons," she told him. "You could bring in several long, rectangular tables and have folding chairs. The kitchen is off this way."

Hillary led them to it. It was small but adequate. Where a kitchen table had most likely stood, she pointed and said, "You could put shelving here and store art supplies or even use one of the bedrooms for that. Notice it's got a nice farm sink where students could clean their brushes."

She showed him the single bathroom in the narrow hallway and two small bedrooms on either side of it. An idea began forming, and Keaton pushed it aside for now.

"Is it for rent or sale?" he asked. "I didn't see a sign in the front yard."

"The owner passed away two weeks ago. Her nephew in Del Rio was her only heir. He came to the funeral and contacted me afterward. Took a few pieces of furniture with him, and I had a donation truck come and pick up the rest yesterday. He prefers selling it. I was going to put it on the market for the weekend."

She named what she had decided to list the property at, and Keaton thought it a fair price.

"Could you do me a favor and hold off on listing it? Give me a day to think it over?"

She smiled. "I can do that for my favorite client. Something tells me I'm going to make another sale."

He walked her back to her office and then returned to the square, where he drove his truck to the gas station where Collin worked. While he was there, he filled the tank first, paying at the pump, and then went into the garage. Collin was changing a tire and glanced up.

"Hey, Keaton. You said you needed to talk to me. Did one of my paintings sell?" he asked eagerly.

"Not yet, but my gut tells me you're going to break out soon, Collin. In the meantime, I have a proposition to offer you."

Collin stood. "I'm open to anything."

"Layne has been pushing me to offer group art lessons at the gallery. There's really no room for that, though, and I don't have the time or inclination to teach. I was hoping you might want to take on a few classes, say, two nights a week. Maybe even a Saturday or Sunday afternoon. I know the weekend slot would cut into your painting time, though."

"I could easily handle the two nights a week if we could fill the slots. If you're paying me to teach these lessons, that is. Money's tight, and I could really use the extra income."

Keaton decided to broach Collin with the idea that had come to him.

"I just saw a house off the square where the lessons could be held. It's a two-bedroom. How would you like to live there, rent-free? You could take one bedroom as your own and use the other as a studio. The remainder of the house could be used for the lessons."

Collin's face lit in surprise. "Are you kidding me? I wouldn't have to pay any rent—*and* I would have a studio to call my own? I'm in. All in. Hell, I'll even teach that afternoon weekend class if it has enough people to make."

Though he didn't need the money, he didn't want to hurt Collin's pride, and so he said, "We could split the fee we charge for the lessons. I'd be responsible for providing all the art supplies. I can do a little research online and see what might be reasonable to charge for a group lesson. So, my role is to provide the space and supplies, while you do the actual teaching."

Collin whistled low. "This is amazing. I actually think I would be a pretty good teacher. My mom says my best quality is patience. When do we start?"

"Let me lock the deal down on the house. It's sitting empty now, and the new owner is eager to sell. That'll give us time to do some research on how to price the lessons. We'll need to decide how many lessons to offer in a session. One or several."

"It should be a series," Collin said firmly. "Maybe four weeks. Six. We could have a drawing class and a painting one. I'll start looking into that, and I'll make a list of the basic supplies we'll need to start up."

"Since you're the one who'll be teaching, you can have free rein on what kind of classes. Maybe sketching and painting could be offered separately. Let's get together in a week and talk things over in more detail."

Collin took Keaton's hand and pumped it enthusiastically. "Thanks for giving me this opportunity. I won't let you down."

Keaton returned to his truck and pulled out of the gas station. Usually, something of this magnitude would be something he discussed with Layne, but he knew she would be on board with buying the house. He also didn't want to keep Hillary waiting, so he dropped by her office again.

"Back so soon?" she asked.

"Collin is willing to teach the art lessons. I made him an offer which included living in the house, rent-free, so he could also use part of it as his own art studio."

She bit back a smile. "I suppose that means you need to purchase the house in order for him to live there and give lessons."

"Exactly. Let's get the paperwork rolling."

She went over a few basics with him, things he was already familiar with, having recently purchased his own house.

"That's pretty much what you need to know. Let me contact the owner with your offer. I'm sure he'll accept it. When he does, I'll draw up the papers." Hillary smiled. "You're becoming a real part of this community, Keaton. Tell Layne I think the idea of offering art lessons is brilliant. I hope they'll be for both children and adults."

"I'll need to work that out with Collin, but I hope we can service both age groups."

He left, stopping at his gallery first, wanting to check on things since he hadn't been there in a couple of weeks. It wasn't a day it was open, so he had the place to himself.

Going into his office, he fired up his computer, opening his bank records. He could swing paying for the house outright without having to carry a mortgage since the price was so reasonable. He scrawled a few notes to himself on a pad of paper, knowing he would need to talk to his banker. The pen ran dry, and he tossed it in the trash, opening the lap drawer to retrieve a new one.

It was then that he saw the pair of concert tickets Stacy had gifted him for Christmas. With everything that had been happening in his life, he had completely forgotten about receiving them.

And the concert was this coming Friday night.

Keaton removed the tickets from the drawer and decided to go home. Layne should have finished her grocery shopping by now. He would ask her about driving to Houston to see Case perform. Or they could even fly since it was at least a five-hour drive from the Bay to Houston. That might be a better use of their time.

The concert would also be the perfect opportunity to ask her to marry him. A romantic getaway. Just the two of them.

He wondered if he should buy her an engagement ring and decided that they should pick one out together. Houston would have a better selection of stones and settings. Excitement filled him, knowing they would be starting a new chapter in their lives. Though their time together had been short, they had helped one another to heal from the heavy hurt in their hearts. He would go through all the pain of Frankie's betrayal again, knowing that it had changed his path, bringing him to Driftwood Bay.

And Layne.

Keaton opened the door and exited the gallery, locking it again. When he turned, the sidewalk was blocked.

A old woman stood in front of him, so gaunt that her clothes dwarfed her. He caught a scent he immediately recognized and knew she was a drug user. Deep wrinkles lined her face, and her thinning hair reminded him of straw. She wheezed and started to speak, and he caught sight of her decayed teeth, something he'd learned was called meth mouth.

"Keaton?" she croaked.

"How do you know me?" he demanded.

Then he looked into her bloodshot eyes. Azure eyes.

The same as his.

His gut churned. "Honey?" he asked hoarsely. It was the name she had told him to call her. She had given birth when she was barely seventeen and had refused to think of herself as a mother.

"It's me," she said, nodding. "Aren't you gonna give your mama a hug?"

"I want nothing to do with you," he said coldly. "You gave me up."

"I'm sorry," she whined, beginning to cough, a deep cough that let him know she wasn't well. "I was young. And God knows, damn stupid."

"Do you know how awful my life was?" he demanded, his temper rising. "I went from foster home to foster home. I never found a family. I was beaten. Lied to. Starved." Keaton paused. "Then again, I guess that wasn't much different from when I lived with you."

Her eyes narrowed. "Well, you're doing pretty good for yourself now. I read about you. You're a fancy artist. You have this store. You make a ton of money."

Now, everything became clear. He knew exactly why she had tracked him down. "I'm not giving you any money, Honey. You'd just buy drugs with it if I did. I don't owe you squat."

Her cheeks mottled a dark red, her anger obvious. "You *do* owe me. I brought you into this world. I need help, Keaton. You're the only one who can give it to me."

Eying her steadily, he said, "You would be the last person I would ever help. You were nothing but an incubator. You may have given birth to me, but you never loved me. You only love getting high, and I'm not going to give you money to do that."

Out of nowhere, she slapped him. Hard. Shaking her head, her voice full of fury, she said, "You were worthless from the start. Always crying. I hated you. I hated having you. You ruined my life, you son of a bitch."

Keaton looked at her a long moment. She had never taken responsibility for anything. He realized he didn't hate her. He was merely indifferent to her.

"Go, Honey. There's nothing here in Driftwood Bay for you."

"You'd toss out your own mother," she snarled, then seemed to think better of it. Softening her tone, she added, "Oh, just spend a few hours with me, baby. I've been through hard times. Just talking to you would help. I could come home with you. Stay a while."

He almost laughed aloud at her pathetic attempt to try and play on his sympathy since the anger hadn't worked.

"I never had a mother. Least of all you," he replied, stepping around her and walking away.

He got into his truck and started the engine, needing Layne more than he ever had. Keaton pulled away from the curb, turning his truck for home.

And never glanced back at her in the rear view mirror.

Chapter Twenty

Layne headed to the grocery store, thinking how a mundane task such as stocking their kitchen appealed to her. Her mother would have had a good laugh, knowing Layne had always lived on take-out, ordering the few groceries she needed, such as coffee and creamer. It was nice she could think of Mom and not tear up.

Her life had changed for the better. Although she missed her parents deeply and wished they could have been able to get to know Keaton, she knew she was better off now with the life she was building with him in the Bay. Moving yesterday to the house sitting on the water, it felt as if she had truly come home. With Mila living here and Piper returning soon, Layne had her chosen sisters for life nearby now, and their support would be invaluable.

She entered the grocery store, snagging a cart and moving up and down the aisles. She was already familiar with the store's layout, thanks to the trips she had made here with Keaton. She liked how he was teaching her how to cook. Already, Layne could make several of the dishes Miss Peggy had been known for, as well as basic meals such as spaghetti and meatballs and fried chicken. If it turned out that she wasn't able to find a breakfast cook for the Bay Breeze, she would be able to take over that task herself. Grinning, she thought maybe she could pass along her new knowledge and teach Piper how to cook. Her friend was even more helpless in the kitchen than Layne had been.

As she moved through the store, loading her cart, she stopped and chatted with a few people she knew. It was funny how all she had wanted to do was leave the Bay when she graduated from high school, tired of seeing people she knew everywhere she went and feeling as if everyone knew her business. Now, she embraced the small town and its atmosphere of friendliness.

When she reached home, she punched the remote Keaton had placed in her rental to pull into the spacious, four-bay garage, where she made numerous trips back and forth between car and kitchen, toting in groceries. She placed items in the freezer first and then the perishables in the fridge.

Then she heard the doorbell ring and wondered if Keaton might have actually forgotten his key. She had remembered to put the new key on her key ring, but she hadn't asked if he had done the same. Layne headed to the front door and opened it, only to find Mrs. Perry standing on the porch. Mila's mom held a vase filled with beautiful Gerber daisies and tea roses.

"Hi," she greeted. "Won't you come in?"

"I was hoping to find you at home, dear. I just wanted to stop by and drop off these flowers for you and Keaton."

"That was so thoughtful, Mrs. Perry. Come back to the kitchen. I'm putting away some groceries."

The two women went to the kitchen, and Mrs. Perry set the flower arrangement on the kitchen table.

"Tell me how I can help, Layne."

"Just have a seat. I'm still finding my way in the kitchen, trying to figure out where I want to put everything."

They chatted about the updates which had been made to the Bay Breeze as she put away the final groceries, and Layne said, "We'll be doing a final walk-through today at noon with the contractor who did a good deal of the work."

"I heard Joe and Keaton talking. It sounds as if Keaton had quite a hand in the remodeling process himself."

She nodded. "Keaton worked for a contractor before he began painting full-time. He refinished all the floors in the inn, upstairs and downstairs. Put in new kitchen and bathroom countertops and pulls for all the drawers. He even got me involved in some of it. I helped wallpaper the guestrooms. Joey and his crew handled the plumbing and installing of new toilets throughout the inn, and they also put in a new HVAC system. You'll have to come by and see everything we've done."

"I checked the website and know you'll be putting up new pictures on it soon."

"As a matter of fact, Stacy Reed has already taken the exterior photographs. She'll return today to shoot the interior, and then I'll put those up."

"You know, Layne, it might be smart to hold an open house at the Bay Breeze to let others see the makeover. That could generate some good buzz. Don't ever underestimate word-of-mouth in a small town."

"That's a wonderful idea. I can't believe I didn't think to do that."

Mrs. Perry smiled. "You've had so much on your plate, honey. Losing your parents and your job. Moving back to the Bay. Finding Keaton. By the way, I think the two of you are wonderful together."

"I wasn't looking for a relationship when I arrived here—much less love—but Keaton has saved me in every way. I didn't realize how broken I was until I begin to heal under his gentle touch."

Mrs. Perry stood. "Jack and Lark would have adored him. And they would be so proud of all you've accomplished. Well, I'm not going to keep you. I know you have a thousand and one things to do. I simply wanted to drop by and say hello."

She hugged the woman who'd been a second mother to her. "Thank you for the idea regarding the open house. We probably should do the same here once we get a little more furniture and are more settled."

"Take your time. There's no rush on that. You're back in the Bay now, dear. We'll help take care of you. And Keaton."

Once Mrs. Perry left, Layne checked her phone and saw that Stacy had texted and was already at the B&B. She drove over, seeing Stacy's car was the only one at the inn.

Layne went inside, hollering, "I'm here!"

Stacy appeared, camera in hand. "I just beat you here by a few minutes. I've been playing with opening blinds and testing light levels with and without overhead lights on."

"We're going to meet with Joey later, but come with me now. I want to see everything that you and Sullivan did yesterday."

They went through the entire downstairs and then moved upstairs.

"I can't thank you and Sullivan enough for helping pull things together yesterday. This has saved me so much time, and it'll allow you to take your photos sooner, as well."

"It was a pleasure to have a small part in bringing the Bay Breeze back," Stacy said. "I love everything you've done to it. Jack and Lark would be thrilled at how things have turned out."

"I think they would embrace the changes and updates. Hopefully, it'll draw more guests than previously. I also still feel

I have a part of Dad with me, seeing his paintings hanging on the walls throughout the place."

"I'm going to start downstairs if that's okay with you," Stacy said. "Hopefully, I'll wrap things up before Joey shows up and be out of your hair."

Layne pulled her tablet from her purse. "Meanwhile, I'll try to be productive and work on copy for the website to accompany your photographs.'"

"I think that you should create a tab about your father's paintings. I can photograph each one for the website. It would be something nice to spotlight, and it makes the Bay Breeze more unique than the average B&B."

"Oh, that's a marvelous idea, Stacy. Yes, please do so. Dad wrote the title of each painting on the back side, so I know how to refer to each one."

Layne waited while Stacy took pictures of the common room first from several angles, then she took a seat and opened a new document, working on the wording for the website. She described the various guestrooms and wrote a few stories about each, as well as writing copy for each of her dad's paintings and what they depicted. She also thought to include a tab for the history of the B&B, but she would have to do a little research on that. It also wouldn't hurt to have information about the history of Driftwood Bay, as well as make a few recommendations for activities in the area and restaurants to dine in.

An hour later, Stacy entered the common room again. "I'm all done, Layne. I'll review everything at home. I shot way more pictures than you'll need, but I was trying to get the rooms from every angle. I'll choose the best ones and send them to you."

"Forward all of them if you would. I'd love to see every one of them."

"Then I'll create a master folder with all the photographs I think you should use, with sub-folders of each room. There'll be another folder for the leftovers."

"That sounds good to me. Thanks again for taking on this project, Stacy."

"It's been a pleasure. Photography used to be a hobby of mine, before teaching and my family. It felt good to be back behind the camera's lens."

"I'll definitely credit you on the website for the photos. If you'd like, I can include your email address so that people have a way to contact you if they like your work. Or do you have a website?"

"Keaton encouraged me to claim my domain name when I started up my artwork again. I do have a basic website, which is in its infancy. It would be a good idea if I did have information about my photographs on it, though. You never know if someone else might be interested in hiring me. I'll text you my info."

"Do you have a day in mind for the dinner we owe you?"

"I'm pretty open. With both the kids tied up with school and extracurriculars, they're rarely home. Just look at your schedules and let me know what's convenient for the two of you. And despite being a guest, I'll definitely bring the wine."

After Stacy left, Layne went back to writing her descriptions. She fleshed out more of her brief history of the Bay Breeze, as well as noting something about each of the guestrooms. She opened a new document and listed information about her dad's background and the artwork he had created which filled the inn. She listed the names of the landscapes hanging on the wall, already knowing each of them by heart.

Deep in thought, she suddenly sensed a presence nearby and looked up, thinking Keaton or Joey had arrived.

Instead, Jeremy Riggs stood in the doorway.

Shock reverberated through her, followed quickly by anger. "What are you doing here?" she hissed, the sight of him sending chills through her.

"I was hoping for a friendlier greeting from you, Layne," he said, entering the room.

She shot to her feet. "Why would you come here? I suppose you want to scrawl more obscene graffiti."

Guilt flooded his handsome face. "That was pretty childish of me. I was angry with you. You had blown up our entire relationship. And you blocked me everywhere. You didn't even respond to my email."

"I believe you are the one who ruined things between us. You need to leave, Jeremy. We have nothing to say to one another. I don't want you here."

He glanced around. "You've done a lot of work to the old place. I barely recognized it when I pulled up." His gaze met hers. "I'm here to apologize, Layne. I was a world-class ass to you. We had something good together, and I ruined it. I'll freely admit that I'm the one who screwed things up. Yes, I called you out for working so much and never being around, but I know you were doing everything for us."

Jeremy gave her his heart-stopping smile. "I've missed you, Layne. And I still love you. That hasn't changed."

She glared at him. "You think you can waltz back into my life and speak empty words which you don't mean? You don't love me. You only love yourself. I'm thinking you want me back because you don't want to have to pay for everything. I was your golden ticket. Well, this goose isn't laying anymore golden eggs for you. Get out. Don't bother coming back."

He strode across the room, quickly closing the distance between them, grabbing her upper arms and squeezing tightly.

"Let go," she said through gritted teeth. "If you don't leave now, I'm calling the police. You're trespassing."

"The door was open. It's a public place. I just came in to find out about a room."

Before she knew what was happening, his mouth slammed against her. Disgust rose through Layne, and she kneed him hard in the groin. He yelped, stumbling back, a stream of expletives coming from him.

Then Keaton was there. She saw him quickly assessing the scene. He spun Jeremy around and landed a solid punch to the center of his face. Blood spurted immediately from her ex's nose, giving her immense satisfaction.

Jeremy's hands flew to his face. "Who the hell are you?"

"I'm the man who loves that woman. If you don't get out now, you're going to find yourself with more than a broken nose."

Layne saw the wild look in Jeremy's eyes, and he threatened, "I'll press charges against you. You assaulted me for no reason. My nose is broken."

"And I'll let the police know that Keaton was protecting me," Layne said. "That you sexually assaulted me."

"It was one kiss, Layne," Jeremy protested.

"One unwanted kiss," she retorted. "One uninvited kiss. You forced it on me. I didn't want it. I don't want you here in the Bay. You better leave now before we call the police. In case you don't remember, one of my best friend's dad is the chief of police. I'm like a daughter to Chief Roberts. He'll know I'm telling the truth and that you're a creep and a liar."

"Bitch," he said menacingly, wiping his forearm against his bleeding nose. Jeremy looked to Keaton. "You're welcome to this cold fish. She's worthless in bed."

Jeremy stormed out of the room—and hopefully from their lives.

Keaton hurried to her, throwing his arms around her and

drawing her close. Layne realized now just how upset she was, but his presence had a calming effect on her.

He stroked her hair. "Are you all right? Did he hurt you?"

"I'm fine. Just a little shaken." She looked up at him. "I did get in one spectacular knee thrust to his balls, and that felt amazing."

"You aren't the only one to have an unwanted visitor from your past this morning." He kissed her brow.

"Who on earth would've come to see you?" she asked.

"The woman who gave up her parental rights to me. Honey. Frankly, I thought all the drugs would have killed her by now."

"What on earth did she want?"

"What do you think? Money. I don't know how she knew what I was doing or where I lived, but she showed up at the gallery, looking for a free ride."

Layne kissed him softly. "Well, we've had quite the morning, haven't we?"

She heard the front door opening and tensed. Then Joey appeared in the doorway.

"Hey, you two. Ready to do that walkthrough?"

Her gaze met Keaton's, and they both smiled.

"Ready whenever you are," she told the contractor.

"Then let's start at the top and work our way downstairs," Joey said cheerfully.

They followed him up the staircase, Keaton threading his fingers through hers. Ghosts from their past had confronted them, but Layne knew they would always stand strong.

Because they had each other.

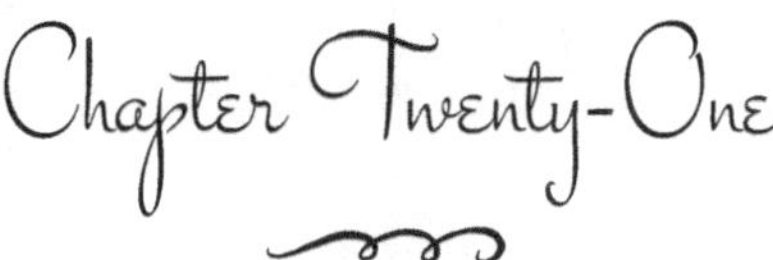

Chapter Twenty-One

They spent a good hour with Joey, who walked them through every task his crew had completed.

"We could never have finished the reno as quickly as we did without your contributions," Keaton told the contractor.

"You've done lovely work," Layne added. "I'll definitely recommend you to anyone needing a construction project done."

"You put us to work at a slow time of year for us," Joey said. "We were grateful to have a small part in restoring the Bay Breeze."

"I'll be putting up the pictures on the website soon," Layne said. "I'm looking to open in three weeks, so look at your calendar. I still want to have you and your wife as complimentary guests for a weekend."

Joey beamed. "I'll talk to her about it. We'll need to farm the kids out to my mom and dad. I'll text you about it."

Once Joey had left, Keaton pulled Layne into his arms for a slow, delicious kiss.

"We did it," he said. "Your parents would be really pleased at how things turned out."

He watched tears mist her eyes. "I wish they could've been here to see it. To meet you. Let's head home. I'm hoping Stacy will forward her photographs soon, and I want to go through and have you help me choose which ones to upload to the website."

"I know you want to get that up and running ASAP, but mentioning Stacy reminds me of something. I haven't been to the gallery much, especially since things are so slow, but I went in today and found concert tickets which Stacy gave me for Christmas. I'd stuck them in a drawer and had forgotten about them."

"What group?" Layne asked.

"It's a country artist—and I don't even know if you like country. He's playing in Houston. A guy who was a part of my construction crew years ago. Case Wellborne."

"You *know* Case Wellborne?" she asked, clearly familiar with the name. "He's amazing. So talented."

"He was one of the painters. A damned good one, by the way. Case was always humming or singing while we worked. He began playing weekend gigs. As he grew more popular, he started traveling through Texas on weekends. Finally, he quit Frank Peterson's construction crew to earn a living by making music."

Keaton paused. "In a way, Case was my inspiration to keep painting. I hoped that one day I could follow my art and make a full-time living from it, just as he did his music."

"I'd love to go see him live," she said enthusiastically. "*The Devil Dancing in the Moonlight. The Bridge to Another Heart.* He's put out some really great songs."

"Good. I'm glad you don't mind going. The thing is, we were going to drive up next weekend to see Piper's last performance. Would you rather fly to Houston and save all that time in the car? It would eat up five or six hours each way."

"That's a great idea. Things are going to be getting really busy around here. We could be there in a little over half an hour if we fly, where it would take five or more to drive. That's ten hours, there and back."

They walked out to their vehicles, and he said, "I'll arrange the tickets. Pick a hotel close to the venue. So clear all day tomorrow and Saturday, too. We can fly back early Sunday morning."

"Will do," she said, allowing him to open her car door and getting in.

As Layne drove off, Keaton got into his truck. He had no idea how to contact Case and then thought about DM-ing him. At Sidney's urging, Keaton had created social media accounts, mostly to stake a claim to his name. He had only made an occasional post of a painting to Instagram, and he followed no one. Still, it seemed the only way to get in touch with Case. If the singer responded, that would be terrific. If not, they would still enjoy attending the concert.

He found Case's Instagram handle and opened his DMs, typing a message.

Hey, Case. Keaton, your fellow painter, from a long time ago. Bringing my girl to your Houston concert tomorrow night. Doubt you'll get this or if you would even honor a fan request, but I thought it was worth a try. If you would dedicate *Marry Me Before Sundown* to Layne, I'd appreciate it. You can text me at 972-555-4672.

Keaton sent the message, thinking Case probably received thousands from fans each day. Most likely, he had a social media manager who monitored his accounts for him and would probably blow off the message. Still, he had made the effort.

He opened an airline app, skimming through available flights to Houston tomorrow, and reserved two seats for them on a one o'clock flight out of Corpus. He booked return flights for Sunday morning, wanting to give them all day Saturday in Houston to shop for engagement and wedding rings. Keaton planned to ask Layne to marry him at the concert. He was glad to know that she liked Case's music.

Then he arranged a hotel room for Friday and Saturday night near the Toyota Center, receiving an immediate confirmation. By now, he had also gotten an email with their boarding passes, so he downloaded those to his wallet.

The trip taken care of now, he drove home. As he approached the sprawling property, he couldn't help the pride swelling within him. This was his forever home with Layne. This was where they would make a family and he would create art.

He pulled into the garage and cut the engine. His phone rang, the number unknown. For a moment, he thought to let it go to voicemail, afraid it might be Honey. He decided to answer anyway. It he heard her voice, at least he would know to block the number.

"Hello?"

"Keaton? It's Chief Roberts. Got a little situation on our hands that I wanted to make you aware of."

The chief's words caused Keaton's stomach to sink.

"Does it involve a woman named Honey?"

"Yup. That's the one. She was caught shoplifting on the square. She's been hollering to high heaven, demanding to talk to her son—which I assume is you."

"She may have given birth to me, Chief, but Honey washed her hands of me years ago. Renounced her parental rights when

I was young. I haven't seen her in over twenty-five years. Until this morning, when she appeared at the gallery wanting money and I sent her on her way. I don't want to have anything to do with her. She's a stranger to me."

"I hear you, son. She's on parole for selling meth. Looks like a user herself. Don't worry. I'll take care of things. You don't have to see her or talk with her. She'll be going back to prison for parole violations. I just wanted to touch base with you."

"Thank you, Chief Roberts. And just a heads up to you, Layne's ex from Dallas, Jeremy Riggs, also showed up today at the Bay Breeze. We convinced him to leave, but I just wanted you to know in case he decided to hang around and cause a little mischief. He spray painted Layne's garage in Dallas with an expletive after they broke up. I'd hate for him to do anything to the Bay Breeze."

"Pulling up his driver's license picture and vehicle registration now," the police chief said, all business now. "I'll send out the info and make sure my guys know to be on the lookout for him. We'll keep an eye out, Keaton."

"Appreciate it, Chief.'"

He went inside the house, relieved to know that Honey wouldn't be bothering them anymore. Layne was sitting at the kitchen table, pouring over her tablet.

She smiled up at him. "Pull up a chair. We can go through these photos together." Picking up a pen, she turned her notebook to a fresh page. "I'll make notes of the ones we like best."

They perused the folders Stacy had created for each room at the B&B, noting the number of shots which appealed to them. He told her that she didn't want a cookie cutter layout, so they were careful to choose a variety of photographs of the various guestrooms.

"Now that we've made our choices, I can slide them into

the templates I've created. I'll be needing your opinion again once that's done and I've added the copy I wrote."

"Then I'm going to go and get a little work done."

Keaton retrieved his sketchpad and went to sit outside on the deck. He believed he would do a lot of sketching here, looking out over the water.

Layne joined him, asking, "Do you mind if I look at what you've been sketching? I don't want to invade your space or break up your routine."

He had never had anyone to share his work with at any stage, but he decided he wanted her involved in every aspect of his art.

Handing his sketchbook to her, he dragged his chair beside hers. Together, they went through each page, viewing the sketches he'd been working on.

"As fabulous as I think your oil paintings are, you could actually sell your sketches. Maybe compile these into a book and detail your process."

"It's a thought," he agreed.

"You were meeting with Collin today. How did that go?"

"Well, a lot happened this morning. We own another house now."

The look on her face was priceless. "What in the world are you talking about?"

Keaton explained how the space on the square wasn't going to be available, after all, and how Hillary had taken him to a house on the market.

"It's in decent shape. I'd like to have it painted inside to brighten it up a little. Joey can handle that. Anyway, it has one large room which had served as a combination living and dining room. We can bring in long cafeteria-style tables for the students. It has two bedrooms. To sweeten the pot, as well as helping out a cash-strapped Collin, I offered for him to live in the house, rent-free. He can take one bedroom for himself and use the other one as an art studio for himself. I know we don't need the money, but I told him we'd split the fees we'd charge for lessons."

"Good idea. I know you really believe in him. This will give him a place to work, as well as some additional income."

"Exactly. I did say that I would provide all the supplies for the students. We can put some shelving in the kitchen, and students can go there to get what they need. Clean their brushes at the end of a lesson. Collin is looking into the curriculum. Deciding what to teach in the classes. Stacy mentioned about having lessons for both kids and adults, which isn't a bad idea."

"I like that, especially having lessons for kids. Who knows? You might find the next budding artist to come out of Driftwood Bay."

"If this idea catches on—and I think it really could—Collin might be able to give up his job at the gas station and teach lessons, both group and individual ones, and paint fulltime."

"We need to think about designing a website for this venture," Layne said enthusiastically. "Painting Plus? Painting by the Bay? I need to think on it."

He laughed and leaned in, capturing her mouth for a sweet kiss. "Let's go work on dinner first."

Her eyes lit with mischief. "And maybe other things after dinner?"

Keaton looked at her innocently. "Oh, right. We need to pack for our quick trip."

"You are incorrigible, Maxwell. But oh, so sexy."

He ran a finger down her arm slowly. "After we pack? I'll let *you* pick tonight's activity. We have a lot of rooms to christen in this house, Layne."

"That we do."

She stood. "Right now, you need to feed me. It just hit me that we never ate lunch. I'm starving."

As he followed inside to the kitchen, Keaton knew he was starving not only for food.

He would always be hungry for Layne.

Layne said, "I'm in need of comfort food." She began pulling out the ingredients for one of Miss Peggy's easy, go-to dishes. "Hope tuna casserole is good with you."

"It's always a good time for tuna casserole."

"Let me handle it. Open some wine for us and go relax."

He found a bottle of pinot noir and opened it. Fetching two glasses, he poured wine into both of them and then checked his phone, on the off-chance Case might have replied to his message.

To his surprise, Case—or someone working for him—had actually responded. Eagerly, he sat at the table, reading the message.

GOOD TO HEAR FROM YOU, buddy. Janine and I always think of you fondly, especially every time we put a new baby into that cradle you made for us. We've had four of them sleep in it now and may or may not be done.

Would love to see you and Layne. The tickets I can get you are better than anything you bought. I'll give my manager your number. He'll text you where to come around seven and have backstage passes for you. We'll get in a quick visit before the show starts. Looking forward to catching up with you.

THIS WAS FAR MORE than what Keaton had expected, especially because he hadn't been friends with Case, merely friendly with him. He decided this part would be a surprise to Layne.

"What are you grinning about?" she asked, putting the casserole into the oven.

He took a sip of wine, calming himself. "Just got the confirmation for the hotel. I also booked flights for us." Keaton smiled. "Things are really shaping up for this weekend."

Chapter Twenty-Two

As they boarded the airplane in Corpus, Layne looked forward to having this brief getaway with Keaton. Their lives had been a whirlwind ever since she had arrived in the Bay, and she knew once the Bay Breeze reopened in a couple of weeks, things would only grow more hectic.

She was pleased with how the renovations to the inn had helped update it while retaining its charm. It had been fun selecting furniture for each room, as well as choosing other pieces to decorate the B&B. Some had come from Keaton' gallery, art representing local talent, while some knickknacks had come from several shops on the square. Thankfully, Piper would take on the job of managing the inn and its guests for the spring and summer, giving Layne time to secure a more permanent innkeeper. She doubted her friend would want to make the management job hers, but if she did, so much the better.

Layne had followed Keaton to Corpus in her rental car, turning it in at the airport before they checked in. He told her it was time to shop for something she could keep, and she supposed that was one of the reasons they were staying in Houston tomorrow. A large city would give them plenty of car dealerships to visit. Although she knew he had booked them on a flight back to Corpus Sunday morning, it would be easy to cancel her ticket if she had a new car to drive back.

He stored her carry-on in the bin above them. She hadn't brought much with her. For tonight's concert, she would simply wear what she had on now, jeans and a shirt, with a light jacket. She had packed something to wear for tomorrow, along with pajamas and toiletries. She would wear her jeans again with a fresh shirt she had brought for the flight home on Sunday.

After he sat and buckled his seatbelt, Layne said, "I'm really excited about the concert tonight. I haven't been to a live event in ages."

"Do you enjoy going to concerts? Or even plays?" he asked.

"Both." She frowned. "I haven't made play a priority in a long time. Maybe we can choose one live event to go to once a month in Corpus. Or even San Antonio. It's not that far away, and they draw better acts."

He took her hand and kissed it. "You've already made me fall in love with San Antonio, same as I fell in love with you. I'm ready to go back anytime you are."

"Well, we probably won't be going far for a while, not with you needing to get back to painting and me helping Piper with the Bay Breeze. She doesn't know how to cook, so I told her I'd handle breakfast each morning for the guests. That means I'm committed daily to providing that meal. I do want to arrange with Seaside Sweets to have fresh cookies every afternoon for those staying at the B&B. Piper can pick those up, though."

"You need to teach your friend how to cook. I've taught you, and look how fast you've caught on. You're already offering to cook breakfast every morning."

"I guess I could try to give her lessons," she agreed. "Piper is really smart. She picks up things fast. Like the piano. One minute, she was hitting a couple of notes. The next, she was playing chords and then entire songs."

"I'm looking forward to seeing her perform," Keaton said. "It's too bad she doesn't have a teaching certificate. If she did, she could take over her mom's position in choir and drama at the high school. Maybe they could hire her on a provisional basis until she could earn the certificate."

"Piper doesn't have a degree," Layne explained. "She'd need to finish that before she would eligible to earn an alternative teaching certificate. She dropped out of college after two years because she had the chance to tour in a musical production. The lure of performing live, coupled with money and travel, was just too much for her to say no."

"I know you've got two degrees, but college isn't for everyone. Look at me. I'm proof that you can succeed without going to college. Of course, I'm one of the lucky ones. If I hadn't gotten the breaks I did, I'd still be doing blue collar construction and remodeling jobs."

She leaned her head against his shoulder. "I'm so glad you were able to quit and follow your dreams, Keaton."

Layne couldn't help but think of her own dad and how he'd put his artistic dreams aside to marry and run the Bay Breeze. She hoped their kids would be able to chase their dreams.

It surprised her that she was thinking about having kids with Keaton. He'd never mentioned them, but her heart told her that he would be a fantastic dad. She told herself not to put the cart before the horse, though. They were just now living together. Hopefully, they would talk marriage down the road. And then kids.

The flight to Houston's Hobby Airport went off without a

hitch. Layne was glad they could bypass the luggage carousels as they headed for the car rental counter.

"Where's the concert being held?" she asked as they waited in line.

"The Toyota Center. The Rockets play their home games there."

"So, we're talking a big arena."

He nodded. "Huge. I remember going to see Case in some dive bar that didn't hold twenty people. His wife was there. Janine. She was pregnant and his biggest supporter. Janine was always the one who encouraged him to give up the day job and concentrate on writing and performing."

"Were you close?"

"Not really. You know me. The lone wolf. But we worked together for a few years. Talked some. He would sing, both other people's songs and his own. It made the jobs go faster."

"Wouldn't it be great if you could see him?" she asked.

Keaton chuckled. "I don't think the seats Stacy bought are on the floor."

She slipped her hand through the crook of his arm. "It doesn't matter. This is going to be such a fun experience. One of many we'll have over the years to come."

They reached the front of the line and were given the keys to a dark green SUV. Keaton put directions into his phone and drove them to a Marriott.

As he handed the key to the valet and they headed inside, he told her, "We can walk to the concert tonight. The arena is about ten minutes from here. The car is more for running around tomorrow."

"I like hearing that we're so close. I hate getting stuck in traffic after a concert. Sometimes, you're in it longer than the actual concert ran."

They checked in, going to a room on the seventh floor. It took less than five minutes to unpack.

Layne went and wrapped her arms around his neck. "How would you like to kill time until the concert?" she asked coyly.

Keaton gave her a lazy smile. "Why don't you show me what you have in mind?"

Slowly, she began unbuttoning his shirt, kissing his chest after she undid each button and peeling back the material. When she reached the last one, she pushed the shirt from his broad shoulders, neatly placing it on the nearby chair.

"Wouldn't want it to get wrinkled," she purred.

He returned the favor, his lips nuzzling her neck, sending lightning bolts shooting through her. No matter how much time passed, she knew she would never grow tired of his touch.

Greedily, they kissed, removing the rest of their clothes, sinking onto the bed and making love. As he thrust into her, her hips rising each time, she thought every day with him was a new adventure.

They dressed afterward, and Keaton said, "I'm hungry. Let's set out toward the arena now. I'm sure we'll find something along the way where we can stop and grab some dinner."

Two blocks down, they stumbled across a Korean noodle restaurant. Keaton ordered *jajangmyeon,* a noodle dish with pork and vegetables swimming in a black bean sauce. Layne opted for spicy garlic shrimp noodles.

"My mouth is on fire," she admitted, finishing her entrée.

"Then we need to order something to cool it down." He glanced at the dessert menu. "How about this *makgeolli* ice cream? Says it's mildly sweet with the delicate flavor of Korean rice wine."

They asked their server about it, and she explained that it was light, between a sorbet and a full, creamy ice cream.

"Okay, one order of it and another of the yaksik," he said, referring to a sweet rice dessert.

They split the desserts so they could each have a taste of both, and Layne couldn't decide which had been better.

"It's nice to know you'll try a new cuisine," she said, recalling how set Jeremy was in his ways when it came to eating.

"I love Korean food," he told her. "I ate a lot of it during my construction years. Miss Peggy learned how to make a few Korean dishes from a neighbor and taught me how to prepare them, too."

She squeezed his thigh. "You are just like an onion, Keaton Maxwell. I peel back one layer, and I learn something new about you every day."

He signed the bill and slipped his credit card into his wallet. "Oh, you have so much more to learn about me."

Layne laughed. "We'll start with if you know all the lyrics to the Case Wellborne songs we'll hear tonight. I'm betting no."

"That's a bet you'd win. I'm familiar with a lot of his songs, but I don't know the lyrics by heart."

"Well, I do. I'll be singing in your ear all night long."

They left the restaurant and headed to the downtown arena. Instead of joining the lines in front of the building, Keaton led them to the side of the structure.

"Where are we going?" she asked. "Or will my man of mystery keep that a secret?"

"You'll see."

They came to a side door where security guard stood. Keaton approached him and gave their names. The guard consulted a list on a clipboard he held and then radioed someone inside.

"What is going on?" she asked.

"From this point on, I don't really know. It'll be as much a surprise to me as it is to you," he admitted.

The door opened, and a man in his mid-fifties emerged. He was bald with a salt-and-pepper beard and dressed in jeans and a T-shirt.

Offering his hand to Keaton, he said, "Dusty McGraw."

"Keaton and Layne."

"Put these on," Dusty said, handing them two lanyards. "Come with me, folks."

Layne was baffled at where they were going as they followed Dusty inside the arena. The halls were busy, full of people scurrying about. Everyone moved with purpose.

Dusty stopped at a door and opened it, motioning them in. They walked through the first room and into a second one, filled with sofas. A long table laden with food was along one wall.

"Get yourself a drink. Something from the buffet," Dusty suggested. "Case'll be out when he can."

"Thanks," Keaton said as the older man left them.

Grabbing his arm, Layne asked, "We're going to *meet* Case Wellborne?"

"I think. I hope. I sent him a message that we were coming to the concert tonight. He said his manager would get us in. That's who Dusty was."

Others now joined them, and they met the band's drummer, a bass guitarist, and the keyboardist. All three had women with them and were friendly. Layne learned two were wives, while the drummer had been with his girlfriend eleven years. While she would never push Keaton into marrying her, she hoped they would tie the knot sooner than that.

Then Case Wellborne emerged from another door, followed by a woman with fiery red hair. He looked around and broke out into a smile.

Keaton and Layne both came to their feet, and Case shook hands with Keaton.

"Good to see you, brother." He glanced to her. "And this is Layne?"

"Yes," she said, her heart beating quickly. "So nice to meet you."

Case slung an arm around the redhead who joined them. "This here's Janine. My way better half. You know Keaton. This is Layne."

"Nice to meet you," Janine said. "Your guy made a cradle for us before we had our first baby. We were dirt poor. Ready to use a drawer in the dresser as a crib. Keaton carved up a sweet piece of maple and sanded and painted it. We've brought home four babies from the hospital, and every single one of them has slept in that cradle by our bed for their first few months."

Layne felt her throat swell with emotion. "That's wonderful." She looked to Keaton, who seemed embarrassed by Janine's praise.

"Glad you've gotten good use out of it," he said humbly.

"Let's sit," Case suggested, and they moved to open spots on the sofas.

"I'll fix you a plate, hon," Janine said, bustling off.

"She's always taking care of me," Case said. "We've been together since eighth grade. Janine believed in me when no one else did. She's the one who found the early gigs for me. Booked me into bars and dive joints on the weekends. The places became a little larger. The turnout grew. She told me to quit painting and start writing more music, so that's what I did."

Case turned his gaze to Keaton. "Always listen to your woman. Because they're right—even when they're not."

They laughed at his joke, and Layne thought how down-to-earth the singer was.

"You've really had a great career," Keaton said. "I still

remember you singing while we painted. When I heard *Drinkin' Makes Me Drink You In* on the radio, I couldn't help but smile because you'd sung it enough while we were working together."

"You haven't done so bad for yourself," Case said. "I don't know nothin' about art, but Janine looked you up after I told her I'd heard from you. You're a painter now, Keaton. Not of houses. Of real pictures people hang on the wall." He grinned. "And you charge a pretty price from what Janine says."

Keaton shrugged. "You know those Highland Park wives. They'll pay whatever you ask if they like it enough."

"You're being modest," Janine said, handing her husband a plate and setting a beer down in front of him. "You've gone from painting rooms to producing gorgeous landscapes. Mountains. Woods. The sea."

"Whether he knows it or not, I drew inspiration from this guy," Keaton said, indicating Case. "I was painting every Sunday back then. Honing my talent. When Case left the construction crew—and then I started hearing his songs on the radio—I thought if he could make it, so could I. Took me a little longer, but I'm happy with what I do now."

"Are you still living in Dallas?" Case asked.

"No. I moved to the Gulf Coast back in the spring. Near Corpus. I own a gallery in Driftwood Bay. We have a house there, right on the water." he added, entwining his fingers with hers. "Layne's just inherited a B&B in the Bay from her folks. You should come stay sometime. The beaches are pristine. The fishing is good. Lots of great places to eat."

"Oh, Lordy. The kids would love that," Janine said. "What's it called?"

"The Bay Breeze," she said. "We'd love to have you come and stay. It's got four guestrooms, all with en suites."

"Maybe when this tour finishes," Case said. "We go

through the end of July. Have to be finished because the two older ones are in school. Janine doesn't like to tour without the kids, and I don't tour without her. I focus more on recording now during the school year."

"Then you'll need a vacation," Layne declared. "Come stay at the Bay Breeze. Or even with us. Our house is large enough for your whole family."

"You do not want that zoo, honey," Janine said, laughing. "But I'm thinking Mama and Daddy could come and stay with the kids for a few days in early August. We could sneak down and have some time to ourselves." She smiled up at her husband. "Maybe make another baby?"

Case laughed. "You see why I have to keep making music? This woman'll keep popping kids out as long as she can."

"You love every one of them, Case Wellborne," Janine chided playfully.

The singer grinned. "Not as much as I do you."

Case kissed his wife, and Layne felt Keaton squeeze her hand.

"Give me your number, Layne," Janine said, handing over her cell. "I'll text you about when we could come stay at your B&B. Just the two of us this time around."

She input her number and returned the cell. "Text me so I'll have your number, and I'll send you the website. You can choose whatever room you like, free of charge."

Dusty appeared. "Case, you need to go warm up your voice."

"Excuse me, folks," the singer said, rising. "Gotta go earn a living. Babe, get them settled, would you?"

Layne learned that they wouldn't be using the tickets Stacy had given Keaton. Instead, they would be sitting in the front row. Janine took them to the seats on the floor, just a few feet from the stage.

"It was great meeting you, Layne," she said. "I'll be in touch."

Keaton grinned at her after Janine left. "Front row. All I can say is—wow!"

"You certainly know how to treat a lady," she said, kissing him. "And Case and Janine are really nice. That's so sweet, you building a cradle for them."

He looked sheepish. "I'd forgotten about doing that. I knew they were strapped for cash. We'd ordered some wood for a project, and the customer changed her mind halfway through. My boss let me buy what was leftover at cost. By then, I wasn't painting much anymore. I'd moved into cabinetry and found I had a real talent for it. I built the cradle and gave it to them. It wasn't long after that when Case left."

"Well, I think it's terrific they've used it for all their kids when they were babies."

The lights blinked, signaling that the concert would be starting soon. Layne had gotten online and read where Case didn't have a warmup act.

Two minutes later, the lights dimmed considerably, with stage lights coming up. The crowd began buzzing, and the air filled with electricity. The band took the stage and began playing, and she recognized the tune. When Case came walking out, she sprang to her feet, squealing like a teenager.

For the next hour, the country singer and his band rocked the house. Layne danced and sang, her heart light.

"He's played so many of my favorite songs," she told Keaton. "I'm having a wonderful time."

"We're gonna slow things done a touch," Case said, taking a seat on a stool, a microphone in front of him. He picked out a tune on his guitar strings, and she knew what song would be played next.

In a husky voice, Case said, "This here is a song for my old buddy Keaton. He wanted it dedicated to Layne, his lady."

Tears stung her eyes as *Marry Me Before Sundown* unfolded. She turned to Keaton, who slipped an arm about her waist and took her right hand in his, swaying back and forth with her as Case sang the ballad. Keaton's gaze never left hers, and in it, Layne could feel all the love he had for her pouring from him.

When the last note sounded, he dropped to one knee, holding her hands in his.

"Marry me, Layne. Make me the happiest man alive."

"Yes," she told him. "You're the only one for me."

He came to his feet and took her in his arms as thousands of fans cheered the proposal.

Keaton broke the kiss. "Sundown has already come today. And we can't get married tomorrow by sundown. I've already checked. We need a license and have to wait seventy-two hours. But I want to marry you, Layne. Soon. I've never wanted anything more than to be your husband. Whatever sundown we choose."

"Then let's go home and get us a license," she told him. "I'm ready to be Layne Maxwell."

They kissed again, the concert happening all around them.

Keaton broke the kiss and waved at Case as he took Layne's hand and led her from the arena. She wasn't like Piper, who devoured romance novels. Layne had never really believed in a true happily ever after.

Until now.

She was going to get one.

With Keaton Maxwell.

The love of her life.

Chapter Twenty-Three

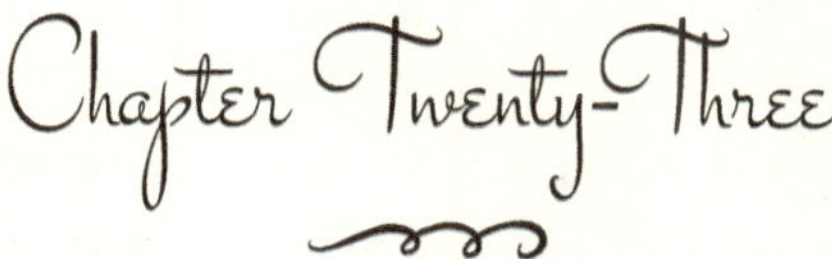

Keaton rinsed the conditioner from her hair, and Layne enjoyed the feel of his fingers massaging her scalp. Actually, she liked the feel of his hands anywhere on her body.

He turned off the showerhead and opened the glass door, reaching for a towel. He stepped out, toweling himself off and then wrapping it around his waist. The towel hung low on his hips, and she was thinking about pulling it off when he shook his head.

"You've got that look in your eyes, Miss Larson. Don't even think about it."

He held open a towel for her, and she moved toward it, letting him slip it around her. He handed her another towel, which she wrapped around her head.

"You aren't going to be able to call me Miss Larson much longer. In about two hours, the wedding ceremony starts. So let's say, in two hours and fifteen minutes, give or take, I'll be Mrs. Maxwell."

He frowned. "Are you sure you want to change your name

to mine? You've built a terrific professional reputation as Layne Larson. It's got a real ring to it."

She shook her head. "I still have no profession. No idea what I want to do. Sometimes, I wonder why you're even bothering to marry me. I'm just as much a mess as I was when we first met."

Keaton slipped his arms around her, kissing her softly. "The first time we met, you were a top business executive in Dallas, oozing smarts and confidence. That was at Carson and Mila's wedding. I was really attracted to you right away."

"And the second time we met, I cried more that day than I ever had my entire life."

He kissed the tip of her nose. "Yet despite your red eyes and even redder nose, I still found you incredibly sexy." Keaton framed her face with his hands. "You're about to reopen what I believe will be a very popular B&B. Even after the reno, you still have a good chunk of money from the separation package and the sale of your house in Dallas. Today's ceremony is just that. A ceremony. We're already committed to one another. What's mine is yours, and vice-versa. This house is paid for. My art is bringing in money. We're fine. Take all the time you need to figure things out," he encouraged.

Layne had been surprised to find that Keaton had placed her name on the deed to the house he had bought. She'd tried to give him cash. Not an entire half of what the purchase price had been, but she wanted to pull her weight. He had refused, telling her not to worry about it. She hoped she would decide what she wanted to do soon.

He was right about the Bay Breeze. Once she'd placed the pictures Stacy had taken on the website, a slew of reservations had poured in, many from longtime guests who were eager to return to Driftwood Bay. They would have the grand opening this weekend, and Piper was pumped to be in charge. Her friend had come in and gotten her feet wet as Layne had given a crash course in the running of the B&B. Piper added some good ideas to how things were already set up, plus she had taken to the cooking lessons Keaton had given her.

Since most of the inn's guests only stayed three to four days, Piper said she would rotate four days of different breakfast items, then she would start at the beginning of the list again. She had mastered scrambled eggs, along with bacon and sausage. Then Piper had conquered French toast and pancakes. It had taken her several tries before the consistency of her oatmeal was good enough to serve, but she was comfortable with preparing all those items.

Piper had suggested a small fridge be placed in the dining room, along with a toaster. That way, they could stock the fridge with cartons of yogurt, milk, and juice. Guests could also prepare their own toast or English muffins. Because of this, Layne and Keaton would not need to drive over every morning and prepare breakfast for guests, and he had convinced Layne to go on a honeymoon. They would leave in two weeks for Italy and France, two countries she had yearned to see for as long as she could remember. Though neither of them had ever been abroad, Keaton somehow had the passport process expedited, so nothing was holding them back.

While he shaved and dressed, Layne put on her makeup and blow-dried her hair.

"Go," she told him. "Piper is already horrified that we spent the night together and woke up in each other's company this morning. If you see me in my wedding dress, we'll never hear the end of it from her."

Keaton kissed her lightly. "I'll see you when the ceremony starts. Love you."

"Love you more," she said, nudging him out the bedroom door and closing it behind him.

She wouldn't let Piper's superstitions invade this perfect day. Layne looked out the window, seeing blue sky and ample sunshine.

Then a knock sounded lightly on the door. Thinking it might be Piper or Mila, she hurried to answer it, only to find Keaton standing there. He held a frame in his hands.

"I forgot that I wanted to give this to you," he apologized. "I thought at first I'd paint it for your birthday. Then as a wedding gift. Finally, I decided I would just combine the two occasions since your birthday is soon."

He turned the painting around so that it faced her. Immediately, her throat tightened. Tears stung her eyes.

It was the view of the bay from their backyard. He had captured the varying hues of the water, so well that you couldn't tell where one color ended and another one started. Two seagulls flew across the sky above the water. Along the shore, two Sandhill Cranes stood close to one another, looking across the water.

"We're the cranes," Keaton told her. "They're monogamous and usually mate for life. They build a nest together. While the female lays the eggs, both parents incubate them and raise their young as a team."

He smiled, tears misting his eyes. "That's how I think of us, Layne. As a team. They're us. We're them."

She took his face in her hands and pressed a fervent kiss against his lips.

"Thank you. For painting this for me. Really, for us."

"It's the first of what I hope will be many paintings which you inspire. You are my muse. My love. My life."

They kissed again, and she heard the doorbell sound.

Breaking the kiss, she told him, "Go answer that. And take the painting. I want everyone coming today to see it and hear the story behind it."

"Will do."

Layne closed the door and took a deep breath, letting it out slowly. Keaton made her feel cherished beyond words. She knew his art spoke for him, and the painting he had just gifted to her was a physical embodiment of their love for one another.

Another knock sounded on her door. This time when she answered it, Mila and Lily stood there.

"Hey, you two. Come on in. I love your dress, Lily."

"I practiced throwing fake rose petals," her flower girl confided. "I'm really good at it."

"I knew you would be."

"You look pretty, Miss Layne."

"Why, thank you."

"Okay, you've seen the bride, Lily. Go back and stay with Daddy."

"And Gran and Pops," Lily said, referring to Mila's parents.

The little girl skipped down the hall, passing Piper, who then joined them.

"Let's get you ready," Piper declared.

Within minutes, her friend had worked her magic, and Layne's makeup looked perfect with the simple, A-line cream dress. It had a V-neckline and capped sleeves and struck her just below the knees.

"I really like this dress," Mila said, helping Layne into it.

"I didn't see the point of a traditional wedding gown that would cost a fortune and never be worn again," she said. "This dress is classic. I can wear it for years to come. Unless I have kids down the line and it doesn't fit me anymore."

"Speaking of kids," Mila said, her hand going to her belly. "I know it's too early to be telling people, but you two aren't just any people. You're *my* people. My sisters. And aunts-to-be."

Layne and Piper squealed, and they quickly went in for a group hug.

"I knew I needed to come back to the Bay for this very reason," Piper said matter-of-factly. "With both of you getting married, my gut told me that babies would appear pretty quickly. Does Lily know?"

"No, we're not going to tell her just yet. Carson said we can wait until I'm beginning to show. Maybe when you can touch my belly and feel the baby kick. That will be more real to Lily."

"She'll make for a perfect big sister," Layne assured her friend. "When are you due?"

"Mid-October. Not great with volleyball season, but I'll work it out." Mila squeezed both their hands. "Oh, this is really something I've wanted. Watching Carson be such a great dad to Lily, I just know he'll be terrific with another one."

Piper glanced to Layne and smiled knowingly. "When will you start popping babies out?"

She couldn't help but blush. "We've talked and want them. We just haven't discussed a timeline."

"Go for it," Piper said. "I've told you that the Bay Breeze is in good hands. It's the last thing you should worry about. Besides, you have this incredibly large house. It's only right you fill it with the laughter of children. You and Keaton are great together, Layne. I can't see you with anyone else."

"Me, either," Mila seconded.

Layne went and fastened her mom's pearl earrings onto her earlobes. She brushed the tips of her fingers against the rounded pearls, saying, "I feel like Mom is here with me today. Dad, too."

"They would've loved Keaton," Mila said. "I feel as if they're watching you, and I know they approve."

A tap sounded at the door, and Mila answered it. "Hey, Mom."

Laura Perry said, "Everyone is here, Layne. We can start whenever you're ready."

"I'm ready now. I've been ready to marry Keaton ever since he asked me."

Mrs. Perry chuckled. "I love how his proposal went viral. Millions of people have seen Case Wellborne dedicate his song to you and Keaton dropping to one knee."

She smiled. "Case texted Keaton and said that sales for *Marry Me Before Sundown* have gone through the roof. The song is over five years old, but radio stations are playing it again. It hit number one on several music streaming platforms. Case also said at every concert since Houston, concertgoers begin chanting for him to play it."

"I read online where eight more couples have gotten engaged at his concerts while he plays it," Piper said. "That is *so* romantic, just like one of my romance novels."

"Come on, ladies. I don't want to leave my man waiting any longer than I have to."

They left the bedroom and moved down the hall. Dr. Perry waited in the great room.

"Ready to make that walk to your groom?" he asked, offering his arm to her.

"Ready and eager," she replied.

The others opened the doors to the deck, while she and Mr. Perry waited a moment.

"I don't want to make you cry, but your parents are here with you in spirit, Layne. They loved you more than anything."

"I know," she said softly.

"Keaton is a fine man. You'll build a good life together in the Bay."

With that, he stepped forward, leading Layne out onto the deck and down the steps. She was barefoot since they would speak their vows directly on the beach, and she enjoyed the feel of the sand as they moved toward the man she loved. A handful of others were present, but she only had eyes for her groom. Keaton watched her coming, beaming at her.

Dr. Perry handed her off, and she joined hands with Keaton, their gazes holding.

"You are so beautiful," he told her. "Inside and out."

"Ready, lovebirds?" asked Chief Roberts, who was licensed to perform weddings and would serve as the officiant at their wedding.

As they spoke their vows to one another, contentment washed through Layne. Though she had gone through some difficult times, those were behind her now. With Keaton by her side, she believed she could do anything. Whatever that would be, he would be right next to her, cheering her on.

"I am pleased to say that the two of you are now husband and wife. Keaton, you may kiss your bride. Just don't take too long," Chief Roberts teased.

Her new husband slipped his arms around her and gave her a sweet, lingering kiss. Their first as man and wife.

When he broke it, he asked, "Would you care to go inside, Mrs. Maxwell?"

Grinning at him, she batted her lashes. "I'd be happy to go anywhere with you, Mr. Maxwell."

They led their guests inside. The reception's food was a potluck, and everyone had brought different, favorite dishes to serve. Seaside Sweets Bakery had baked the wedding cake, however, and once everyone had finished their dinners, Layne cut the cake, Keaton helping to guide her hand. They distributed pieces to everyone, with Mila and Piper dishing up scoops of Blue Bell ice cream to go with the cake.

Piper put on some music, and they danced to everything from old Motown hits to the Cotton-Eyed Joe. Then the beginnings of *Marry Me Before Sundown* began, and Keaton swept Layne into his arms as everyone allowed them to dance to the song by themselves. Keaton held her close, humming along, and love for him poured through her.

When the last verse and chorus ended, Piper spoke up. "I think it's time to tell the newlyweds goodnight."

Their guests quickly left, and Keaton scooped her into his arms, carrying her to their bedroom. He set her on her feet, his fingers gently caressing her face.

"I love you so much in this moment, but I know my love for you will grow stronger with each passing day." He swallowed. "Thank you for coming into my life, Layne. Thank you for being who you are and wanting to be with me."

"Thank you for saving me," she said softly. "You've given me back my confidence. You've become my best friend. I can't wait to see what life brings to us, in this house, living in the Bay."

Keaton kissed her, and Layne knew this was the start of the best years of her life.

Epilogue

Keaton and Layne stood on the footbridge, feeling the mist from Cameron Falls lightly brush their faces. They had just finished hiking along a trail next to the falls, seeing the Canadian Rockies in all their glory, with Cameron Creek running below.

"I think I could move here," Layne declared, her face flushed from the hike.

And happiness.

He understood what she meant. "You say this everywhere we go, babe," he gently teased.

"But I mean it about Canada," she protested, smiling. "All right. You've got me. Yes, I seem to be taken by all the places we visit." She leaned over and kissed him. "The world calls out to me. And my partner in crime."

She lifted her camera and took a few shots of the falls, and he knew he would also use her photographs—and their travels—for inspiration.

Neither of them had really been anywhere when they got married, and they had made travel a priority in their marriage.

The first part of their honeymoon had been spent in the idyllic countryside of Tuscany, though they had managed stops in Rome and Florence before spending two wonderful weeks soaking up the Tuscan sun and eating like royalty. They had left Italy for France, first visiting Paris for three days before leaving the City of Lights for the Loire Valley. Again, they had drunk in the pastoral beauty, as well as enjoyed sampling regional wines and eating rustic meals.

It was on their honeymoon that Layne began her photography journey. She had that artist's eye, inherited from her father, and she framed photos and captured scenes, seeing things no one else did. Her photographs, both black and whites and in color, brought scenes to life. She had self-published a book of photos taken on their honeymoon, which had done incredibly well, leading to her current career. Wherever they traveled, she always had a camera in hand. Her photographs now commanded top dollar. Her travel blog was popular with tourists. Both these ventures still gave her time to be a mom to Allie and Bryan, their two children. Their children followed in their mother's footsteps, playing soccer, though Bryan also enjoyed playing right field in baseball. He had his mom's innate sense of numbers, while Allie liked painting with watercolors and singing in the choir.

Though they enjoyed bringing their kids on vacation, they always tried to take a trip every now and then with just the two of them. This late September trip to Waterton, where the prairies of Alberta met the Rocky Mountains, was proving especially fruitful. Yesterday, they had hiked through Red Rock Canyon, a fairytale landscape of scenic red and green argillite rock formations shaped by water over the centuries. He had filled almost half a new sketchbook, while Layne had taken hundreds of photographs.

The day before, they had rented canoes and paddled

around Cameron Lake, which was at the end of Akamina Parkway. Not only had being out on the water given them spectacular views of the Rockies, but they had also seen wildlife along the shore as they paddled at a leisurely pace. They had brought a picnic lunch and eaten it as they floated on the water, both inspired by their surroundings. He'd scribbled madly, turning page after page in his sketchbook, telling his wife that he would need to study some of the photos she took to fill in gaps.

That's what he had done since their honeymoon. Keaton tried to sketch what he could, but he counted on the pictures Layne took to help him fill in the blanks of his pictures and memory. The trip to Italy and France had proven to pack a punch for him professionally, and he spent the next two years using inspiration from what they had seen to do several series of paintings. Sidney had gleefully accepted all his landscapes, getting top dollar for each painting in the various series. Keaton had become fulfilled in his professional life, but it was his personal life and contentment with his wife and children that truly gave him purpose.

"Ready to go?" Layne asked.

"Lead the way."

They strolled through Waterton village, a place where everything was reachable by foot in a matter of minutes. As they walked along the sidewalk, they saw a deer coming down the center of the street. Layne stopped to snap a few pictures of him. She also stopped in front of a B&B, where a doe and her two fawns were sitting in the front yard, basking in the sunlight. The tame wildlife had been a pleasant surprise when they first arrived several days ago, but they had soon adjusted to it. Everyone in town gave the wildlife space, and people and animals existed in harmony.

"Where to next?" he asked as they continued strolling along the main street.

"We haven't been down to the International Peace Park Pavilion yet. I want to see it. Let's cut over to the shoreline and walk along it."

Waterton Lake and Glacier National Park in Montana sat adjacent. Together, they formed the world's first international peace park. He slipped his hand around his wife's and they walked along the marina's seawall, pausing when an elk appeared. Keaton guided them to a bench and they sat, watching the elk move leisurely toward the water. Layne silently took pictures of the magnificent beast, who after pausing for a drink, strolled off.

"Hey, we can see our hotel from here," he said, pointing in the distance to the Prince of Wales Hotel standing on the bluff.

She stood, taking several shots of the iconic hotel, saying, "These will be a nice companion to the photos I've taken from the hotel, looking down on Upper Waterton Lake."

He stood and joined her, slipping an arm about her waist. "I'm ready to sit beside those huge windows and enjoy the peaceful view." Grinning at her, he added, "With a cup of tea in hand, of course."

"Don't forget the scones and clotted cream," she reminded. "I'm so glad I've turned you into a tea drinker."

"Well, I'll never give up my morning coffee, but you've convinced me that a cup of tea during the day can be soothing for the soul."

Layne put her camera in her backpack and slung it over her shoulder. "Let's go back to the hotel. I've gotten plenty of pictures."

"For now," he teased. "I have a feeling when we take our sunset trail ride tonight, your camera will appear again."

She laughed. "I may just use my cell phone. I haven't been on a horse in a long time. I think I'll need to keep both hands on the reins most of the time."

He saw the look of contentment on her face as she gazed across the water.

"Keaton, I think I can finally put into words what happened when we met."

She faced him, those moss green eyes still as mesmerizing as they were all those years ago, drawing him in.

"I felt like I was drowning—and you built me a boat. It was a boat for two. Sometimes, you've done the hard work and rowed for the both of us, but I hope I've done my fair share of helping steer our boat and getting it to where we are today. The boat has magically expanded, incorporating Allie and Bryan. One day, we'll need to build them a boat of their own. Put them in it. Hand them the oars. Then nudge it out to sea, so they can be on their own."

Layne blinked back tears. "I know that's not for years, but when that time comes and our chicks leave the nest we've built, they'll be fine. And so will we."

She tenderly touched his cheek. "Because we have each other."

"I'm yours for this life—and all the lives to come," Keaton said.

He kissed her, thinking of the adventures still ahead.

And how he wouldn't want to experience them with any woman but Layne.

Also by Alexa Aston

COASTAL DREAMS

Second Chance on the Shore

The Art of Healing

Crafting Love

Tides of Trust

THE STRONGS OF SHADOW CREST

The Duke's Unexpected Love

The Perks of Loving a Viscount

Falling for the Marquess

The Captain and the Duchess

Courtship at Shadowcrest

The Marquess' Quest for Love

The Duke's Guide to Winning a Lady

CAPTIVATING KISSES

An Unexpected Kiss

An Impulsive Kiss

An Innocent Kiss

An Unforeseen Kiss

An Enchanting Kiss

An Urgent Kiss

An Unforgettable Kiss

A Promising Kiss

The Lyrics of Love

Finding Home

HOLLYWOOD NAME GAME

Hollywood Heartbreaker

Hollywood Flirt

Hollywood Player

Hollywood Double

Hollywood Enigma

LAWMEN OF THE WEST

Runaway Hearts

Blind Faith

Love and the Lawman

Ballad Beauty

SAGEBRUSH BRIDES

A Game of Chance

Written in the Cards

Outlaw Muse

KNIGHTS OF REDEMPTION

A Bit of Heaven on Earth

A Knight for Kallen

SUDDENLY A DUKE

Portrait of the Duke

Music for the Duke

Polishing the Duke

Designs on the Duke

Fashioning the Duke

Love Blooms with the Duke

Training the Duke

Investigating the Duke

SECOND SONS OF LONDON

Educated by the Earl

Debating with the Duke

Empowered by the Earl

Made for the Marquess

Dubious about the Duke

Valued by the Viscount

Meant for the Marquess

DUKES DONE WRONG

Discouraging the Duke

Deflecting the Duke

Disrupting the Duke

Delighting the Duke

Destiny with a Duke

DUKES OF DISTINCTION

Duke of Renown

Duke of Charm

Duke of Disrepute

Duke of Arrogance

Duke of Honor

About the Author

USA Today and Amazon Top 100 bestselling author Alexa Aston lives with her husband in a Dallas suburb, where she eats her fair share of dark chocolate and plots out stories while she walks every morning. She enjoys travel, sports, and binge-watching—and never misses an episode of *Survivor*.

Alexa brings her characters to life in steamy historicals, contemporary romances, and romantic suspense novels that resonate with passion, intensity, and heart.

KEEP UP WITH ALEXA
Visit her website
Newsletter Sign-Up

MORE WAYS TO CONNECT WITH ALEXA

OLIVERHEBERBOOKS

A small press bound by the belief that every voice matters.

Sign up for our newsletter to learn about new releases and more.
https://oliver-heberbooks.com/subscribe/

Follow us on social media:

facebook.com/oliverheberbooks

instagram.com/oliverheberbooks

amazon.com/oliverheberbooks

youtube.com/@OliverHeberBooksPublisher